MRS D'SILVA'S
DETECTIVE
INSTINCTS
AND THE
SHAITAN
OF CALCUTTA

Glen Peters was born in Allahabad, India, to a family originally from the city of Lucknow. His early childhood was spent living in a railway colony near Calcutta. After his family immigrated to the United Kingdom in the 1960s he attended university in London where he graduated in chemistry and was president of the students' union. He pursued a career in engineering management and become a partner in an international accounting firm. The idea of fictionalising some of the stories of his youth came to him during a sailing holiday when the starlit skies triggered childhood memories of the night skies over Calcutta.

He is founder of Menter Rhosygilwen, a Pembrokeshire-based rural arts regeneration venture.
www.rhosygilwen.com

Mrs D'Silva's DETECTIVE INSTINCTS AND THE SHAITAN OF CALCUTTA

Glen Peters

PARTHIAN

Parthian
The Old Surgery
Napier Street
Cardigan
SA43 1ED
www.parthianbooks.co.uk

First published in 2009
© Glen Peters
All Rights Reserved
This edition published in 2011

ISBN 978-1-906998-39-4

Cover design by www.theundercard.com
Typesetting by Lucy Llewellyn
Printed and bound by Gomer Press

Published with the financial support of the Welsh Books Council

British Library Cataloguing in Publication Data

A cataloguing record for this book is available from the British
Library

CONTENTS

THE PICNIC

Calcutta had seen better days. Once the capital of the Raj, with magnificent Victorian architecture, large green spaces and a thriving commercial hub, it was now sliding slowly into decay: a metropolis of open drains, overpopulation and political mayhem.

'It's that bloody *shaitan* devil again,' swore Mr De Lange as he read the front page of the *Sunday Statesman*, which was reporting another series of general strikes called by the Workers' Revolutionary Movement. 'I'd get that blighter Dutta up against the wall and put a bullet in his head if I had my way.' But Mrs De Lange, who had heard her husband's rants many times before, drew his attention to the approaching railway station.

The rickshaw wallahs at Bandle station always rejoiced on the day the sahibs arrived for their picnic at the shrine of Our Lady by the Hooghly, a tributary of the great Ganges. Anglo-Indians were charged the sahibs' rate and were considered a soft touch when it came to fare haggling. The fact that this community of mixed European and Indian descent were still considered 'sahibs' a decade after the British had departed India showed how they were regarded by their fellow citizens.

On this particular day the group was made up of four families drawn from an assortment of households at the railway colony in Liluah, which was about ten minutes by the slow, ponderous electric train from Howrah, Calcutta's main station. They'd boarded this Sunday with their free family passes and were loaded with numerous shiny aluminium tiffin boxes. These were stuffed with *roti*, many different aromatic vegetables, the fluffiest yellow Basmati rice and, as a special treat, Joan D'Silva's fish curry *molu*. Joan's ten-year-old son Errol had been looking forward to the trip for days, thanks to the promise of a ride on the new electric train.

Mr De Lange was the assumed spokesman of the group; he was the senior foreman at the railway workshops and commanded the greatest respect in his community. Once, during the religious riots of '47, he had sheltered a dozen Muslims in his house, armed only with one cartridge in his double-barrelled shotgun.

Top of the social pile of course were the Shroves, who considered themselves superior Anglo-Indians because they were by far the whitest of the four families. If it hadn't been for Mrs Shrove's passion for fish curry *molu* she would not have joined this group as she and her husband Bernard preferred mixing with the officers at the Railway Club, which was closed to lower-ranking employees.

To cries of 'Mum, the rickshaw's spilling the gravy over

2

my Sunday dress' and 'Uncle, did you remember to bring the rounders bat', they bounced along the pothole-riddled, dusty road to the shrine, propelled by a dozen or so sinewy, loincloth-clad cyclists, each one intent on reaching his destination first. The twenty-minute journey drew longing looks from shopkeepers and pavement dwellers, as if they knew of the culinary celebration in store.

The shrine was a peaceful place, set in about fifty acres of palm trees and a grassy *maidan* overlooking the silted waters of the Ganges as it neared the end of its long, life-giving journey from the Himalayas. The *maidan's* surface was of the finest-blade grass, kept in peak condition by the ceaseless efforts of local devotees, who worshipped daily at the feet of the Lady. It was said that she had once appeared to fisherfolk out of the early morning mist, clad in a white sari.

They were far from real pilgrims. For them this was a day out to enjoy each other's company, for the adults to gossip and yearn for the good old days and for the teenagers to tease, flirt and play games. But above all else it was a chance to indulge shamelessly in the culinary specialities of their best cooks.

They were soon setting out sheets of matting under a large shady palm tree. The Primus stove that had been carried by one of the boys was pumped up, and its deep-blue coral flame produced enough heat to bring the food to the right temperature with a profusion of smell and taste. The bubbling fish *molu* gravy gave out a powerful aroma of the freshest spices, which Joan's cook had spent hours cutting and grinding the day before, and all was ready for the performance to begin.

This was no ordinary picnic; it was theatre. As recipients of these delicacies, the picnickers were both audience and actors. They formed a big circle under the palm tree and sat comfortably with legs crossed in a very Indian way. But in a most non-Indian way they used spoons and forks instead of fingers, emulating the half of their ancestry that was British, to which they hung on so precariously.

The picnickers saw themselves as different from, and superior to, the rest of their fellow citizens. They spoke of Britain as 'home', had tailors fashion garments featured in the latest London magazines and brought in the New Year with 'Auld Lang Syne', singing words the meaning of which none had a clue.

Today's play was in two acts; the first produced by Joan. She had tied her jet-black hair in a ponytail with a ribbon of the brightest red silk, matching the colour of her summer blouse and showing off her olive complexion. Her tense, expectant face resembled that of a director on a first night, with front-row critics poised to pan the performance.

But the party hadn't eaten since seven that morning and the build-up to the first bite of the afternoon had set stomachs rumbling. If they had been offered cold stew, they would have appreciated it. Joan gave a characteristic little shake of her head as she doled out spoonfuls of fish over small piles of yellow *pilau* rice. 'It's something small, really, to get you going,' she said. '*Challo*, let's eat.'

A few dazzling red chillies swam in the turmeric-infused gravy that seeped into the rice, creating little rivers of a deep-gold liquid and leaving no doubt that the first morsel would assail the senses. Those last in the serving order were almost delirious with desire.

The aroma of the steaming piles of food wafted towards the riverbank where a distant pariah dog sniffed the air and trotted towards the group, her collection of skin and bone buoyed by the prospect of sharing in Joan's fish *molu*.

The culinary foreplay over, a few minutes passed as the serious business of eating went ahead. Joan tensed at the continued silence. Her stage-director nerves were on edge and she fidgeted with the red ribbon in her hair. Had she committed the heinous crime of not adding enough salt to the gravy? Perhaps they thought the fish not fresh enough? Damn that fishmonger, he'd said that the fish had been caught the night before. She never did trust the one-eyed rogue.

It was a definite taboo to ask outright. Were they using silence so as not to offend?

'Joan, that was the best fish *molu* I've had in years,' said Mr De Lange suddenly, a man not usually profuse in praise. Soon all the picnickers were joining in.

'Joan, did you buy the fish from the one-eyed fishmonger? It was so fresh.'

'Joan, was that your mum's recipe?' The accolades started to flow.

Joan began to breathe again as she answered all the questions in turn, pausing to eke out as much as she could of the rice and fish from the tiffin cans. As she sat down again for the rest to finish off their second helpings, she said a quiet Hail Mary to Our Lady of Bandle, and the emaciated dog looked on in dismay.

The fishmonger was forgiven, her own reputation intact and, judging by the gushing praise, the day might be hers despite the formidable culinary competition that lay ahead. They'd be talking about her fish *molu* all the way back home.

Talk about food dominated most conversations amongst Anglo-Indians: before meals, after meals and between them. Most events were recalled by the food that had been served at the time rather than the circumstances of an occasion. 'Lovely patties they had at Ernest's funeral', or 'terrible dry cake at that Marchant son's wedding', and 'such big fat prawns they were catching during the floods last year'.

'Shall we start a game of rounders, Mum?' asked Errol, wanting to take a break from the ceaseless attention to eating.

'No, baby, I don't think everybody is ready yet,' said his mother. 'See, Aunty Shrove is serving the next round of food and uncle is pouring the lemonade.'

The Shroves were carefully unpacking kebab *pongas* from the tiffin boxes and laying them out on a serving dish. These were succulent cubes of marinated lamb, cooked on charcoals and wrapped up in unleavened *paratha* bread: perfect picnic fodder over which they had laboured for two days.

Every year they dominated the picnic Oscars.

'Darling, I can never get my meat so tender' and 'Bernard, how do you manage to stuff those *parathas* and keep them so lovely and thin?' were the regular comments. One or two families always wanted to know if the Shroves were going on the picnic before they'd commit to coming; their kebab *pongas* a bigger inducement than the quality of the company.

But this afternoon, the huge success of Joan's fish *molu*

had satisfied even the most demanding appetites and the picnickers seemed quite content with their lot.

Then someone called out, 'It's one o'clock, time for *Musical Band Box*.'

Most Anglo-Indians within a hundred miles of Calcutta would tune in every Sunday to this musical interlude on All India Radio, with Pearson Sureeta's gravelly voice introducing the hits from the English-speaking world.

The Beatles hadn't quite arrived. This was the age of Dean Martin, Nat King Cole and teen idols like Cliff Richard, whose song 'Move It' was played over and over. The transistor radio had just arrived in India, and those who could afford it were abandoning their crystal sets, cat's whiskers and valve radios for this portable music-maker. And of course Mr De Lange had the latest model.

Like its owner, it was a chunky affair. Its green Rexene covering, with three gold plastic knobs, was the height of fashion. De Lange produced it proudly out of the purple knitted cover his wife had made to protect it from the smallest scratch. He switched it on and, without having to wait for the valves to warm up or to tune the receiver, they were listening to Connie Francis telling her boyfriend that lipstick on his collar had told a tale on him, quickly followed by Cliff Richard putting on his dancing shoes.

'I knew his mum,' said Joan. 'She was a Webb, from Lucknow. They got out in '47. Wouldn't want to know us now.'

'What about Bathgate?' said De Lange. 'They had two sons, one fair and one dark, when they went to England. The fair one, Johnny, completely disowned the dark brother and the rest of the family within a year of landing there. He works in TV now, I believe.'

For the next half hour food was going to take a back seat as most of the picnickers, big and small, had taken to their feet and were dancing in whatever way came naturally. Some twisted, others shook and the older ones waltzed in approximate timing to the music. When it was Chubby Checker's turn to go 'round and round', the parents were brought back to the ground with moans of 'whatever will they think of next?'

The radio kept the group amused as the teens flirted and the adults' antics risked slipped discs and angry spouses. A couple of teenagers used the cover of *Musical Band Box* to slip away into one of the empty cloisters of the cool, shady shrine to grope and discover forbidden parts of each other's bodies in their clumsy, hasty way.

Sureeta was signing off with one of his favourites, 'Memories Are Made of This', when Joan spotted her son running up the riverbank looking as though he was being chased by a boa constrictor. He flung himself into his mother's arms with a faint sob.

'Errol, darling, what's the matter?' she asked, not having noticed Errol wandering away from the group in the first place and not having seen the boy in such a distressed state for a long time. He was sucking on his thumb, something he hadn't done for five years, and he buried his quivering head in his mother's bosom like a two-year-old.

'Ma, it's... it's...' His voice faded and all he managed was another half sob. By now the other All India Radio listeners had gathered around him, anxious to find out what was the matter with the boy.

'Ma, there's a woman...' he stuttered again.

'What woman, darling *beta*, tell your mummy,' said Joan reassuringly.

'There by the river, a dead body of a woman,' he blurted out finally.

'Darling, a dead body, are you sure?' asked Joan, stunned.

Errol, entranced by the trains trundling over the Hooghly bridge, had gone to the river's edge to get a better view of a locomotive belching black smoke and pulling a half-mile-long array of trucks and wagons destined for some far-off shunting yard.

As he got to the top of the steep bank, he'd caught sight of what looked like the naked body of a woman lying in the long grass, with the brown murky waters of the river lapping up to her breasts. Errol had never seen a naked woman in his life so he strained to get a closer look, but suddenly lost his step and slid down the grassy slope.

His sudden descent came to a halt a few feet from the body and he saw, to his horror, a face with gouged-out eyes and a mouth that had been virtually eaten away, revealing a chilling, skeletal smile. Two scavenger birds took swiftly to the air, their feast disturbed. Flies hovered around the body and maggots crawled everywhere. He froze for a moment, not quite believing what he was seeing; then his eyes wandered to the bottom half of the torso and saw that most of the stomach area and ribcage had been torn out, as if the body had been attacked by wild animals.

Errol had taken a few seconds to recover from the first shock and then had turned and clambered up the slope as fast as his short legs could carry him, arriving in his mother's arms a minute later.

De Lange stiffened and remembered his seniority in the group. He was, after all, head foreman in the Carriages and Wagons division of the Indian Railways, while the others were mere chargemen or shift supervisors. He took control.

'*Achha*, I'm going to take a look around now. Everybody wait here and please stay quiet. Errol, *chullo*, come and show me where this body is.' De Lange motioned to the boy, who looked nervously at his mother.

'I'm going with him,' she said, putting her arms around her son and beginning to walk towards the riverbank. De Lange didn't try to separate them and merely followed, keeping pace with the young Errol who was still shaking with shock as he part walked and part ran towards the scene of his discovery.

As the reconnaissance group moved towards the river, the picnickers fell silent in strict adherence to De Lange's command. It was Bernard Shrove who spoke first, a few minutes later: 'It's these *ghats*. These days they are not cremating them properly. They just dump them in the river half burnt and go off to do another job. Chappie in my shops told me.'

'Well, I read a report in *The Statesman* last week that said there was a series of young girls committing suicide by jumping into the river because they didn't want to be married off to some small, fat fellow,' volunteered Mrs De Lange.

'I heard from one of the officers at the club,' said Mrs Shrove, 'that these *goondas* lured one of the convent girls into a Lindsay Street brothel. When she tried to run away they had her beaten up to such an extent she was in a coma for days. What is it coming to, this country? Our lovely picnic ruined. I'm glad we're off to Australia next year.' She looked grumpy, annoyed about her twenty uneaten kebab *pongas*. Two days of preparation down the drain because of the inconsiderate discovery of a dead body.

De Lange's normally steady, moustachioed expression twisted into a grimace when he saw the corpse. The young woman lay on her side, her face partially hidden by the grass at the edge of the water, one arm stretched above her head and her hollow stomach eaten by scavenger birds, revealing the yellowing bones of her ribcage. Her long black hair covered part of her face, some of which had also been consumed by avian hunger. The unbearable smell of rotting flesh defied anyone to spend more than a few minutes near the victim.

Joan turned away with a pained look and covered her son's eyes with both her hands, saying, '*Chullo, beta*, we must go back now to aunty and uncle.' She walked the boy, still in shock, back up the riverbank to the grassy field towards the gathering, which was again sitting in silence.

De Lange followed, holding a handkerchief to his face as if still trying to mask the smell of the corpse. The birds resumed their macabre feast as he disappeared from sight. '*Achha*,' he announced to the group as he made it up the bank, slightly out of breath, 'we have a body of a woman all right and it's in a very sorry state. I will have to report it to the authorities now.'

'Oh no, now we'll be here all day,' protested Mrs Shrove. 'What about all those *pongas*?'

'Dammit, we're Christians, aren't we? We can't leave the sacred body of a human being here in that condition.

She's a child of God and we have our duty,' he shot back with a combination of moral and admonishing tones.

'But what if the police suspect foul play? We'll be called by the magistrate and get mixed up with crooks and villains,' wailed Joan, seeing a harmless picnic entering the uncharted waters of a criminal investigation.

De Lange was having none of these protestations and marched off with great purpose towards the small administrative office behind the basilica to find a telephone.

An hour later, down the grass field rolled a police Jeep with four policemen in it, their crumpled khaki uniforms looking like hand-me-downs from another century. Three wore tin hats and carried 303 rifles that probably hadn't been fired in decades. The fourth, the senior man of the group, distinguished by his red-banded cap, was the first to descend from the vehicle.

'I'm Inspector Basu,' he said, surveying De Lange and scratching his balls at the same time. The heat of the midday sun and the Jeep ride had taken their toll.

The inspector's patch covered a vast area and his small contingent of constables was heavily in demand, not only for recovering dead bodies but also for dealing with the dark underworld of gangsters, dacoits and the wave of sometimes-violent political unrest sweeping Calcutta, the state capital of West Bengal.

An hour later Inspector Basu had the situation under control. He called De Lange to join him by the Jeep, where he was finishing off a conversation with someone on the police radio. The police officer looked satisfied with his work so far, having despatched the tin-hatted constables to stand by at the scene of the discovery.

'This is the situation I'm seeing, Mr De Lange,' he said. 'The body of the female is of a condition where I cannot rule out the circumstances of suspicion. There are being no clear signs of burning to point to the cremating option and the position of the arms is telling me that the person may have been in some distress at the time of death.'

De Lange listened intently, as serious as if he were receiving a telling-off from his general manager. 'Yes, inspector, I see: a very bad fate to befall a woman so young. May her soul rest in peace.'

'Mr De Lange, I'm sorry to have to report to you that we will be wanting to get the statement from the person who first discovered the body,' said Inspector Basu in a most self-deprecating manner.

'But that was little Errol, he's only ten, a minor. That can't be correct,' said De Lange indignantly.

'I'm sorry to have to say this then, sir, but we will have to be taking his mother or the next closest relative to the *thana* jail for the making of the statement. It is correct police procedure from British times you see, Mr De Lange,' he said, as if to legitimise the idea for the Anglo-Indian group spokesman. The two men walked back to the group of awaiting picnickers.

When Joan found out she had to go to the *thana* jail, she was furious. 'But we have nothing to do with this!' she erupted. 'You can't drag us off to the *thana* against our will. When are we going to get on our way?'

Inspector Basu's face broke into a smile as he said, 'Miss D'Silva, do you remember me? I'm Basu.'

'Basu?' she repeated, not absolutely sure why the

inspector was being so familiar with her.

'Basu, miss, the father of my son Beelu who is in standard four at Don Bosco. Who you are teaching English in a very excellent way.'

De Lange was the first to react. 'Ah, inspector, Mrs D'Silva is a very good teacher and I hope all goes well in Beelu's exams this year,' he said with a smile that seemed to say enough for the message to land with the inspector just where it had been intended.

'*Achha*, hmm! Yes, oh good afternoon, Miss Joan, it's very good to meet you. My son is a very intelligent boy. I hope he will be a doctor one day and go to London.'

'Oh, not a policeman like you?' said De Lange.

'No, this is a very dissatisfying job. Everybody is hating the policeman. Bad people, good people, important people, everybody.' Basu was beginning to sound morose.

'Look, inspector,' said De Lange, aiming to capitalise on the sudden empathy. 'Are you sure you can't get Miss Joan and her young son to make a statement tomorrow? They are very shocked by today's events and also very tired. She would very much appreciate being able to go home now.'

'I suppose in the circumstances pertaining at this time I may be allowing this but I am bending the rules, Mr De Lange.'

'Thank you, Basu,' piled in Mrs Shrove, giving the man a tight squeeze of his hand and a firm slap on his back. 'Would you and your men like a *ponga* kebab in appreciation of your diligence and hard work?' she added, desperate to shed a few of her creations.

'No thank you, miss, I'm vegetarian and so are all my

men. But you can be going now. Sorry, Miss Joan, for the distress I'm causing your son.'

'Thank you,' said Joan. 'We hope to see you at our sports day soon, inspector. Do come by and say hello.'

The tin-hatted subordinates looked longingly at the piles of *ponga* kebabs lying on the small picnic table as Basu barked orders at them to get back into their vehicle.

'Are you sure they wouldn't like to try one, inspector?' asked Mrs Shrove once more, in her astonishingly insensitive way.

'Definitely no, miss,' came back the final firm refusal.

That night Errol awoke from a nightmare. He'd seen the corpse again in his school, by the pond where the boys threw stones to see how many times they would bounce off the surface. Joan took him to her bed for the rest of the night, comforting him with the assurance that he would be OK next to her.

IDENTIFICATION

Xavier Lal had become concerned about his young wife, Agnes, after she failed to come home for several days. She had gone missing a few times before but those times she said she had spent the night with her student friend Philomena from Calcutta College because, she said, she had missed the last tram home. Xavier hadn't minded as he didn't much care for the company of his wife's young friends, so he didn't want her to bring them home with her. He was twice her age and not able to share in the small talk of college affairs or the heated discussions of the students' intellectual ideals.

It was the newspaper article he saw about the unidentified body of a woman found in Bandle that prompted him to go to the Howrah *thana* and report his wife missing. Women went missing every day in Calcutta, usually because they might have overstepped what was allowed in their narrow lives of servitude. Other times they were just unhappy with their miserable existence and had decided to end it all by jumping off a bridge, or into the path of an express train, or by setting fire to themselves. But Xavier had never imagined Agnes would meet her end in such a tragic way. It was always something that happened to others and she seemed such a resilient sort of girl, with a mind of her own.

The police had issued the description of the woman in the vaguest of terms: height and length of hair and so on, but it was the mention of a six-inch scar on the left shoulder, one of the few parts of her body that had not deteriorated, that made Xavier think it might be his wife.

Not that he had seen much of her without her clothes on. In the two years they had been married they had not slept together, and Sister Theresa, who had been responsible for the union, had told Xavier that love would come to them eventually in God's own time. And while God took his time, Xavier slept on the only bed and Agnes made herself a comfortable 'field bed' on the floor.

Xavier had been a convert to Christianity in his twenties and discharged his religious duties with solemn regularity. Morning mass, the Angelus, benediction, confession, you name it, Xavier made sure he ticked every box. Sister Theresa, the head of the Loreto convent, was impressed. So impressed that she took it upon herself to make sure Xavier got a job as a waiter at the Grand Hotel, pulling her long strings that stretched into the most influential parts of Calcutta society.

When Xavier had come to her and said that the manager of the hotel thought a man of forty should have a wife, it was Sister Theresa who had introduced him to young

Agnes, probably one of the best-looking girls at the convent. The nun was glad that one of her flock would be finding a good home. One less mouth to feed, one more soul saved; another success for the sisters of the poor.

Xavier went to the *thana* with some trepidation, for no one voluntarily stepped into a police station. Members of the public usually went there only in chains. Some went to see relatives behind bars, but most sensible people stayed well away.

There was only one place on earth worse than the inside of the Howrah *thana* cells and that was the mortuary buried deep in the basement. The stench of decomposing bodies and the condition of the corpses brutalised the senses of most mortals. Yet, while Xavier clutched a handkerchief to his face to suppress the smell of rotting flesh that was making his stomach churn, the man who called himself the 'morgue superintendent' went about his business in a most matter-of-fact way.

Xavier did not have to look long at the highly disfigured body to know it was that of his wife. Yes, the scar was there, and one side of her face that had lain in the river mud had been protected from decomposition, making her instantly recognisable to her husband. He nodded and the superintendent covered the body with the stained white cloth to keep away the flies.

Xavier had seen some horrid things in his life on the streets of Calcutta but the Howrah mortuary beat them all. It was not that he had many feelings towards his wife; it was more the shock of seeing the repulsive remains of a once-beautiful woman laid out on a marble slab that caused him to sit down on the steps of the police station and put his head in his hands in an effort to obliterate the memory.

Xavier gave the police a picture of Agnes for publication. It was one he found amongst her things in their shared bedroom. The next day Joan saw Agnes on the front page of *The Statesman* with the headline 'Bandle Girl Identified'. It was one of those pictures taken in a photographer's basement studio off The Esplanade. The photographer had lit his subject sensitively as she held a film-star pose, her head leaning back, her face looking sideways at the camera. Her long black hair glistened in the studio lights, falling carelessly down her back, her Jane Russell-style blouse exposed her neck and shoulders, and her dark lips were half open in a sultry expression, rounded off by those partially closed eyes, which oozed desire. The backdrop was a jungle scene with a Bengal tiger looking at the camera and competing for the viewer's attention.

One of Agnes's college friends had encouraged her to have the photo taken for a Bombay studio that was looking for attractive young Anglo-Indian women to star in forthcoming epics, no previous experience required provided they were good-looking. Several copies of the picture were posted to addresses in Bombay, but Agnes never received any replies.

The same morning that Xavier went to identify the body, a police Jeep sent by Inspector Basu picked up Joan D'Silva to take her to the police station, a mark of the great respect that she was owed as the teacher of the senior policeman's son.

The Jeep was an open-top vehicle and Joan held her hair in a blue scarf to protect the expensive perm she had had earlier in the week at the Chinese hairdresser in Sudder Street. This was a six-monthly affair which Errol hated; he had to wait for three hours or more in a salon full of women sitting under large electrical coils of wire that fried their hair into tight curls. Joan would buy him a *Classic Illustrated Comic* of one of the famous books by Dickens or one of the Brontës, and Errol passed the time taking in the stories of great authors.

At the police station Joan was ushered into an administrative office where half a dozen Corona typewriters chattered away, their carriage bells tinkling every few seconds as the lady stenographers copied transcripts of statements and records onto official-looking forms, backed up by several layers of carbon paper.

'Madam, you are coming to give statement?' said the office *babu*, who appeared to be the man in charge.

'Yes, it's on behalf of my son, he originally discovered the body,' said Joan.

'Your son is not here?'

'No, he is a minor and the inspector said that it would be OK for me, his mother, to make a statement on his behalf.'

The *babu* scratched his head, not having had someone make a statement on someone else's behalf before. He took details of the time, the location, the state of the body, the position it was in and how Errol happened to be at the scene at the time. When he was satisfied that he had all the details, he handed them to one of the stenographers, who assembled several sheets of carbon paper with official-looking forms and began her task of copying the *babu*'s handwritten record. She seemed to rattle along the keyboard at frightening speed for it was only a few minutes later that Joan was being asked to read the neatly typed forms and sign each copy, the last one being barely legible.

'Thank you, madam, now the inspector would like to see you,' said the *babu*.

Basu greeted Joan like a long-lost friend. 'Mrs D'Silva, good morning. How are you?'

'I'm fine, inspector, thanks for sending the Jeep to pick me up. You saved me a lot of time. Now I can get back to the school for your son's English class,' said Joan, smiling and looking around her to see if she was supposed to be sitting down.

'Oh, please be sitting down and are you having a cup of Marsala tea?'

'Yes, that would be nice,' she said, a little surprised by the hospitality she was receiving at the city's most loathed establishment. 'Tell me, inspector, where are your enquiries heading with the Bandle Girl?'

'Not very good, Mrs D'Silva, I'm sorry to say. Yes, we have identified her now, but we are not seeing the death motive. Nobody is being able to help us. Her husband is saying that it is not possible that she is taking her life but we are not finding clues as to how she may have died.'

'Her husband? Can't he give you a clue? Do you suspect him?'

'No, he is working every evening at the Grand Hotel. I don't think he is implicated. Mrs D'Silva, I'm sorry to be saying this, but girls like her are going missing every day and no one cares. If we are following up all the missing persons I would need many hundreds of men.'

'But, inspector, it's terrible to accept such awful crimes,' said Joan, raising her voice a little.

21

'I'm agreeing, but such is the poor status of the woman. It is only that you found the body and called my department that we now have to investigate. Many others are not bothering.'

'Well, I'm beginning to feel a personal responsibility for finding out the real cause of her death. When is the coroner's enquiry?'

'At the end of this week, and you must attend as you are a key witness in the discovery of the body. Judge Bhattacharya, our senior judge, has decided he will preside over the enquiry. That shows how important a case this is becoming. It must be because the girl was from Sister Theresa's Loreto convent.'

'Don't worry, I'll be there,' said Joan, leaving the policeman in no doubt that he would be seeing a lot of her until the mystery of Agnes's death was actually solved.

THE CORONER

The coroner's enquiry into the death of the Bandle Girl was to be held at the Court House, Number 21 Dalhousie. The nineteenth-century building had once been a grand edifice to some aspect of British Raj administration. Its crumbling, peeling exterior, a dark shade of dirty brown mixed with green stains from rainwater and other city pollution, now projected quite another picture: that of a city in decay.

Joan and Errol had travelled to the enquiry from Howrah by tram, a mode of transport that Errol preferred to buses, probably because they ran on tracks and he did adore anything that moved on rails. Also you could usually get a seat on board a tram.

Buses were run by private operators and they liked to cram people in until passengers were hanging out of all the openings on the vehicle. The conductors must have been on commission for the number of tickets they could sell on each journey: sardine canneries could have taken lessons on how to pack an impossible number of creatures into a confined space.

Ladies and small children usually got to sit down in comfort. Bengalis maintained a high standard of manners, giving up their seats despite having to endure the alternative discomfort of standing, squashed to the extent that their ribcages hurt each time the bus hurled itself around to avoid stray cows or slower vehicles. Joan was never sure why even transvestite *hijiras* also got preference as ladies, for it was clear that they were men really and everyone knew they were.

She preferred taking a taxi to avoid the sweat and smell of a full bus. 'You end up dirtier than the *dhobi*'s washing at the end of the journey,' she would say to justify the extra cost of the taxi fare.

But today was not an outing to have fun or go to the New Market for a shopping trip. This was a serious piece of official business for which the school had given her time off. The comfort of the tram made her feel that the decision had been a good one, and she knew that she was quite a few rupees better off than if she'd taken a taxi. Errol, too, seemed to be happy, watching the driver working the control lever that regulated the speed and the foot-operated bell, warning those on the track ahead of their impending doom.

'*Babujee*, I'm here to attend the coroner's hearing with my son,' she said to an official who sat cross-legged on a chair, chewing betel nut, when she and Errol arrived inside the main office of the court. *Babus* were the cogs that turned the wheels of administration and bureaucracy here, slowly and in their own time. They rushed for no one and Joan was not about to be an exception.

'The name?' the official replied, looking bored.

'Joan D'Silva and this is my son, Errol. Here is the letter from the District Coroner's office,' she said, handing him the piece of paper she had received. He viewed it through the bottom of his specs.

'*Achha*, go to room three at the top of the steps,' he said, waving the palm of his right hand as if he was pushing around a pile of rice, looking for dead weevils.

Errol followed his mother up a wide set of stone steps and past a woman sweeping up the previous day's litter of monkey-nut shells and bits of paper. The walls had been painted green at some stage in the last ten years, which combined with the smell of disinfectant and the single neon light at the top of the stairs to further the dingy effect.

Room three was a large, teak-panelled room with a few black, Rexene-covered chairs for visitors and press and two tables at the far end. One table was for the coroner and the other for the district magistrate, the police inspector responsible for the enquiry and the support staff.

Joan spoke to the official, who ticked her off the list along with Errol. There were a handful of others in the room, press people she assumed, always on the prowl for a scoop, and a nun, clearly distinguished by her habit of the order of nuns from Loreto.

Inspector Basu, when he entered the room, was the first person she recognised. His uniform was pressed for the occasion. He looked a lot less crumpled than the last time Joan had seen him. He smiled at her in recognition. Joan had dressed with the intention of looking authoritative and businesslike. She wore a brown safari trouser suit which her *durgee* had tailored for her a year earlier, when the Chief Minister had come to her school on a special visit. She sported a beige-rimmed sun hat and just a hint of make-up. Her husband had told her once, 'Joan, you have enough natural beauty, you don't need to add any more.' And yet Joan was caught up like other women in the magic of Max Factor and its clever advertising.

'Ah, Mrs D'Silva: good to see you this morning.' Inspector Basu raised both his hands together in a *namaskar*. 'Master Errol, how are you?'

Errol offered a shy smile to acknowledge he was fine. It was all rather like going to visit the doctor: a long wait, the smell of disinfectant and having to sit with people you didn't know. He could chat away for hours about trains and trams and the quality of continuous welded track, but the system of governance and enquiry left him very fed up.

'Now, just as we were talking in the *thana* last week, I'm thinking to remind you of the main points,' said Inspector Basu, wishing to ensure everything was wrapped up on this case by midday, as he had far more important crimes to solve. The inspector ran through the main points the coroner would want to elicit from Joan. She would have to answer for Errol, as he was a minor and not able to speak for himself, but he would have to agree with everything that his mother said before it was accepted as an accurate record.

The coroner entered on the dot of ten o'clock, with a small entourage of officials. He was a middle-aged man with a receding hairline, dressed immaculately in a white linen suit, a red carnation in his lapel. 'Please be standing for Judge Bhattacharya,' called the official. The presence of such a high-ranking judge for such a minor inquiry was unusual and the inspector sat on the edge of his seat with his hands clasped tightly together. Basu and Bhattacharya were not the best of friends; the latter was a member of the prestigious Bengal Club and part of Calcutta's intellectual elite; the former from the poorer end of the middle class, struggling on his meagre public servant's salary. The inspector was not looking forward to this.

When everyone had been asked to sit, Bhattacharya spoke in a businesslike manner. 'The purpose of the inquiry this morning is to establish the circumstances surrounding the death of what the press have been referring to as the Bandle Girl. I hope this won't take long and waste too much of our precious time. Inspector Basu, as the investigating officer, could you lay out the evidence for us?'

'Certainly, sir,' said Basu, getting to his feet. 'On the afternoon of the twenty-third of November, 1960, my *thana* received a telephone call from a Mr De Lange to report the finding of the partially destroyed body of a young woman by the banks of the Hooghly river, adjacent to the Bandle Catholic shrine.'

Basu gave a full account of how the body had been found and the position in which it lay. Then Joan had to give her firsthand account of how Errol had happened to wander off from the group.

'So am I to understand, inspector, that this was the first sighting of the body?' said the coroner.

'That would be correct, sir. We have no other sightings of this body prior to the day of the twenty-third of November.'

'I find that extraordinary. The forensic examination

27

reveals that the girl died at least seven days earlier. Inspector, did you not seek to interrogate any of the fishermen or boatmen on the river to establish whether they may have seen the body?' said the coroner, making Basu feel uncomfortable.

'Sir, no. This is a very desolate spot of the river and we did not make any further enquiries.'

'Well, that's a pity!'

Basu was getting a public telling-off. He began to perspire a little.

'Let us hear from the husband of Agnes Lal. Mr Xavier Lal, please come forward.' The court official translated the instruction into Hindi and Xavier, wearing an open-necked *kurta* and a gold chain around his neck, came forward to speak.

'Mr Lal, how long had you been married to the deceased woman?' asked the coroner.

'Two years,' replied Xavier.

'And in these two years have there been any disturbances to your relationship?'

The court interpreter had to think about the way he might phrase this in Hindi. The sentence didn't translate easily; in fact what came out was 'Have you been disturbed by your wife in this time?'

Bhattacharya picked this up as his command of Hindi was excellent, and he translated the question directly for Xavier's benefit: 'Did you have a harmonious relationship?'

'Yes, it was a peaceful one. She may not have cooked all my meals when I got home at night but we did not fight,' he answered.

He said that when he returned home on the night of the

28

fifteenth of November his wife was not there. This was not the first time she had not been home when he got back from work, so he went to bed expecting her to return later in the evening, but by the next morning she still had not appeared.

'So why, Mr Lal, did you not report your wife missing until several days later?' demanded Bhattacharya.

Xavier Lal looked at the inspector nervously. 'I just thought she might come back. Wives go missing for days sometimes and then come back. It is when I heard that an unidentified body had been found by the river that I went to the police.'

'I find this quite unusual, Inspector Basu. Mrs Lal had no family of her own, having been brought up by the Loreto orphanage, but she had the people at the convent and her husband. Why was she not reported missing earlier?' Bhattacharya said. 'Sister Theresa,' he motioned to the nun in the front row to come forward. 'That's all for now, Mr Lal.'

Sister Theresa, dressed in the full habit of the Loreto order, moved swiftly to take the chair next to the coroner.

She was somewhere in her sixties, though it was very difficult to tell as she was totally covered from head to toe. She had come to Calcutta at the age of fifteen from County Kerry in Ireland, given by her family to do good work for the missions. She came to a Calcutta at the peak of the British Raj. During the war years, Calcutta had provided much of the logistical support for the army in Burma and further east. After partition refugees had flooded into West Bengal and the nuns of Loreto had been very busy saving souls from the suffering of life on earth and hereafter.

She had grown to be both a woman and a bride of

Christ, working at the orphanage in Howrah. The orphans were usually abandoned babies left at the door by mothers who couldn't afford to keep their newborn, or stand the shame of an unwanted pregnancy. Others were brought to the orphanage by hospitals where the mother had died in childbirth and the newborn girl child was rejected by the father's family.

'Sister Theresa, please tell us when you last saw the deceased?' said the coroner.

'Oh, every Sunday for mass at eight o'clock, until I saw her picture in the papers as the missing Bandle Girl. All our girls keep coming back to mass unless they move away or the devil takes them,' said the nun in a soft lilting Irish voice which she still kept, even after fifty years in India.

'Did she ever speak to you about her life, her marriage? Did the young woman seem troubled at all, sister?' asked Bhattacharya.

'Oh, not really. But then few of our girls complain because of the care we take in finding them good husbands for their future lives,' she said in a voice designed to leave one in no doubt.

'So the marriage of Agnes and Xavier Lal was arranged by your good self, sister?' the coroner probed further.

'To be sure now. Xavier had an excellent job as head waiter at the Grand Hotel in Chowringhee. He was a good Catholic and he made his intentions to find a wife known to us. Agnes was sixteen, had passed her basic school exams and needed to move on. We introduced them one Sunday after mass and they both seemed to be happy with the match. I made the arrangements two weeks later for Father Ambrose to perform the nuptials in our chapel of the Blessed Virgin Mary. You know, we...' she was in full flow when the coroner interrupted.

'Sister, was no consideration given to the considerable age gap between the two?' asked Bhattacharya, the evidence confirming his suspicion that the nuns were not the best matchmakers in the world.

'Sir, if you are implying that we had no concern for the girl, then you would be wrong. Our first consideration is always whether the man is Catholic and Xavier is indeed a fine Catholic man. Our second consideration is whether the man can provide well for our orphan girls, who need to be protected from the horrors of poverty in our city. Thirdly we ensure the candidate is of good conduct. Mr Bhattacharya, I put it to you, are not these the three most important considerations before we allow people into holy matrimony?' Sister Theresa fought back.

The coroner was not going to take on this feisty nun, one of the pillars of the establishment and a personal acquaintance of the Chief Minister. 'Very well, sister. That will be all.' Sister Theresa arose and moved briskly back to her seat, her starched skirts swishing as she went.

The inspector presented more forensic evidence concerning the approximate time of death, the inconclusive findings about its cause and the general state of health of the woman before she met her end.

'So you can confirm, inspector, that there is no evidence of foul play, that is, death caused by others?' probed the coroner.

'Well no, sir, not exactly. The forensic report is inconclusive on this because of the advanced deterioration of the body,' said Basu, sticking to his guns.

Next it was the turn of Philomena Thomas, the only friend from the convent that Agnes seemed to have kept since she had left the orphanage. Philomena was also eighteen and, like Agnes, they were both abandoned babies.

She took the witness chair dressed in a white frock with puffed half-sleeves and a knee-length skirt that billowed ruffles of chiffon: a sort of cross between a communion outfit and a party dress.

Ex-residents of the Loreto often wore hand-me-downs, and they hung onto these for many years after leaving. Joan looked at her with some pity. She would never have been seen dead in something like that at eighteen. Sister Theresa looked at Philomena with a scowl.

'I last saw Agnes at the Coffee House on the Strand on Saturday the fourteenth of November,' she said in response to a question from the coroner. 'She seemed to have fallen and hurt the right side of her face. It was bruised and she was a bit shaken.'

'Did she happen to mention whether there were any difficulties in her life at that meeting or on any other occasion?' asked the coroner.

'Well, actually, when she was with me and the other girls of the Bachelor of Commerce class from our college she was always happy, joking about our school days and about some of the boys in the class. She was the most beautiful person, so there was Eve teasing going on all the time with her, you know, rude whistling and comments of a sexual nature. She would never speak about her husband, but it was common knowledge that their marriage was not consummated.'

'Not consummated?' repeated Bhattacharya, surprised

at this revelation. 'Is that what she said to you?'

'Well no, not precisely, but judging from our conversations she was quite unaware of some of the things that a husband and wife do, if you see what I mean,' said Philomena, looking uncomfortable and gazing down at the floor.

'You mean that their marriage was without sexual relations,' said the judge.

'Well, sir! Well, I couldn't say precisely. I don't think so,' she replied, apparently getting more uncomfortable by the second. Bhattacharya began to realise that she might shut up completely if pushed any further.

'Do you think she may have had reasons that would have led her to take her own life?' he asked directly, apparently trying to eliminate the chances of foul play.

'Not actually,' said Philomena, 'my only concern about her circumstances was that as a child bride, would she ever be happy? There was always talking behind her back. Some of the boys at college joked about her needing help with sex and things, but I don't think Agnes ever noticed. Somebody said that they saw her once in Lindsay Street, you know, where men go for fun with ladies.'

Joan watched the expression on Sister Theresa's face at this revelation: the nun's cheeks reddened as she straightened her back and glared at Philomena. Bhattacharya too looked uncomfortable, shifting in his chair more than once. A couple of the men from the papers scribbled furiously.

After a long silence, Bhattacharya asked Philomena to stand down, accompanied by murmurings from the courtroom.

'Inspector Basu, this case is puzzling me more and

more,' he said. 'You have no sightings of this woman around the time of death, we have no reasons to suspect foul play and there are no suspects in this case. We know that the woman was a Catholic and that Bandle is a popular shrine where people of her religion go to seek solace. It seems likely that she may have been disturbed by her unconsummated marriage or even have entered some other hopeless relationship and decided to end her misery. Do you have any theories that you have investigated to answer this point?'

Basu rose. 'That is definitely a perplexing question. Bandle is being a popular shrine for Roman Christians, sir, and it is very possible that she visited there on the day she went missing to pray for some peaceful resolution to her distress, upon which she decided to take her life.'

Sister Theresa got up from her seat and raged, 'That is absolutely absurd. We Catholics are taught of the mortal sin of taking your own life and there is nothing but a future of burning in hell with the devil for those that commit the sin of despair.'

'Please, sister, do sit down. Your comments, although helpful, are out of order,' said the coroner firmly.

'I will not sit here and let you come to a conclusion of suicide when that is clearly not apparent from these findings,' she barked and then sat down.

'Inspector, I am coming to the conclusion that to grant a verdict of death by taking one's own life is illogical given the evidence brought to the court this morning,' said Bhattacharya, leaning forward and adjusting his ICC club tie. 'And what is more, inspector, I don't think you have discharged your duties well in this case. I find an insufficient

34

depth to your enquiries and a lack of witnesses.'

Joan saw Basu getting glummer by the second as he received his telling-off. Police relations with the judiciary and civil administration had never been very good. Most of the judges were considered to be far too *pukka* and into their British ways, with their gins and tonics and days at the races. And the judiciary regarded the Bengal police as bumbling, incompetent boy scouts, quite often open to corruption to inflate their meagre salaries.

Finally Bhattacharya delivered his verdict, which drove in a painful blade and twisted it until it hurt for many of the people there: 'I'm afraid I have to record an open verdict in the case of the death of Agnes Lal,' he said. 'I'm recommending that the police continue in their investigations until a suitable reason for the death of the victim can be deduced. And I'm putting on record my displeasure at the unsatisfactory way in which this death has been investigated.'

Everyone in the court knew that the case would remain among the many hundreds of unsolved, mysterious deaths that the police never had time to unravel. The daily toll of missing young women, added to all the other unsolved crime, was a fact of life in this overcrowded, decaying city.

THE NEWCOMER

The next day's papers were full of the Bandle Girl story, with the same picture of Agnes Lal as a prospective film star. The caption read 'The Loreto girl who died from unknown causes'.

There were also pictures of Inspector Basu putting on a brave face and saying that the search for the truth would go on according to the coroner's instructions. Joan too was quoted as having found the body with her son Errol.

The teachers' room was buzzing with rumours about the story. The teachers had their own common room and Phillip John, the newcomer, was receiving his initiation. With the exception of Punditji, the Hindi teacher, and now Phillip, it was an all-female staff group.

'Good God,' said Mrs Shrove, 'how on earth could that nun have married the poor girl off to some fat, ugly waiter more than twice her age?'

'Ridiculous!' said another.

'Phillip, what do you think, as a man? Would you marry

a girl less than half your age?' asked Joan, who had had little reason to speak to him since he joined the staff contingent.

Phillip seemed completely unprepared for the question and hadn't followed the case, being new to the area. He looked up from the corner of the room where he sat and said, 'It all depends really.' There was a hush around the common room. They were waiting for more, but nothing further came from Phillip's mouth. Was this the limit to the communication skills of the newcomer?

'Depends on what?' said Mrs Shrove, ready to demolish the man's standing right from the beginning.

'Well, if there were a genuine bond of affection between myself and the girl...' That sounded much better to the women, who thrived on the romantic short stories in the overseas edition of *Woman's Own* and the novellas of Daphne Du Maurier. 'Love knows no bounds. Isn't that what they say?' He was winning their admiration now with every syllable he uttered.

'So is there a Mrs John in the making?' came a very sudden question flying in from some corner of the room.

'Well no, not at the moment,' he said with a faltering smile. Joan thought he showed an attractive degree of modesty.

Eligible, educated Anglo-Indian bachelors in their mid thirties, with a respectable job, were few and far between. And many mothers with daughters of marriageable age would have been desperate to find a way of introducing Phillip to their families. He was attractive too, six foot three when he didn't hunch his back. Most unusual of all were his green eyes, which seemed almost fake, set deep in his brown face.

It was not uncommon to find children of every hue and colour within the same Anglo-Indian family: the result of a few hundred years of intermarriage since the Portuguese first landed in India. Under British rule, young Anglo-Indian men were generally guaranteed a job, and educational achievement was never a top priority. After independence, this privilege being lifted, employment became just as scarce as it was for every other Indian; and while women became secretaries or teachers, young men struggled to make a living.

The few who did break through this vicious circle clearly stood out from the crowd and Phillip was one of these, a point that had not gone unnoticed by Joan or the other female teachers.

The school bell sounded at four o'clock and children rushed out of their classrooms in the usual mêlée that marked the end of the school day. Parents, *ayahs* and rickshaw wallahs all mingled at the school gates to pick up their charges and take them home.

Phillip had packed up his things and was walking towards the gate himself when he saw Joan coming out at the same time. 'Enjoy the day?' he said, as if to make some friendly contact away from the throng of the other women in the teachers' common room.

'Oh well, I've had worse,' she said casually. 'What about you?'

'It's one of those settling-in phases when everyone is testing you out, the boys, your fellow teachers, the principal. But it's not a bad place so far,' he said neutrally.

'You were put through the mill a bit in the common room this afternoon, I'm afraid.'

'Not at all, part of the initiation,' he answered, now walking alongside her out of the gates.

'Listen, where are you lodging at the moment, Phillip? Come over and have a cup of tea. I only live at the north end of the school,' she offered.

'I'd like that. Be good to get in on all the gossip,' he accepted with a mischievous smile, which Joan liked.

'I'm not sure I can tell you all the gossip – you'll have to talk to Mother Shrove for that – but I'm sure I can give you the beginner's guide.' She found the idea of him wanting to learn the ropes from her amusing.

Joan lived in a small block of flats built by the school to house the few single teachers: women like Joan who had for some reason lost their husbands, or indeed never married. Her flat was a small, single-bedroomed unit that she shared with Errol. He slept in the same room as her, which was not ideal for a boy of ten, but compared to the other options that Joan faced when she lost her husband George, this was luxury.

The Father Rector liked Joan and her dedication to the school. So when she had to leave the railway quarters three months after George's death, she was offered a flat that happened to have come free when one of the female teachers got married.

'So you're lodging in the railway colony then?' she asked, pouring a cup of freshly brewed Darjeeling.

'Yes, it's a large room with a bath, which is ample space for me. The main resident, Mr Jones, is a bachelor and the house is far too big for him. You said you have a son?' said Phillip, seeing a framed studio picture of Errol, aged five, with his father, George, and Joan.

'He's ten going on eleven and mad about trains. I'm afraid I can't give him much support in that department. I think he is staying back for a catechism class today. Father Rector says that he's way overdue for his first holy communion.'

'Hmm, I'm quite a train buff myself. My dad was a mail driver. Is that your husband in the photograph too?' asked Phillip. He was trying to complete the picture.

'My deceased husband. I lost him in the Doon Express crash of 1955,' she explained. 'We were a very happy family.' Joan looked at the photograph with a sad smile and Phillip caught a quick glimpse of beauty in her brown eyes and long eyelashes as she blinked a few times to push back a tear.

He knew something too about loss and told Joan about the death of his mother from diphtheria before he was ten and the death of his father while he was still in his teens. His grandmother had brought him up at the family house in northern India, by the foothills of the Himalayas.

'How did you come to be at Don Bosco's?' asked Joan, her curiosity rising steadily.

'Oh there just comes a time when you have to move on, you know,' he said vaguely. 'I was getting into a bit of a rut in the school at Darjeeling. All the boys were the privileged sons of rich parents who didn't really want to learn and didn't appreciate how lucky they were.'

'I do love this school because it just isn't that. I think you will be very happy here,' said Joan.

The front door opened and Errol came through, his usual dishevelled self at the end of a school day. With his tie at the oddest angle, his shirt hanging out and looking as if he hadn't washed for a week, he gave Phillip a quizzical look.

'*Beta*, do you know Mr John? He joined the school teaching staff this term,' said Joan, making the introductions.

'Hello, young man,' Phillip chimed in, but Errol kept quiet, preferring to smile shyly in response. 'Your mum tells me you like trains. Are those the steam-driven ones or the diesels?'

'Oh definitely the steam ones, sir,' Errol shot back instantly, his shyness gone.

'I hear the diesels are faster though and can pull more carriages,' said Phillip.

'Well yes, sir, but the steam engines work on coal of which there is plenty in India. Also if they get a good head of steam they could easily beat a diesel,' replied Errol.

'Errol, go and change now, have a bath and wash off some of that mud. Would you like something to eat?' said Joan, suddenly the fussing mother.

'No, Ma, I'm fine.'

'You haven't been eating that *chat* from the *puchka* wallah have you? I've told you you'll catch some horrible disease if you do. He stands by the *nallah* and never washes his hands or anything,' she went on in an admonishing tone which Phillip all at once found familiar.

Errol disappeared into the bedroom to escape any further questioning from his mother. He couldn't resist the delights of the *chat* wallah, as unhygienic as the street food was.

A round with the *chat* wallah would usually begin with about half a dozen *puchkas*. These crispy, hollow *puris*, stuffed with chickpeas and potato, spiced with cumin, coriander and chillies and dipped into a vat full of tamarind water, perched temptingly on the *chat* wallah's

41

stand. Popping the *puchkas* whole into his mouth caused an explosion of flavours for Errol, until the chillies forced him to stop the process and recover.

Errol had become the *chat* wallah's best friend and the wallah would offer him an extra *puchka* for free, or if Errol had a friend with him, the wallah would allow them both to eat for the price of one. And Errol sailed through it all without the slightest harm to himself.

'Well, it's time I was going,' said Phillip. 'I've got some private tuition to give at six and I don't want to be late.'

'It was a nice chat,' said Joan. 'Do come round any time if you want. We're nearly always in.'

'Thanks, I'll take you up on that.' Phillip seemed grateful for the invitation. He was quite used to being invited to homes but it was usually with strings attached, as someone wanted to introduce him to a daughter. Although Anglo-Indian women had considerable autonomy in choosing a love-match for themselves, their mothers were always anxious that they played a part in making sure the men seeing their daughters were suitable candidates. So Phillip was frequently invited to tea or to birthday parties or to lunch after mass on a Sunday. Although he'd never had the opportunity to indulge in irresponsible behaviour in his teens or his early adulthood, he often felt the urge to sabotage these parties so he wouldn't be invited again. But he never did.

Errol came back into the room just as he was leaving. 'Errol, perhaps you and I could go down to Liluah station and watch the trains sometime,' he said. 'What do you say?'

The young boy's eyes lit up like oil lamps at *Diwali*.

THE COFFEE HOUSE

'Anil, what are you doing here?' asked Joan, seeing an old pupil of hers from Don Bosco's at the Coffee House, the newly opened meeting place for the middle classes in Calcutta.

She knew she'd seen the boy recently and tried to remember where.

'Ah, miss, good morning, how are you?' said Anil Sen.

'I'm fine. Weren't you at the coroner's inquiry a few days ago? You were wearing that checked shirt at the time. I remember.' Joan saw past pupils frequently but seldom recognised them as they grew quickly from boys to young men just months after leaving school.

'Yes, miss, I was in the same B.Com class as Agnes,' said Anil, impressed by the directness of his ex-teacher.

'How are you and how are your college studies going?'

'It was good until the tragic death of Agnes, miss,' said Anil with a sadness creeping into his voice that Joan interpreted as something deeper than the accidental loss of a college friend.

'Anil,' she said, concerned, 'can Errol and I join you and you can tell me all about your studies and your lovely family too? That nice sister of yours, now, what was her name?' Joan paused.

'Anita,' said Anil. 'She is doing fine, still at the convent.'

The convent at Bali, a few miles from Calcutta, was popular for the education of the daughters of Bengalis of a certain social standing. The French nuns there not only taught in English, the essential ingredient for a girl's future prospects, but also gave pupils a second European language, so important if they intended to travel abroad.

Errol was in the highest of spirits at being in the Coffee House. He could brag to his cousin Ken about being there and having his favourite, the Tutti Frutti, an extravagant ice cream affair brimming with syrups of all colours, bits of fake cherry and sprinklings of sweet sugary candy.

'What will you have, Anil?' asked Joan.

'The coco milk, please, miss,' said Anil, without looking at the brightly coloured plastic menu, his knowledge clear evidence of many visits.

They waited a while for one of the harassed waiters to come to their table. Anil was uneasy but Joan sensed he wanted to talk.

'The result of the coroner's enquiry was very unsatisfactory, don't you think?' she said, attempting to draw out his interest in the case.

'Yes, miss, very unsatisfactory, as you say. Such a tragic thing to happen to her.'

'What was she like in the class at college?' Joan probed further.

'She always had a peaceful face, miss. Also she was extremely good-looking, we used to say she should be in Hindi films, and all the boys used to be Eve teasing her,' Anil replied, verifying Philomena's words in the court house.

'But I'm sure you didn't, Anil, did you now? You were such a well-behaved boy at school.'

'No, miss, no,' he lowered his voice so as not be heard. 'We had become friends, so to speak, but no one knew. It was a close secret between us.' He paused to get a reaction from Joan.

'Anil, what do you mean close friends? How close? She was a married woman, Anil.' Joan was leaning forward to get an explanation, surprised at the candid nature of the young man's disclosure.

'Miss, he was an AC/DC, you know, both ways, except probably more DC. Agnes discovered that Xavier was having a relationship with one of the boys at the college,' Anil said, defending himself.

Joan retreated into an embarrassed silence for a while and looked down at the table. A dozen thoughts raced through her mind: the despair of the young woman, still in her teens, landed in a desperate marriage with no way out. As an orphan she would have had no family to turn to, and the nuns would not have entertained her return to the orphanage no matter how temporary and whatever her reasons might be.

The waiter arrived and orders were placed, Errol asking for an extra topping of chocolate syrup. He had been preoccupied so far with the surroundings rather than the conversation. The ice cream machine that oozed out the yellow vanilla substance absorbed his attention and he wondered if he could make ice cream like it at home. The whoosh of the Italian coffee maker every few seconds also made him think of steam and engines. Together, these two wonders of Italian culinary science created a fine spectacle for a boy of ten.

Errol had never quite liked Anil at school, as he was one of the bigger boys who always pinched his cheeks and called him 'fatty, fatty boombalaty', a rhyme made up to annoy and tease him. Errol had always been on the porky side thanks to a bit of overfeeding by Joan in his early years. Even now he would drain a huge bowl of porridge every morning. This was no ordinary lean Scot's recipe; it was prepared with full-fat buffalo milk and then topped with sweetened Nestlé's Dairymaid condensed milk. School meals were usually out of a tiffin box laden with *parathas*, kebabs and all sorts of other rich, bodybuilding foods, ensuring that the precious *beta* would not go hungry.

In her more reflective moments, Joan wondered what it might have been like to have had more children, but deep in herself she was quite happy with just Errol. Other Anglo-Indian women of her age would by now have at least half a dozen children, and she enjoyed the relative freedom to come and go, with Errol attaching himself to one of the other families in the apartment block when she needed to be out by herself.

'But I still don't think she took her own life, miss,' said Anil to break the pause in the conversation, already interrupted by an overloud whoosh from the coffee maker.

'Why do you say that?' said Joan, who had begun to believe the suicide theory.

'I just don't believe it. You know, the times we spent

46

together. The plans we made.' Tears were beginning to form in the corner of Anil's eye. He rubbed it hard.

'This is all very sad and must be a big blow to you,' she said. 'I'm so very sorry. I do hope that one day someone gets to the bottom of this. The coroner has kept the case open, so you never know,' she added reassuringly, knowing in her heart that Inspector Basu would probably have to be coerced into getting at all enthusiastic about investigating the case further when he had dozens of unsolved abductions and deaths every week to occupy his force.

The waiter arrived with the Tutti Frutti and the hot drinks. This gave Anil a moment to regain his composure and Joan an opportunity to try to lift his spirits.

'Well, it's the new term now and we have a new teacher at Don Bosco's, a man,' said Joan.

'Ah, miss, is he a brother?'

'No, a layperson who has joined us from one of the schools in Darjeeling. His name is Phillip John,' said Joan.

'Do you like him, miss?' asked Anil innocently, trying to get an early approval rating of the new male teacher.

'Well it's too early to say; he's only been at the school for a few days. But look Anil,' she said, still wanting to help, 'if you ever want to talk about anything, please come and see me. You know where I live. Or call by the school one day after your classes are over. Losing a friend is hard, and particularly in such a tragic way.'

Anil hesitated. 'Well, miss, there is one thing.'

'What is it?'

'We'd, that is Philomena and I, we'd really like you to help us uncover the truth behind Agnes's death. No one would take us seriously really, we're just students. But you're a well-loved teacher at Don Bosco's and the school has a lot of respect in the community. We'd like your help with the inspector, with the judge and all those important people who just wouldn't talk to us.'

'I think you're overestimating my influence, but I'll see what I can do. I do find it unfair that someone so young has died without anybody even knowing why.'

Errol had got to the end of his Tutti Frutti and there were people queuing to get tables, such was the popularity of the Coffee House. It was time to go home. Anil's request for help played over and over in her mind as she and Errol caught the number 54 bus back. They stood all the way as a group of *hijiras* monopolised the ladies' section and no one gave her a seat.

HARTAL

Philomena Thomas had managed to escape the match-making of Sister Theresa. She had left the orphanage at sixteen to become nanny to the family of the managing director of Guest Keith Williams, an engineering firm with a range of manufacturing facilities in Calcutta.

Having been taught to cut her own hair, she had a short, black, uneven mass that looked like it had never been brushed or combed in its life. She had always been the athletic type and although the nuns did not encourage boyish behaviour in their girls she would frequently go for a sprint at break times, do press-ups and all manner of things that she'd read about in the 1948 *Annual for Girls*, which featured the women athletes competing in the London Olympics that year. Her strong, muscular legs could outrun any boy and she longed for the chance to further her physical training.

Philomena was transported from an austere life with the nuns to a comfortable one in a large bungalow in the smart Calcutta district of Alipore, where her duties consisted of accompanying the managing director's two children to school in the morning in a chauffeured Ambassador, bringing them back at four o'clock and helping them with their homework.

That gave her plenty of time to further her own education, for Philomena believed that she was destined for great things. India, the place of her birth, was a fledgling country, rich in opportunity, and she intended to be a part of the glorious new age despite being a woman, without an extended family and without the vital connections which opened the country's most impenetrable doors.

She decided to enrol on the bachelor of commerce course at Calcutta College, and she funded the tuition out of her small nanny's salary of a few hundred rupees a month.

Bengal festered with political intrigue, with several campaigning parties vying for power as they walked down the pathways of the new democracy. The parties split roughly along two lines: those that supported Nehru's Congress, quasi-Gandhian point of view, and those that took the Marxist line.

The state of Kerala boasted the first-ever democratically elected Marxist state anywhere in the world, and this had made some communists pause and reflect on the advantages of gaining popular support through the ballot box rather than the gun.

Philomena decided to join the Workers' Revolutionary Movement of Bengal after her first week at college when she went to a meeting in the students' union. The Movement wished to bring down the current establishment by all means at its disposal and this had caused an ideological split away from the main Communist Party.

'How can you join such a party, Phil?' Agnes had said. 'They don't believe in God.'

'The Movement has its own interpretation of the Marxist doctrine, Aggie. Many of us come from different religions but we don't let that contaminate the main ideal of the equal distribution of wealth and the destruction of the capitalist model. You know many say that Jesus Christ was a Marxist.'

'But Phil, the big communist nations just seem so bloodthirsty. Look at what Mao is doing to the middle classes and the academics in China; look at Stalin, purging millions of his own countrymen. You don't propose that, do you?'

'Well, not killing people because that is not the Indian way. But certainly we need to use our own weapons such as strikes, *hartals* and fasts to bring about a revolution here in Bengal. The multinationals will kill India if we don't. This is new, twentieth-century colonialism.'

'Philomena, you work for the managing director of one of the biggest multinationals in India.'

But Philomena managed to put this and her Catholicism to one side in pursuit of her political ideals.

The firm of Guest Keith Williams was involved in heavy and light engineering and had been established by British owners in the early part of the century. They built, repaired and maintained equipment, locomotives, ships and everything that involved mechanical engineering. They considered themselves an important part of the building of this new nation. While many established British

51

companies had sold their operations to private Indian interests, Guest Keith had no intention of doing so, despite several approaches from a wealthy, family-owned firm.

Charles Smith was the new managing director at Guest Keith, not an old-colonial India hand but a distinguished engineer, who qualified at Imperial College in London and joined the company in the English Midlands. This was his first major management job, and the Calcutta head office was being used as a testing ground for bigger things elsewhere.

In his opening address to his employees, he had written thus:

Dear friends,

> *I'm delighted to have been asked to take on the job of managing director of this splendid company here in India and I hope that I can fulfil my ambition to continue to make this a rewarding place to work.*
>
> *I know that we face a number of challenges in the years ahead and I hope that you will join me in addressing and solving the most difficult issues. I see three issues that we must tackle in the coming year with our best endeavours.*
>
> *I'm aware that our productivity has fallen way behind other units of the company and if we cannot improve our position we will not enjoy the levels of investment that are necessary to sustain our future.*
>
> *That means cutting our levels of absenteeism, working in more flexible ways and cutting out job demarcation. It also means that we need to restrict*

*excessive wage demands every year unless we can
actually increase our productivity. And finally, it
means equal opportunity for all based on merit and
not class, caste or religion.*

*Please consider my office always open to those of
you who have ideas on how we can do this or indeed
disagree with my proposals.*

> *Best wishes and regards,*
> *Mr Charles Smith,*
> *Managing Director*

By any standards this open approach was unusually
enlightened. In India such openness was unheard of. How
did this person combine the ideals of capitalism,
Gandhism and Marxism into a single mantra? Was he a
serious businessman? It soon became apparent he was.

One of his early actions was to issue instructions to the
personnel department that no future wage negotiations
could take place with the unions unless they were linked
to productivity improvements to pay for the increases.

He then asked that strict caps be put on absenteeism,
with eventual dismissal if the problems persisted, and
finally he instructed that any mention of caste, religion or
other personal background be struck off all employment
forms or data records when people were being considered
for a job or for promotion.

It was not long afterwards that Mr Kuldeep Singh, his
personnel manager, was knocking on his door. 'Sir, I'm
having to report much hooting from the union
representatives.'

'Come again, Mr Singh, hooting? I'm not familiar with that term,' said Smith quizzically.

'Hooting, sir, angry exchanges, you know, threats of violence and even *hartal* for the company if you don't withdraw your comments in the newsletter,' said Singh helpfully.

'Bring the ringleaders to me, Mr Singh, and I will explain to them why we need to work together. This is not an "us" and "them" situation. This is the twentieth century.'

'Sir, most respectfully, this is not being the twentieth century here in Bengal. These are nasty *goondas*, sir. They are receiving encouragement from other companies too, sir, to make our life very difficult,' Singh tried to explain.

Kuldeep Singh, a Sikh veteran from the Indian Army, had taken up a second career in commerce and personnel management after his unit had been disbanded following the disastrous Burma Campaign.

He knew the shop steward and some of his close cohorts were not just union activists, but indulged in other unsavoury practices to supplement their income at the company. Then there was the rumour that other firms had infiltrated the union to help bring down GKW. The union reps never seemed to do any real work and the company had allowed them to continue in this role for fear of destabilising the work force irreparably.

The workers, just content to have a job, mostly ignored their union representatives but dared not vote against them for fear of recriminations. And so the status quo had continued until Charles Smith came to take over the running of the company in India.

Philomena was leaving the Smith home one afternoon when the chauffeured car was stopped outside the gates of the bungalow by a chanting group of flag-waving men with Workers' Revolutionary Movement of Bengal banners that read 'GKW out of Bengal'. They stopped the driver and asked him not to cross the picket line.

The chauffeur did not dare drive through the crowd unless there was a police escort to protect him: he and his family would live in fear forever. So he complied with the instructions of the crowd, to many cheers, and went back into the bungalow with Philomena in the car. Philomena, too, was secretly thankful she hadn't had to cross the lines.

There remained the problem of going to pick up the two children from Don Bosco's School by four o'clock. There was only half an hour to get to the school. Mrs Smith was away for a ladies' tea gathering at the Alipore club, so Philomena had to act alone to bring the children safely back home.

Shielding herself from the sun and from identification by the picket lines, she slipped away to catch a bus and pick up the children. The road was long and heavily potholed and the bus stopped every few minutes to pick up passengers: passengers often accompanied by their livestock.

At the school Joan noticed the Smith children standing at the gates looking quite sorry for themselves. All the others had now departed with their rickshaws, parents, aunties, uncles or servants.

The children stood at the gates looking lost but as well groomed and clean as they did first thing in the morning. Terence was seven, blond and blue eyed, and Oliver, darker haired and slightly taller than his older brother, had just turned six. Both boys were something of a novelty at the school as they were the only 'foreigners' on the register. They were aware of their unique status and stayed close to each other most of the time, more out of security than a genuine yearning.

'What's happened, boys?' asked Joan in a soothing voice, seeing that they seemed anxious. 'Has your car not arrived?' She got a couple of silent shaking heads.

'Come with me into reception and sit down with the *chowkeedar* for a while. I'm sure it will be along in a minute. The traffic is so bad these days,' she added reassuringly.

Joan called the Smith home and failed to get a response, so she decided to take the two children back with her until the driver arrived, telling the *chowkeedar* to send the driver over to her flat to collect them.

It was gone six o'clock when there was a knock on her door. Joan was rather taken aback to find Philomena standing outside.

'Mrs D'Silva?'

Joan nodded.

'I'm so sorry it's late but I've come to collect the Smith children. There was trouble with some pickets and we couldn't get the car out of the drive.'

'Oh, I see. Well that's OK then. I've been getting them to do a bit of homework to pass the time. Do come in for a minute. Will you have a quick cup of tea? It must have been a long journey on that terrible number 54 bus.'

'Well I shouldn't really but I will, as I've asked the *chowkeedar* to call a taxi and it might be a while. So thank you.'

Joan boiled the kettle while Philomena went over to the children and told them that everything was fine and

56

that they would be home soon. They seemed quite content to be with one of the teachers and Errol had joined them to finish off his homework.

'Weren't you at the coroner's enquiry the other day, Philomena?' said Joan, not forgetting the name and the clumsy, old-fashioned dress, or Anil's request for help on his and Philomena's behalf. The girl nodded.

'I don't believe I've seen you with the children before.'

'No, I usually pick them up at the school gates. But I've heard about you, Mrs D'Silva.'

'Oh yes, from whom?' asked Joan, though she thought she could guess.

'From Anil, whom you taught when he was at Don Bosco's.'

'Ah, so the three of you, Agnes, Anil and yourself, were all in the same class.'

'That's right, Mrs D'Silva.'

'But I thought you told the coroner that Agnes didn't know anyone really well other than yourself.' Joan was curious.

'That's correct. Agnes and I were close friends and we both tried to keep it that way.'

Joan felt uneasy. Could it be possible that the girl didn't know of the relationship between Anil and Agnes? Who was she trying to protect?

'Tell me, Philomena, do you think Agnes took her own life?' asked Joan, wanting to get to the point.

'Mrs D'Silva, I was a good friend of hers. We both shared an unfortunate start in life but were united in our ambition to make something out of our lives, unlike our parents who abandoned us. She was not a quitter but she had a lot of problems. Xavier was an unsuitable husband for her and she was trying to make an independent life here in Cal. Because she was so beautiful, she believed that she could get all she wanted out of men and sometimes it went too far. That's all I can say at this time.' She gave a little shudder and fell silent, but immediately there was a knock on the door; the taxi had arrived.

'I don't understand,' said Joan. 'What did she do to compromise herself?'

'That's all I can say, Mrs D'Silva,' repeated Philomena as she backed out of the door and took the boys home.

Industrial relations at GKW worsened. There were more walkouts and demonstrations and then the increasingly militant arm of the Workers' Revolutionary Movement reached out to grab the opportunity being presented to it. Custom and work practices in most companies were grossly inefficient and privately owned groups stayed out of Bengal due to the worsening state of labour relations, combined with the personal risk to management.

Philomena went to a meeting at her college one evening when the steward of the company's union branch came to address the activists. Speaking in Bengali he set out the case for a mass demonstration and *hartal* to teach GKW's new managing director a lesson.

'Brothers and sisters, the curse of the multinationals is increasing every day and now is the time to curb their unlimited power. The new managing director, Mr Charles Smith, thinks he can propagate his imperialist ways but we need to prove him wrong.

'He asks us to cut our wages to maximise the profits of

the company that go back to England and make his bosses very rich. Can you, comrades, let this man make us slaves for nothing? Is this why we fought for our independence from the imperialists? Are we going to let our children starve for the good of the foreign capitalists?'

There were shouts of '*nahi, nahi*!' after every question. The convener then read out a motion that asked all those gathered to support a one day *hartal* against all multi-nationals in Bengal and to get all members to picket every GKW workshop and facility so as to bring the entire company to a stop for one day, and to repeat the action until Charles Smith was recalled to England.

'Does anyone wish to speak against the motion?' asked the convener.

No one seemed likely to oppose the motion until a hand went up in the middle row and Philomena stood up.

'*Didi*, please come to the front and state your objection to the motion,' said the convener in a condescending tone.

'Comrades, for those of you who don't know me, I'm Philomena Thomas. I grew up in an orphanage, had nothing to call my own and still have nothing. Last year I was taken on by Mrs Charles Smith to look after the family's children.'

She paused to get the group's attention and then continued.

'Please forgive me for speaking out against this motion as it stands, but I believe it is an unfair representation of a man and what he stands for. I'm definitely for curbing the power of the multinationals, but Mr Smith in my mind is a force for good here in Bengal.'

There was a shout of 'traitor' initially from the steward

and then many more joined in. The convener called the meeting to order, 'Please could we give our *didi* a chance to put her case.'

She continued, 'I have had many discussions with Mr Smith. I have heard him speak passionately about human rights, the need for all workers to earn a decent wage and the role of women in modern society.' There were more shouts from the floor but Philomena was going to finish her speech. 'I think it is not the right thing at this stage to campaign for his removal but rather to encourage him to negotiate his position. I fear that the company may replace him with a much harder man who will eventually close the company and then so many of us, comrades, will be jobless. Please consider the consequences.'

The steward was on his feet immediately. 'Comrades, don't be intimidated by this woman, who lives with the enemy of the proletariat. Vote for the complete motion.'

The convener then asked Philomena, 'So what is your amendment, *didi*?'

'I move that the sentence relating to the removal of Mr Smith be struck from the motion,' said Philomena.

'So there it is, comrades. As I assume the steward of GKW does not accept the amendment can we first put the original motion to the vote,' instructed the convener.

'Those in favour?' To Philomena's surprise not all the hands were raised. In fact quite a few remained down. 'Those against?' A number of hands went up. 'Abstentions?' And there were many more hands than had been raised previously. The convener had been counting the votes all the time.

'I have the result now. Thirty-one in favour, twenty-eight against and forty abstentions. I therefore consider the motion carried.'

There were shouts of support, applause and some booing. In the commotion Philomena went up to the convener and asked for a recount.

'I have been asked for a recount and according to the constitution we have to grant this in view of the close result,' he said.

To everyone's surprise, at the recount the motion was rejected by ten votes and Philomena's amendment carried unanimously. At eighteen, she was suddenly being noticed by a number of her fellow party members, not least the leader of the Movement who sat on the sidelines, observing the proceedings.

TRAINS

'Good morning, Phillip,' said Joan after mass one Sunday in the Parish hall. This was the occasion when Father Rector kept a tally of how many of his teachers observed the Lord's Day. Don Bosco's Catholic church was the only one for miles and so excuses for non-attendance had to be few and far between.

There was the usual chat between parishioners, and Father Rector circulated among them like a shepherd with his flock, enquiring after their well-being. The De Langes and the Thomases from the railway colony were there, as were Mrs Shrove and her husband and their daughter Audrey, a striking young woman of around twenty with the looks and dress sense of Ginger Rogers.

Phillip couldn't help casting an eye towards her at every opportunity as she talked to family friends. Tea had been served and the buzz in the hall was positively carnival-like. Audrey seemed a woman at ease with herself and the company around her. She smiled effortlessly and conversed combining charm with concern for the people she talked to.

Phillip tried to manoeuvre himself into a situation where he could get an introduction to Audrey but De Lange had pinned him down into a discussion on the worsening situation in Ladakh, where the Chinese army appeared poised to take over most of the Indian state at the foothills of the Himalayas.

'The Americans could be telling these beggars that they'll bomb the living daylights out of the chinks unless they pull back. Instead, Nehru keeps sucking up to the commies in Moscow,' he fumed.

The politics of the sub-continent consumed many column inches in the newspapers and were the heated subject of countless discussions in teahouses, homes and the work place. *Babus* in offices sipped tea procured by their peons and pontificated for at least an hour every morning on the worsening situation before they got around to processing any of the mountains of paperwork for the benefit of expectant citizens waiting for the slow wheels of officialdom to move in their favour.

By the time Phillip had extricated himself from the conversation about the war in Ladakh, Mrs Shrove was saying her goodbyes, and both Audrey and her father had climbed into a large black Citroen limousine to be driven back home. Phillip watched them drive away.

Mr Shrove's ancestors came from Bedfordshire but he had been born in India like his father and several generations before him. He had never visited England, was the first to marry an Anglo-Indian woman and had decided to stay on after independence, continuing in his role as the district manager of the Eastern Railway Carriage and Wagon division. His seniority got him the best house in the colony and a chauffeur-driven car, which enabled the family to live like Rajas, a lifestyle that would not have been achievable in dear old *Blighty*.

Phillip turned back into the hall. He noticed Errol smiling at him. 'Would you like to go and watch some trains this morning?' he asked.

Errol immediately jumped at the idea. 'Ma, can I go with sir to watch the trains please? Please?' pleaded Errol.

Joan was more than pleased for her son to have a bit of male company and agreed immediately. 'Come and have some *chota hazri* with us before you go,' she offered to Phillip.

They ate a bellyful of omelettes and *rotis*, smothered with jam and washed down with cups of tea, sweetened with condensed milk. They talked about the school and the various teachers in the common room and Phillip fished around for more information on Mrs Shrove and Audrey.

'Oh she means well, does Mother Shrove, but she can upset a few people with her la-de-da ways. I mean who would call their husband "Bunny" for God's sake? And she's always talking about the officers' club on Gardiner's Road where they live.'

'Sir, can we go to watch the trains now,' said Errol after he had finally finished his second *roti*.

'Sure, let's get ready. I'll take you on my cycle.'

There were shady palm trees at the local stop on the main line from Howrah. These had circular benches around the base and made an ideal spot to sit and watch the trains.

'Have you heard of James Watt?' asked Phillip.

'No, but what a funny name, sir,' responded Errol, now fully relaxed with the teacher.

'Good pun, Errol. Have you done puns in class?'

'No, what are they?' asked Errol.

'Well you just cracked one. Watt is a name of a person and also used as a question. Get it?' asked Phillip.

In the distance, the roar of a Winnipeg bullet-nosed locomotive signalled the approaching 'three down' Dehra Doon mail. Train routes were numbered using even numbers for outward or 'up' trains and odd numbers for returning trains – so the Doon express was known as the 'four up three down mail'. It was travelling at full throttle with steam billowing out of its pistons. Every muscle in Errol's body tensed with excitement as the train came close then thundered past the platform, making the ground quiver.

'Errol,' asked Phillip during a lull. 'Do you like your school?'

The response was slow in coming, 'Sometimes, sir. I like my science classes but can't do arithmetic very well, and don't understand Mr Sen. And I don't like it when the bigger boys pinch my cheeks and call me fatty. I like writing stories and essays and reading them back in the English class.'

'Well, you know, I didn't like my school very much. The Christian Brothers used the cane a little too much so it made me dread going to classes. I had to leave eventually,' Phillip confided. 'Look, I could help you with your arithmetic. Would you want me to?'

Errol wasn't quite sure how to respond. He'd come to watch trains and being distracted by a conversation about school was not quite what he'd bargained for. 'Thank you, sir,' he said eventually, thinking that this was an offer he shouldn't refuse.

When Errol told Joan that he would be staying back after school she was thrilled. Errol also told her how much he'd enjoyed the trains and wished that Phillip would take him again.

The following week Phillip showed Errol how to do long division, multiply fractions and the finer points of the lowest common denominator. He took time with Errol. He made him practise the solutions again and again until the boy became fluent at working out the answers.

The fog of arithmetic began to clear and soon Errol was getting the magical ten out of ten for his homework. His confidence began to build as his schoolwork improved in all subjects. Joan also noticed an improvement in his general behaviour, his increased confidence and more friends coming back with him after school.

Phillip began popping around to Joan's flat at least a couple of times a week for tea after he had given Errol a lesson. At each meeting they talked more openly about their lives, likes and dislikes.

'That's enough about me,' said Phillip one evening. 'I hardly know anything about you.'

'I can't say my life has been as tough as yours. About the most difficult time I had was losing George,' she answered. 'Not being able to say a proper goodbye to someone you have loved so much was difficult. The pictures I saw of his body for identification gave me nightmares for months after,' she added with a soft sadness in her tone. 'He was a lovely man and I was so lucky to have spent a brief part of my life with him. I doubt I'll ever find anyone else as understanding and as kind as him. He was going up country to the workshops at Burdwan and had to pack in a hurry. Our goodbyes were brief as I expected him back in a couple of days. I read about the disaster in the newspapers the next day: more than a hundred were feared dead and reports were still coming in. When I saw the telegram man approach on his red bike later that day, I knew it was bad news even before he got to our bungalow with the wire. *Mrs D'Silva. Husband feared dead. Please report to Railway Police Howrah,* is all it said, in that abbreviated official tone.'

Phillip and Joan were sitting out on the small veranda of the flat on a couple of cane armchairs. He leant over and held her hand, and she accepted. Neither of them spoke for a while.

'There were only photographs left. Only photographs,' she murmured softly.

The next day was sports day, an annual event at Don Bosco's School. Teachers, pupils, parents and even relatives attended to watch all manner of activities, from the trivial egg and spoon race to the more strenuous shot putt, long jump and four hundred metre relay. Parents came to be seen by other parents and to rejoice in the perception that to have your son at Don Bosco's was quite a privilege.

Portly Punditji was there in saffron *kurta*; the subject of much good-hearted teasing by the boys about his athleticism. '*Aré yar*, how will I be able to run when I am panting out of breath after two minutes of just walking,' he said to those who asked him to join the relay. The sight of Punditji running around the track was a prize worth capturing on the school's Baby Brownie.

'But Punditji, we'll put you in the strongest team so that the other members can make up the time, and we'll give you a nice long handicap so you can start ahead of everyone,' said Kailash, one of the head boys and Phillip's principal bag carrier. 'Even Mrs Shrove, who is much fatter than you, sir, is entering.'

Phillip, dressed in brilliant starched white, with a whistle around his neck, held the starting pistol; it was actually a toy, with those little red caps that you loaded one at a time and frequently didn't fire because they were damp. This occasion was no exception. The runners crouched in their starting positions. Punditji and Mrs Shrove couldn't even touch their knees so just stood upright.

Finally they were under starter's orders and they were off. Punditji waddled with all his might, *kurta* flying in the air and determination on his face. He was fixed on getting somewhere, but not necessarily on the track, and he wove in and out of Mrs Shrove's path, much to her annoyance as she thundered forwards, her large breasts flying ahead of her.

Audrey, dressed in a lime-green cotton dress perfect for this spring day, laughed out loud at the sight of her mother running.

She had come along to support her mother and to cheer up her rather dull weekend. Audrey was cosseted by her parents for fear she might stray. Their darling

68

Audrey had to find just the perfect man and there was certainly no such person on the horizon in the colony's Anglo-Indian community.

Inspector Basu, dressed now in civilian clothes, had come with his wife, who was wearing a mauve silk sari. He cheered along with the crowd, clapping his hands loudly. '*Challo, challo.*' He was unsure who he was cheering for but felt taken along by the hysteria of the crowd and was glad that the heaviness of his police duties was lifted, at least for a while.

Mr and Mrs Smith, who had come to see their children, Terence and Oliver, participate in their first Indian school sports day, smiled at the fun. Mr Smith looked every bit the *burra* sahib in a white linen suit and Panama hat while Mrs Smith wore a two-piece brown and beige cotton outfit; probably purchased a year earlier from a London department store.

In a pause between the races and other events, lemonade was served by the boys from Standard Seven, the senior class of the school. They mingled with the parents and teachers, carrying trays of glasses containing the cold, cloudy drink. After joining in the parents' race, Joan had eventually caught her breath and joined the lemonade drinkers on the lawn, when she noticed Philomena standing on her own, sipping from a glass.

'Philomena, I didn't see you earlier, did you come with Mr and Mrs Smith?' asked Joan.

'No,' said Philomena, looking a bit surprised to see Joan. 'I came with Anil; he is an old boy and wanted to be here. He's talking to Punditji at the moment.'

Joan looked around to catch sight of Anil.

Just then Charles Smith and his wife walked up to Philomena. 'Hello, Philomena, is this Mrs D'Silva?' Terence and Oliver had pointed her out during the race.

'Oh yes, Mrs D'Silva, please, this is Mr and Mrs Smith,' said Philomena awkwardly.

'Pleased to meet you,' said Joan, shaking Charles Smith's soft, weakish hands and noticing by contrast Edwina Smith's firm grip.

'We've heard so much about you from the boys,' said Edwina.

'Very grateful for your kindness the other day, Mrs D'Silva, when we were having a spot of bother down at the bungalow,' said Charles.

'Oh it was nothing. They're such charming boys. Very good manners and so well brought up,' complimented Joan, choosing phrases that would be music to any parent's ears.

'Mrs D'Silva, I trust you will accept our hospitality some time in return, at our place in Alipore. That's if the unions allow you in,' quipped Charles.

'Certainly, and thank you Mr and Mrs Smith,' Joan smiled politely.

Just then Inspector Basu joined the conversation, 'Good afternoon, Mr Smith. Inspector Basu of the Howrah police division. I have been responsible, sir, for guarding some of your workers from intimidation at your works near Balguri.'

'Ah yes, it's been quite ugly there, inspector, thanks for all your efforts. The union has now been joined by several party members from the Workers' Revolutionary Movement, so we have our hands full. There is talk of calling a *hartal* in the coming weeks which would bring down the whole state I presume.'

'Yes, sir, the hooting has been increasing all the time. The *hartal* will come soon. But you must hold your position, sir. If we are not beating these bully *goondas* our future is not good,' Basu said and Smith acknowledged his supportive words with a nod.

'Thanks, inspector, we've still got a bit of fight left in us.'

Mrs Shrove re-emerged in a bright red flouncy frock that she wore with a large white hat: the whole combination seemed to suit her. Audrey was linking her arm with her mother's, smiling vigorously, and Phillip instantly fell in love.

'Mrs Shrove, congratulations on the run, I swear you look like you've lost a few pounds,' he said, walking up to the lemonade stand where mother and daughter were helping themselves to a drink.

'Oh, darling, do you really?' she said with a mock curtsey.

Phillip was dying for an introduction to this wondrous beaming face that lit up the world for him but none came. They were walking towards Mr and Mrs Smith when Phillip blurted out, 'Ah, Mrs Shrove, would your daughter like to join the egg and spoon race? It's especially for our visitors.'

'Oh, Audrey darling, would you? It'll make you very hot and sweaty,' said Mrs Shrove, in an attempt to dissuade her daughter from straying too far from her side.

'Yes, I'd quite like to Mr... I don't believe we've met,' said Audrey, extending her free hand and breaking away from her mother.

'Ah hello, Phillip, err, John, very pleased to meet you.'

Phillip stuttered out the words, barely remembering his own name and almost forgetting to breathe at the touch of her hand, which he thought was the most beautiful and sensitive he had ever felt.

'I'm Audrey; you're the new teacher, aren't you?'

'Yes, just joined a few months ago and still settling in. But come, let me take you to the starting line for the race and get you enlisted,' he said, attempting to get her away from her mother, who was still heading towards Edwina Smith, whom she was dying to meet.

Phillip's pulse rate calmed down as they walked. Audrey kept up her beaming smile as if the whole world around her was a marvellous place she had just discovered. He felt like a child again.

Joan had noticed that Anil and Philomena had been following her for a while, always keeping just a few yards behind.

'Hello, Anil, I saw Philomena earlier and heard you were here too,' she said, turning round to greet them.

'Miss, I can't keep away from the old school sports days,' said Anil.

'Mrs D'Silva, can we find a quiet place to talk to you?' said Philomena abruptly.

'Why of course,' said Joan, not too surprised by the strange request in the middle of sports day. 'Let's go to the reception area and find a corner where we won't be disturbed.'

'Well,' she said when they were seated away from the hustle and bustle of the sporting activities, 'how can I help you two?'

'Miss,' said Anil, 'we have obtained some additional information about Agnes and Xavier which is quite disturbing.'

'Yes?' nodded Joan, still not really engaged in the conversation.

'I think I told you that Xavier was keeping up this sexual relationship with a boy in our college. He and the boy had a fight a few weeks ago when he started another relationship and this guy got drunk with one of my friends last week. That's when he told him this story that I'm not sure whether to believe or not.'

'And what was the story, Anil?' coaxed Joan.

'He was trying to get Agnes to be a prostitute,' cut in Philomena. 'Apparently Xavier acts as a high-class fixer or pimp, I think they call them, at the Grand Hotel, for rich foreigners who stay there. Xavier knew that he and Agnes would never consummate their relationship so he was encouraging her to make their fortune by sleeping with clients.'

Joan tried not to show her surprise and found herself immediately defending Xavier. 'Are you sure this wasn't just a drunken, jealous lover making mischief?'

'The thing is, miss, we can't be sure and then also we can't ignore it. That's why we really wanted to talk to someone like you about it. You...' Anil was lost for words.

'Yes, I understand. How can we get to the bottom of this?' asked Joan. 'Why don't you tell Inspector Basu? It's his job to follow up these leads.'

'No, miss, then we'll be questioned in the *thana* and maybe even put on the list of suspects. There are some bad people involved in this whole affair, real *goondas* who have influence with the authorities,' said Anil.

'But that's just all wrong,' said Joan.

'Miss, if you were to find some evidence yourself, that would protect us and our sources,' said Philomena. And Anil added, 'Remember, as I told you before in the Coffee House, you are more capable of getting Agnes some justice than us.'

'So you want me to be Miss Marple in all of this?'

'I don't understand,' said Anil, frowning slightly. He had not read Agatha Christie.

'Look, you two, I know Agnes was a dear friend and you want to uncover the truth about her death, but I'm just a humble teacher, a widow, and it's a bad world out there.' She looked at their faces and sighed. 'I can't promise anything, but let me see what I can find out myself.'

Again, Joan felt drawn further into this mystery that seemed to get murkier by the minute. She felt irritated at the growing turbulence the Bandle Girl was causing in her life. It was as though a cyclone of trouble was beginning to swirl around her, picking up the debris of misdeeds, injustice and incompetence by authorities and damage to young lives. There she was, caught in the middle of this circle, wondering if she should stay and fight, or just walk away before it engulfed her.

FORBIDDEN AFFAIR

It wasn't long after sports day that Phillip and Audrey began seeing each other regularly, on the quiet of course, and definitely not with the approval of Ma Shrove or 'Bunny' Bernard, who couldn't see past Phillip's dark skin and teacher's salary. At first it was tennis at the officers' club in the railway colony; later it progressed to badminton and then tea at Firpos in town. But it was at the Metro Cinema that the affair reached its steamy heights.

'Mother dear, I'm off to the pictures tonight with June,' Audrey declared on Saturday morning at breakfast. June was a friend from boarding school who was doing a spell as an assistant secretary to the managing director of P&O in Calcutta.

'Oh, and can I take Citrobelle, Daddy?'

The family had a habit of naming inanimate objects. The Citroën was Citrobelle, Audrey's bike was Tinkerbelle and Bunny even referred to his favourite sofa as Bertha.

'Yes, I suppose so, darling,' said her father; as long as she was taken there by the chauffeur and brought back, they knew she was under some domestic protection.

Very soon Audrey was meeting Phillip every Saturday evening at the Metro for the six o'clock performance after dismissing her chauffeur for the evening. Phillip would buy the best seats at the back of the cinema, somewhere at the end of the last row, which was a favourite with courting couples.

This was by far the darkest part of the auditorium and the couple would snuggle down to watch the adverts. But soon the moving images and accompanying sounds were just a blur. Holding hands soon gave way to French kissing, something Audrey had only heard June brag about. And then the film didn't get much attention.

Full intercourse was never an option, for they had both been schooled in the grievous sin of sex before marriage, and it was a cinema, but they tried as much as they could with their clothes on.

So Phillip and Audrey missed the antics of Jack Lemmon and Tony Curtis trying to woo Marilyn Monroe, and Trevor Howard's simmering love scenes with Celia Johnson. Audrey did, however, cast more than a glance at the young Elvis through the torrid love-making in the back row.

After the film they walked the few hundred yards to the Grand where Pat Tarley, Calcutta's most adored singer, performed in Cabaret till midnight. It cost Phillip a princely sum to get a table at the Grand, especially after tipping the head waiter for 'smoochers' corner', as it was known. That was how Phillip got to know Xavier Lal.

'Mr John, the usual? And how is the young lady?' he would say with a wink.

76

'Do you know that fellow? He gives me the creeps,' Audrey said the first time she met him.

'Oh, he's not a bad chap after all,' answered Phillip, 'just a bit slimy with the charm.'

As Tarley, with her backing quintet, sang those dreamy lyrics to 'I'll Be Loving You Always', close into the microphone, Phillip and Audrey danced, holding each other close in the shadows. The fact that their love was not sanctioned drew them tighter, but there always lingered the belief that it could not go on forever.

As twelve approached Audrey tore herself away with a final long kiss goodnight before meeting her chauffeur outside on Chowringhee for the drive back home before midnight.

Phillip was increasingly distracted from his work. Errol's lessons with him became sporadic and he stopped dropping into Joan's for tea, until one day after school she saw him by the school gates shouting at one of the street vendors for setting up his stall inside the school precinct. Joan thought his behaviour wasn't in keeping with his normally calm, self-assured exterior.

'You haven't been around for tea lately. What's been keeping you?' she enquired in an attempt to establish contact.

'Been very busy with things, you know.'

'Not too busy to come over for a cup of tea, I hope,' said Joan, only barely hiding her desire to find out what was actually going on in Phillip's life.

It was an offer he couldn't turn down. There was no one in the world other than Joan that Phillip could talk to about the state he was in, not in a way that wouldn't be around the school like the flu. So he accepted.

They sat together on the veranda and Phillip told Joan of his romance.

'Well now, I'd never have guessed,' she said, trying to conceal her disappointment. 'You've kept up the secret rather well.'

'Yes, but I'm not sure where it's all going to end.'

'Why don't you just see where it all goes? Go with the flow, Phillip. Time sorts stuff out.'

Joan's homespun counsel seemed to take a weight off his mind and Phillip slept soundly that night for the first time in months.

But everything, as ever, was about to change.

Australia was quoted by many in the Anglo-Saxon world as the new land of hope for people looking to make a fresh start in life. The Australian government promoted this perception as a means of attracting would-be immigrants to the country in the post-war years. They needed to fuel the growth necessary for the country to keep up an improving standard of living, in step with most of the developed world.

Their preference was for white Europeans from England and Ireland but as those pools dried up, they cast their net wider, to Italy, Greece and beyond. At about the same time, many of the ex-British colonies were disgorging thousands of people of British descent who preferred not to go back home to wet old England. And there were many Anglo-Indians who were also seeking a future home where the climate, the language and the culture were not too unlike their own.

Mrs Caruthers was the Australian High Commissioner's agent in Calcutta, appointed to filter out the undesirables amongst the hundreds of hopefuls who applied to emigrate. Colour, or at least a lack of it, was usually high on the list of things that she was looking for, which also included age, dependants and so on. The whiter you were, the better you got on with Mrs Caruthers and the more likely it was that you would be placed in one of the better cities of eastern Australia. If you were an outstanding candidate in all respects other than that you were brown, she just might let you make it to Perth.

So Mrs Caruthers became well known in the Anglo-Indian community as an ogre whom you had to get past to qualify, and she was the topic of many discussions over tea and canasta. The Shrove family went for their interview with Mrs Caruthers well briefed and did not expect a problem. They could trace their parentage back to England for generations.

'So, what is your reason for choosing Australia?' Mrs Caruthers sounded like the head inquisitor of a truth commission. She hadn't uttered a word until then.

'We're looking to settle somewhere where we and our daughter can continue our lives in a way that reflects our own culture. I'm concerned about the way things are going here and that most of our kind are leaving. We don't want to be the last ones left,' said Mrs Shrove in a well-rehearsed reply.

Caruthers scrutinised the three from head to toe. 'Mr Shrove, what work do you intend to do in Australia?' she asked eventually.

'I've been managing the entire Carriage and Wagon

division here in Eastern Railways for over ten years, so I suppose I'll look for something in management. I'm good at getting people to do things, been told I can stay on here if I like till I'm fifty-five. So I think I've been rather well regarded for what I do,' he said.

'Mr Shrove, I don't see any engineering qualifications or university degree. What is your official profession? What school-leaving qualifications do you have? Any Senior Cambridge passes?' probed the inquisitor.

'No, not really. We didn't do that in my day. I just turned up for work at sixteen and they found me a job on the benches doing filing and finishing at the works in Kharagpur. I just went on from there. So I'd look for a role as a managing director of an engineering firm or something in that line.'

'Mr Shrove, you are being very naïve in your estimation of what you might get as a job in Australia. You are going to a literate country, where education counts. At fifty you're only going to get something in your line of work if you have demonstrated the greatest talent in Australia, not here in India, where I'm afraid you might be rather a big frog in a small pond, if you'll pardon the expression. No, I believe you will have to be prepared to do something quite below your current expectations.' Then she turned to Audrey. 'Miss Shrove, what do you intend to do?'

'I'm planning to take my secretarial exams and work in an office, madam,' said Audrey, charming as usual.

'And is there a boyfriend or fiancé here that might follow?'

'No, not at all,' said Mrs Shrove in a flash.

'I was asking the girl,' snapped Mrs Caruthers.

'No, madam, not really,' lied Audrey.

Two weeks later the Shroves received a letter from the Australian High Commissioner noting their application to immigrate to Australia and approving the application, with permission to settle in Melbourne. Mrs Shrove was ecstatic, calling all her friends to tell them the news.

'We're so delighted, darling, to be going to our new sunny home. We can't wait.'

The same day Mrs Shrove had an unexpected caller: June's mother. June was Audrey's supposed companion at the movies and had provided a convenient alibi for her Saturday evenings with Phillip.

'Darling Mildred,' said Mrs Shrove, 'how lovely to see you! We've just had some very good news. We're off to Australia in three months: Melbourne. Can you believe it?' And she shrieked with delight. 'Now tell me your news, we haven't seen you in ages. You *gussa* with us?'

'No, no, dear, nothing of the sort, we've been up in the hills, in Nainital, getting away from this horrible muggy weather,' said Mildred.

'Nainital? What, all of you?'

'Yes of course, dear, we wouldn't risk leaving our June by herself in Cal at her age, dear. She's only just turned twenty.'

'You mean she hasn't been out with Audrey lately? At the weekend?'

'Well no. I can't see how. Why, what's wrong dear, why are you looking so grumpy?'

Audrey's deception was uncovered and, when Mildred left, Mrs Shrove barged into the garden where her daughter was reading a two-week-old edition of *Tidbits* that kept the family in touch with all the London news.

'Bunny, where are you?' she yelled. 'Come here, we've got some talking to do with our daughter.'

'Mummy darling, what is it?' said Audrey with one of her rare frowns.

'You've been deceiving us, for weeks. Who have you been going to the pictures with? Now, tell me the truth.' Mrs Shrove had become deep red with rage.

Audrey had to confess to her liaisons with Phillip. She could not hold the secret back, seeing her mother in such a temper.

'How could you, Audrey?'

'He was very nice to me, Mummy, that's all.'

'That *kala* blighter, black as the ace of spades, how dare he mess with our daughter,' said Bunny, coming up and catching the end of the conversation.

'Think of your future with him, on a teacher's salary and all. What would become of you? Look at all the Anglo-Indian women in this colony and in Cal with their millions of children and not a penny to rub together,' said Mrs Shrove, still red and raging.

'Ma, it was only a bit of fun,' pleaded Audrey.

'Fun indeed! You can't trust people like him and you've no experience with men. Just think what could have happened to you,' Bunny took over the parental savaging.

Fortunately for Audrey the news from the Australian High Commission continued to linger in her parents' minds and it helped to bring the tirade to an early end. But she had to promise never to see Phillip again.

That Saturday evening Audrey failed to appear at the Metro. Phillip was heartbroken. He waited for hours outside the cinema, looking like an abandoned child. The performance of *Bridge over the River Kwai* began and ended but there was still no sign of Audrey. So he decided to walk over to the Grand just in case she had gone there directly, being late for the pictures.

When he got there Xavier said, 'Mr John, are you on your own tonight? No girlfriend?'

Phillip was lost for words, 'I think she has been held up. Perhaps I'll wait for her. The usual please.'

He sat for at least a couple of hours watching other couples dance the way that he and Audrey had done each Saturday night. Every few minutes he closed his eyes and wished Audrey would come walking up to the table and kiss him. He'd read somewhere about the power of mind over matter and tried desperately to put it into practice. The more he tried the worse he felt. A dark cloud of despair descended over Phillip.

Finally he decided to leave and called for the bill. Xavier came over and said, 'Never mind, sir, there are plenty of other nice girls. I'm sure a handsome man like you is not having a problem. You be seeing me, sir, if you need one.'

'And you know lots of "nice" girls, do you?' said Phillip, unable to control the irony in his voice.

'This is being the very valuable part of my job, sir, important men are coming here to the Grand and they are running away, sir, from the *garbar* of everyday living, wives only complaining, business problems and so on. Even the foreigners are escaping from something, sir, I can see it in their eyes. Anglo-Indian girls are coming here too because they know that I can be getting them to escape for one night from their drunken father or mother in so much crowded, miserable places at Elliot Road or McCluskieganj. They are beautiful girls and they are getting a good time. So you see, sir, I'm providing a service.'

'And you get what out of it?'

'Usually, sir, a nice tip from men who are pleased with my introduction. It helps me increase my little income from the hotel. The management are exploiting me, sir.'

'But that's nothing short of being a "pimp", Xavier. You know in English what that means? Anyway it's illegal.'

'Sir, pimp, limp, I don't know. Many people are liking my service.'

Phillip was in no mood to convince Xavier of the error and possible dangers of the way he went about his duties. He paid his bill and left for home.

On Monday morning when Phillip was about to go to school, the postman arrived with a letter addressed to him. The writing on the envelope was in Audrey's hand. He was quick to slice open the fold and pull out the letter. It read:

Dear Phillip,

This letter has been hard to write. I'm really sorry I will not make Saturday night, which you will have discovered by the time you have received this letter. Mother and Daddy have sent me away for the week as they discovered that we had been seeing each other and were not well pleased.

In addition, we have been accepted to emigrate to Australia and given this I thought it would not be practical for us to pursue our relationship because of the additional complications this might cause.

I will never forget our wonderful evenings together and how you made me feel like a woman and going to the pictures again will never be the same. I do hope that you find someone who will do credit to your tremendous sensitivity and generosity of spirit. I'm sure you will.

Remembering you always,
Audrey

FALLOUT

When Phillip went into school, the common room was buzzing with news of the Shroves' intended departure to Australia and, even more interestingly for gossip mongers, the discovery of the affair between Phillip and Audrey.

Nobody mentioned the subject in the common room until Joan did, careful to do so when Phillip wasn't there. She had never liked Mrs Shrove's superior attitude, and although she was privately disappointed when Phillip took after Audrey, she was outraged when he told her about the Dear John letter.

'So are Audrey and Phillip going to be engaged before you go to Australia?' asked Joan mischievously.

Mrs Shrove's face changed to the colour of her lipstick. 'I don't ruddy well think so. Not if I have anything to do with it. The audacity of that man thinking that he was good enough for my Audrey.'

'Most of us think he's rather dishy. What exactly do you have against him?'

'Tell me, what are his prospects for a start, and anyway

they won't allow darkies into Melbourne. I'm not having my Audrey live away from us because of some colour bar. And look at the life that all of you have with your wonderful husbands, those of you that have them. They're happier with their saxophones and drums and parties than with getting a real job.'

'You know, Mrs Shrove, I'm really pleased that people like you are leaving us here in India and joining that lot of depraved sheep stealers and society's rejects in Australia.' Joan had turned up the temperature and the rest stared back at Mrs Shrove for her response, like a crowd at a badminton match, switching their gaze from player to player.

'I've never been insulted so much in all my life. I'm going to report this to Father Rector,' stuttered Mrs Shrove.

'Please go ahead. Good riddance,' said Joan, walking out of the room to her class shaking slightly and surprised with herself for having spoken her mind. She wasn't sure if her outburst was due to the way she felt about Phillip's mistreatment or simply Mrs Shrove's bigotry and prejudice.

When Phillip heard of the exchange he felt better for knowing that someone was on his side. No one had stood up for him like this before, despite the many setbacks in his professional and private life.

'Joan, I heard about your comments in the common room,' he said as soon as he saw her. 'Thanks. I couldn't have said what you did. I'm still smarting,' he told her.

'Oh, it wasn't much at all. I just happen to hate prejudice and hypocrisy. You must feel furious.'

'I've been educated at the University of Hard Knocks

so I'll get over it. Especially with your help.'

'Well I can certainly knock you about a bit,' said Joan, trying to lighten the conversation by punching him on the shoulder. This had the desired effect and they chuckled over Mrs Shrove, her attempt at running on sports day and the look on her face when Joan told her she was going to a land of sheep stealers.

But Joan had other, more disturbing, things on her mind. She hadn't heard from Anil and Philomena in the weeks since her brief conversation with them about Xavier Lal. This was a seedy, unfamiliar world in which she had no experience. She had heard about the reputation of Lindsay Street, but had never been propositioned or harassed when she walked there during weekends. Whatever went on there happened out of sight, behind closed doors.

'Can't say I know much about Lindsay Street myself,' said Phillip when Joan asked him if he knew anything about the world of prostitution in Calcutta. 'Why do you ask?'

'I'm just curious if that girl, Agnes, was mixed up in anything funny.'

'That's quite a leap of the imagination, Joan, from a possible suicide to a prostitution ring bumping her off. But you know, a funny thing happened to me last week. You remember the evening I got jilted by Audrey? Well, that strange waiter with the affected mannerisms at the Grand asked me if he could fix me up. The last thing I wanted that evening.'

'You didn't catch his name at all, did you?' asked Joan, her suspicions immediately aroused.

'Xavier, I think. Tallish guy with red henna hair, very odd. Said he provides a sort of dating service.'

Joan's heart missed a beat at the mention of Xavier. Anil's claims might be closer to the truth than she had thought. How could she find out more? It was no use talking to Inspector Basu as Joan was just a witness to the discovery of the corpse, nothing more. She had to find Anil and Philomena again. She decided to take up the invitation to visit Mr and Mrs Smith at Alipore, in an effort to talk to Philomena.

Errol was only a little older than Terence, the eldest Smith boy, so she took him along the next Sunday for lunch. Edwina Smith was very pleased to see Joan as she looked forward to some company outside the claustrophobic ladies' tea circle to which she belonged.

Edwina was a graduate of Girton, the women's college at Cambridge, where she had studied history. She had very much looked forward to coming to India when she heard that her husband had been posted there. But the reality of being closeted in a bungalow surrounded by ten-foot walls and frequently chanting mobs of people outside was not what she had bargained for.

'Joan, tell me about you. I know absurdly little about anyone here. Even Philomena keeps her life to herself; I've no idea what she does in her spare time,' said Edwina over the lentil soup which had been served piping hot and which Joan found burned her tongue. Philomena, who was at the table, didn't say a word. She was always invited to Sunday lunch as she helped the boys in the afternoon with their homework. Joan noticed that her hair was longer and she had begun to tie it in plaits which made her look more mature, fitting her role as a nanny. Gone too was the hand-me-down, ill-fitting dress, and she now wore a long, navy-blue skirt and white shirt blouse, clearly tailored for her.

'There's not much to say, Mrs Smith,' Joan began hesitantly.

'First name terms please, Joan. Edwina is easier.'

'I'm a single parent as you know. My husband died five years ago. I've been fortunate to find a job as a teacher at Don Bosco's and, although the pay isn't great, together with my widow's pension we make ends meet.'

'Joan, it must be very difficult as a single woman in India?'

'You know, I've been so tied up in getting on with life that it hadn't occurred to me. I have one thing in my favour, I suppose. That is I come from an Anglo-Indian community where women generally have more freedom than if I was a Bengali or Bihari or whatever.'

'Do tell me more about your community. We meet quite a few Anglo-Indians in church but they all appear to work in the railways or seem underemployed.'

'We're going through quite a hard time, Edwina. Independence came as a bit of a shock. We lost our privileged position as the trusted servants of the British. It's going to take a few generations to acclimatise. Many have decided to leave and seek their futures elsewhere, in England, Australia or Canada. I'm not sure they're any better off because from what I hear they have just the same problems there as they have here.'

'That poor young woman we read about in *The Statesman*, the Bandle Girl, I think they called her,' chipped in Charles. 'What a sorry affair. Now she was Anglo-Indian, wasn't she?'

'I don't know, from her photos she looks like one of us.

She was found as a baby by the nuns at the orphanage steps,' said Joan.

'This business of making sure that women are married off in their teens, it's barbaric, don't you think?' commented Charles, the great reformer.

'I'm afraid you have to take into account that being married may be an essential passport to a woman's security, so you can't blame the nuns for what they did.'

'But our Philomena has managed to escape all that for now, hasn't she?' said Charles, sensing that the nanny was ill at ease with the direction of the conversation. Philomena moved uncomfortably in her chair but preferred to keep silent, head down, facing the table. So Joan stepped in.

'If it had not been for your generosity as an employer, I imagine that Philomena would have struggled to achieve the sort of independence she now enjoys.'

The Smiths knew nothing about Philomena's role with the Movement. To them she was a quiet, confident young woman who spent most of her spare time at college. And she preferred to keep up the double-sided life, as it suited her that way. She felt that it was quite normal for people to be a little schizophrenic about their lives. Many of Kerala's avowed Catholics supported the communists who were fervent atheists. Hindus were quite happy to celebrate Christmas and Christians merrily entered into the *Diwali* spirit without examining any potential conflict with their beliefs.

Two bearers hovered around to collect the soup dishes and make way for the Sunday roast, a tradition in the Smith household. 'Darling, would you do the carving please? It's chicken today. So hard to get good beef in this country and pork is rather difficult too. The mutton is impossible to roast.'

Charles disappeared into the kitchen to carve the chicken, an English ritual that the servants didn't quite understand; the cook being quite capable of using a knife. 'Edwina dear,' he was soon calling, 'these birds are blooming scrawny, there's hardly anything on them.'

Edwina excused herself to try to help her husband with the less-than-fleshy birds. Lunch might have to include pieces of meat with the bones intact.

'Philomena, where is Anil?' said Joan in a low tone while their hosts were out of the room. 'It's been days since we spoke and I want to know more about Agnes. You and Anil were her closest friends. If I'm to help, then I need to hear some more about her.'

'I've not seen Anil at college recently so I can't help. If he does come to class next week I'll tell him you want to see him.'

'Yes fine, but you knew her well too. Could we talk? I'm coming to town next Thursday and we could meet at the Coffee House.'

'OK, I'll try and be there. I'll bring Anil with me if he is around,' said Philomena hesitantly. Just then the partially dissected carcases of the two birds appeared, carried by the two bearers with Edwina and Charles behind them.

'Job done,' said Edwina. 'Let's eat.'

They tucked into the roast potatoes and peas with lashings of gravy. Joan was the only one using her fingers to tear the meagre shreds of meat from the chicken bones. The others struggled through with knives and forks. The three boys had eaten earlier and were playing cricket on the lawn, apparently having a lot of fun. Cricket was Errol's second passion after trains, and as he grew older this passion grew stronger. At night he dreamed about playing for India at the Eden Gardens and bowling out the England eleven single-handed. Just occasionally he dreamed about riding the footplate of his own WP7777 steam engine when he was a rich man one day.

'How long are the protests outside going to last?' asked Joan.

'The union is trying to grind Charles down and he won't give in, and there's some local family company, trying to buy out the Calcutta factory,' said Edwina.

'At least we don't have that lunatic fringe of the communists led by Dutta against us,' said Charles. 'They're up for violent revolution and support the ways of Mao.'

'The police want to put Charles under special protection but he's refused so far,' said Edwina.

'Draws too much of a barrier between management and the unions,' said Charles. 'It's just a matter of time before they get to see what we're about. Expenditure twenty shillings and a penny, income twenty shillings equals disaster,' he added, loosely quoting Dickens.

'But Mr Smith, Charles I mean,' said Joan, quickly correcting herself, 'you have to be aware that this is India not England. Your authority comes from your ancestors who were the past rulers and most people still have the perception that what you say must be obeyed. But there are a few, and a growing number, that don't agree and would be prepared to prove that you are just a normal human being and would happily do you harm to prove their point.'

'Well, I can't live my life in perpetual fear, on the off chance that someone might stick a knife in me.'

'Charles,' interrupted Edwina, 'stop being so morbid. Just hear what Joan says and be a bit sensitive and careful.'

Philomena sat quietly through this without a word of comment. Then she arose, 'I'll just go and see how the boys are doing.'

'What do you think, Philomena, before you go,' said Charles.

She stayed standing. There was silence for a few, long seconds and then Edwina said, 'Charles, you've made her feel most uncomfortable. Philomena, please do feel free to leave.'

And with that Philomena left the room.

LINDSAY STREET

Morning assembly had finished and the boys were already seated in class, with Phillip keeping some sense of order, when Joan arrived.

'Oh hello, I got a bit held up,' she said, looking confused. 'Good morning, class.'

'Good morning, miss,' the boys said in unison.

'I noticed that their teacher was absent so I was just taking the attendance,' said Phillip, seeing her confused expression. 'Everything OK?'

'*Hah hah*. Let's talk later,' she said, beginning to regain her composure. Phillip went back to his class next door and Joan began the lesson for the morning.

She was not usually late for class. In the five years she had taught at Don Bosco's she had been late only once before, when she had woken up to find Errol with a high temperature. This morning it had been Errol again; he had been up most of the night with fits of vomiting. 'It's that *chat* wallah, *beta*, I've told you to be careful. You've caught something.'

She had given him a few spoons of Amrithdhara, the wonder herbal cure for all ills, a solution handed down from generations before, and he had been able to go back to sleep and recover from a disturbed night. By and large Errol was quite self-sufficient and took very little looking after. He was used to entertaining himself for hours by building train sets from plywood, cut with his fretsaw and stuck together with glue. With his chemistry sets, cricket, trains and stamp collections, Errol was never short of things to do.

Joan was due to meet Anil and Philomena that evening at the Coffee House and Errol had a personal tuition session with Phillip after school. Joan's curiosity and sense of needing to see some resolution to the Bandle Girl case were getting stronger. What if Xavier had been responsible for the girl's death? That would be morally wrong and, as things stood, he would get off with blood on his hands. And which poor unfortunate might be next? As she had the rest of the day off she thought she would tap into a rich source of information on Agnes: the eyes and ears of the shopkeepers and vendors that she knew in the New Market and Lindsay Street.

Armed with a cut-out copy of the photo of Agnes from *The Statesman*, she arrived at the New Market's main entrance where her faithful rickshaw wallah spotted her and shouted out for her attention. 'Memsahib, memsahib,' came the familiar cry, as indeed did a chorus of a dozen others in possession of the two-wheeled sedans.

Calcutta had borrowed the idea of pulled rickshaws from the Far East and these highly mobile units of transport were mechanically far more efficient than the bicycle variety. You had to be quite agile to climb up on to the seat and then, as the puller lifted the front of the contraption, you were further hoisted into the air as if it were going to topple backwards.

'Rickshaw wallah, *challo*,' she said. In the many years she had known the man she had never got to know his name. Probably like most of his other customers, she addressed him by his job function; indeed this is how most people of his class were known. *Napie* for the barber, *bearer* for the house servants and *malie* for the gardener.

Joan spoke in a pidgin Hindi to the man, which many Calcutta Anglo-Indians developed as their preferred language of communication when not able to communicate in English, their first language. It was a crude form, which ignored the rules of gender, tense or anything vaguely grammatical, but seemed to serve its purpose for procuring goods and services and generally passing the time of day.

However inappropriate her communication system was, she managed to express herself very clearly to the rickshaw wallah when she asked him if he had seen a girl like Agnes around Lindsay Street. The picture of the good-looking young woman had become iconic as one of many unsolved murder cases in the city. The man recognised Agnes straight away when Joan pulled out the picture.

He shook his head as if he had disappointed Joan by not giving her a positive reply. However, he suggested that he take her to the *chameli* mehmsahib in Lindsay Street, who would definitely know. She was the grand dame of the 'ladies of pleasure', as they were referred to by the more elite sections of Calcutta society.

The rickshaw pulled up outside a freshly painted,

three-storey, Regency-style building on three floors, which had been coloured deep red. It was surrounded by a six-foot-high, wrought-iron fence with a gate and a bell. When Joan pressed the button, she had no idea whether the wires were actually connected to a ringing device. However a minute later a top window opened and the face of a middle-aged, red-haired woman, almost certainly in a wig, appeared.

'*Kya hai?*' she enquired of the rickshaw wallah who pointed to Joan to say the memsahib wanted to talk. A few moments later the same face appeared at the front door, looking a little friendlier, but still puzzled. She wore a black, backless lace dress that fell to the floor in an uncomfortable symmetry with the fake red hair that fell to her shoulders.

'How can I help you?' she said in a familiar singsong Anglo-Indian accent.

'I'm really sorry to disturb you but the rickshaw wallah said that you might be able to help me with my search for someone,' said Joan.

'*Hah hah*, a girl that has run away from home to make her way in Lindsay Street, you think. *Achha*, come in, we're not busy at the moment. I was just pouring myself my first drink of the day.'

'Thanks,' smiled Joan gratefully and put out her right hand. 'My name is Joan D'Silva.'

They went up some flights of stairs into a parlour, furnished with faded, balding velvet sofas that had seen plusher days. 'Do sit down,' said the red-haired woman. 'My name is Jessica. Would you like some tea or something stronger? Maybe you could join me in a whisky and soda?'

'No thank you, I don't want to put you to any trouble,' said Joan, still slightly uncomfortable with her creeping Miss Marple role.

'No trouble, but don't mind if I do.' She went out of the room and returned with a half-full tumbler, her black flowing dress trailing behind her as she glided across the floor.

Jessica looked like a woman who'd had a hard life, which her heavy make-up and painted fingernails did nothing to disguise. She smelled of cheap perfume mixed with a forty-a-day smoking habit. She lit a Capstan cigarette and sat on the sofa to hear Joan's reason for calling on her.

'Jessica, you may have heard about the Bandle Girl,' she said, pulling out the picture of Agnes.

Jessica didn't look at the picture; she was presumably quite familiar with the case. 'Oh yes, dear, quite a *tamasha, hah*? Lovely looker, what a shame!'

'You wouldn't have seen her anywhere here on Lindsay Street, would you?'

This time Jessica looked carefully at the picture. 'No *yar*, not really. I don't think she's the type that would come around here for work. She doesn't look the part, too nice or something. It would remind the men of their sister or daughter and put them off their stroke.'

'So what sort of girls come here then, Jessica?'

'Look, what is your connection with all this, by the way?' Jessica was growing suspicious. So far she had seemed pleased to have Joan's company but her questions seemed unusual for someone just seeking a missing person.

'Oh, the case is just a personal interest. I'm always concerned when girls from our community end up badly and when one of the New Market shopkeepers said they might have seen her in Lindsay Street, my rickshaw wallah brought me here.'

'We only attract the girls that can give a man a good time, make them forget their sad lives, look glam, no matter how fake it all is,' Jessica continued, accepting Joan's response without further challenge. 'I remember the days when the Tommies used to come here off the troop ships from Burma and they made a beeline for me because I was the hottest looker in the street. Those were the days, *yar*. Today we just have these desperate foreigners who are looking for a bit of Eastern delight. *Kulfi* with cream *hah*! I have two AI girls working for me at the moment, and you know the Indian men who come here have heard that we have quite a reputation for giving them a good time.'

'Do you know Xavier Lal?'

'*Hah*, *hah*, he's that Indian Christian head waiter chap at the Grand,' said Jessica.

'I'm sorry for asking,' said Joan, 'does he send you men?'

'No, not usually. Girls do pick up men at the Grand and sometimes they come here. I've started letting the top room by the hour, but I don't like doing it a lot because you never know who is coming here.'

'So you're sure this girl Agnes has never been here?' Joan wanted to be certain.

'That is correct, and I know most of what goes on here in Lindsay Street, believe me.'

Jessica poured herself another whisky and soda and talked at length about the good old days which were long gone, and how her clients now included politicians, judges and eminent members of the Bengal Club. But she epitomised discretion, she said, and all their secrets were safe with her.

Joan thanked her for the hospitality she had received and looked out of the window to see if the rickshaw wallah was still waiting for her. He was. '*Challo*, Coffee House,' she ordered, mounting the rickshaw and pleased to be out in the fresh air, away from the stale smell of cigarettes and cologne in Jessica's front room.

The Coffee House was buzzing with early-evening patrons, office workers coming to relax and gossip after work, a few students lingering over frothy cups of Nescafe and the odd couple having a secret tryst before going home to their families.

'Anil, hello, are you on your own?' said Joan, spotting the young man sat at a table for two reading a copy of *The Statesman* that had been left by a previous customer.

'Yes, miss, Philomena couldn't come, she says to be very sorry,' said Anil looking up suddenly.

Joan was a little surprised that Philomena was not with them. 'Look, Anil, you don't have to keep calling me miss, you aren't a student at Don Bosco's any more. You're an adult now.'

'OK Aunty,' was the most familiar form Anil could manage.

They ordered drinks. Joan her favourite chocolate drink, and Anil the same, with cream on top.

'Anil, how close were you to Agnes?' asked Joan when the drinks arrived.

'Aunty, see, we were not lovers or anything but we spent

101

a lot of time together walking in the *maidan*, talking a lot, holding hands. She was a very passionate person, she cared a lot about things, about the poor of Calcutta, about her unconsummated marriage. She never complained, saying that after what she had been through she was prepared for anything.'

'Did she ever refer to Xavier having asked her to go with foreigners?'

'Not quite, she was a stoical girl. The last day I saw her, however, she was quite upset, almost hysterical. I asked her what the problem was and she said that it was a domestic issue and it would pass over. Never did she say what Xavier was asking her to do.'

'When did she find out her husband was a homosexual?' asked Joan.

'Quite early on in the marriage when she confronted him about his affair with the boy from our college. At first he denied it but then he confessed. Xavier was in a marriage he had to go through to keep up appearances, as he was a Christian and his employers expected him to have a wife. He told her this and asked her to accept the fact that he was not interested in her sexually but was happy for her to be his kept wife and to finish her college education. I think the nuns taught her to accept her life as it was and so she did. We just hoped that fate would intervene one day and Agnes and I could spend the rest of our lives together. But we had no great plan to make it happen. We just lived from day to day.'

'And where did Philomena fit into the picture with you and Agnes?' asked Joan, still not sure how the three got along together.

'Philomena introduced me to Agnes. They were friends from the same orphanage, remember. So it was quite hard to separate these girls when they got together. But gradually I could tell that Agnes began to like my company. She would always laugh at my jokes and her smile lit up the room and me inside.'

'And what about you and Philomena, how did you two get on?' Joan was getting into her role as inquisitor.

'We are both interested in politics so we would debate and discuss Marxism, Leninism and whether our country needed to overthrow capitalism. Agnes was more angry about the plight of the poor and the injustices in our society,' explained Anil.

Joan continued to push and probe, but she couldn't fully understand the relationship between the three college students. She had heard Anil's version but suspected there was more to his relationship with Philomena. It looked less and less likely that Agnes had been involved in the prostitution racket in Lindsay Street, so if there was any pressure from Xavier for her to do so, Agnes must have resisted it.

Young Blades

A classroom at Calcutta College served as the meeting place for the Workers' Revolutionary Movement. Most of those attending were students of the college. They were passionate about their politics, and had been active members of the Communist Party of Bengal. Philomena had arrived late because she had been caring for the Smith children. She joined Anil, who had saved her a seat at the front of the room.

The meeting was called to order by a handsome, gaunt, Bengali man in a grey *kurta*. His shoulder-length black hair curled at the ends, complementing the outlines of his thin beard. This was Dutta, their self-appointed leader, addressing the gathering.

'Brothers and sisters, we have reached a time when we need to find a way to step up the fight against the injustice of this capitalist state of ours. The Communist Party, to which we all belong, has failed to take the fight to the streets, into the cities and to the countryside where our other brothers and sisters, the peasants and the workers, are being exploited by the rich landowners and the factory managers.

'I have had the fortune to be in Peking to meet the great Mao Tse-Tung and have seen the fantastic revolution he has begun in order to purge their country of all reactionaries and to give his country back to the people. No one who shares the revisionist ideas of the past is being spared. Academics, artists and teachers are being punished just as much as the rich thieving farm owners.

'Contrast this with the ineffectual Marxist Leninist ways of the Soviet Union where power, elitism and corruption in the Politburo have taken over from the equally abhorrent excesses of the Czar. Our own Communist Party seems to want to be a lackey of this Soviet system which, brothers and sisters, will not achieve our ambition. We will overthrow the imperialism that we have inherited from the British. The peasant workers are being starved out of their strike for better pay. Every hectare, every head of cattle, every cart that moves in that village is owned by one man who has created a monopoly and is perpetuating a mini feudal state. There are many Belubaris in our country and I ask you, brothers and sisters, are we going to become the slaves of these capitalist landlords?'

'*Nahi!*' shouted the room.

'Are we going to stand by while the Communist Party does nothing for the people of Bengal?'

'*Nahi!*'

'We need to start making a difference here in our own city, by bringing the Maoist revolution to our country. Brothers and sisters, show your allegiance to the cause and let's create a complete blockade of the GKW factory this Friday as a show of solidarity to the workers there. Let's show Charles Smith that *we* own this country, not him with his imperialist paymasters. Let's show the nation how we can drive these greedy foreigners from our land.'

The audience went berserk in a frenzy of revolutionary zeal. Dutta's closest followers surrounded their leader, giving him a mixture of congratulatory hugs, handshakes and *namaskars*: Philomena and Anil were among them.

On Friday morning about a hundred 'revolutionaries' gathered outside the gates of GKW, before the morning shift at seven. Dutta was there barking instructions to the mob. 'Link arms, brothers and sisters, and hang on for the sake of the revolution.' The crowd began to grow. The noise level rose like a crowd at a cricket match unhappy about the umpire's decision.

Philomena and Anil were side by side, holding on to each other in the crush of people, against the noise, taut with excitement. 'Anil, I can feel a shiver up my spine. What about you?' she shouted in his ear.

'I think generations of our brothers and sisters after us will respect us for what we are doing. We have to make a stand in our own way. The world is watching us,' he said, hoping that a grand sense of purpose would kill his rising fear of trouble ahead. The crowd began to surge around them.

'Anil, you have a knife?' Philomena noticed the outline of an object, which did not look like a wallet, stuffed into the rear of his jeans.

'Yes,' he replied, embarrassed.

'But, Anil, that's dangerous. Why?'

'Dutta told me to. He said that it was good for at least one of us to carry a weapon for self-defence. In case the capitalist thugs retaliate.'

'Think what happened to Agnes. Just watch out for yourself, OK?'

'I'll be fine. We'll be in this together,' he said, squeezing her right hand and briefly looking her in the eyes.

'Wouldn't it be good if she were with us now?' said Philomena. Anil's expression altered immediately to a frown. 'Anil, were you in love with her?'

There was a sudden lull in the noise of the crowd, as if they all wanted to hear Anil's answer. He said quietly, 'That is pure Hollywood, Philomena. Love, what does it mean for us Indians? Yes I respected her a lot, yes I felt very sorry for her predicament and wanted to do something for her, yes, like you, we shared the same vision for the future of our country. Is that love?'

'It's a good way there. She was also very beautiful and you must have had some feelings towards her?'

'I find it hard to talk about her in that way now she is dead. I hope you understand?'

'I understand,' smiled Philomena. She knew now that Agnes and Anil had been lovers.

Just then the crowd erupted again; the night shift had begun to leave. Dutta's voice became more threatening. 'Come and join us, brothers, do this for your country.' A few workers leaving the factory took the call and joined in. To those that quickly scurried away he called, 'We know where you live, don't be traitors.'

The blockade had now increased by another few

hundred people and not a single worker was able to go through the factory gates to relieve the ones that had just left. One unfortunate got down on his knees and pleaded with Dutta. 'Please, sir, I have a big family; this is our only income; I need this job. They will give us the sack.'

'Brother, do this for the revolution. We all need to make sacrifices for the future. Join us,' Dutta commanded.

'But, sir, that will not feed us, please!' he said, tugging at Dutta's left foot. Dutta kicked himself free.

'Get out of here,' he said in disgust, and the man was dragged away by the crowd, letting out cries of pain as he was punched and kicked.

Philomena's heart reached out to the man. She couldn't see him suffer. It was the capitalist that needed to be hurt, not humble workers like this fellow. '*Achha, achha*!' She barged into the small crowd. 'He's learned his lesson now. Brothers, leave him alone and let him go back to his wife and his children who won't thank us if he dies.'

Dutta was calling them back. One man spat at the man on the ground, cursing as he left; the others just swore at him; one of these gave Philomena a nasty look, telling her she fucked her brother. She helped the injured man get up and walk away from the crowd. His head was bleeding from a gash about an inch long and she used her handkerchief to stem the flow of blood.

There were still no police to clear the gate area and the blockade appeared to be successful. Around eight o'clock Thomas James, the factory manager, arrived in his car. It was stopped at the gates and the chauffeur was persuaded to abandon the vehicle and flee. The manager put on a brave face and began to talk to Dutta.

'Can you at least allow my car through, please? I have no quarrel with you.'

Dutta stared at the man blankly, showing not the slightest sign of any reaction to his request. The look on his face was one of ultimate superiority and control; he was confronting a beaten foe. The crowd began to chant '*jao, jao, jao*' and started clapping slowly at the same time. The chanting rose in volume, intensity and hate until the blockade tipped uncontrollably into a heaving mass with no one in charge. Anil felt himself being pushed forward and back.

Thomas James was no coward. He had been a GKW employee for twenty years. It was his life ever since leaving school at sixteen. A school that had taught him how to box.

A man ran from the crowd and raised his fist to attack. James was ready for him; a quick left hook followed by a jab from the right and the man was instantly floored. 'Would anyone like more of that? *Chullo,*' he said and kept up his guard.

Dutta moved in front of him now. 'You're a very silly man,' he said quietly. 'Do you really believe that you can take us all on? We're fighting for our right to survive; you're fighting for the capitalists. We're here for our survival, our country. You're coming to work to fill the pockets of those imperialists.'

While Dutta spoke, the man who had been brought down was getting up. The crowd urged him on. Thomas James did not see him come from behind, and the man drove a knife between his shoulder blades. James fell to the ground, crying out in pain, and the assailant finished off the job by driving the blade into his stomach. Blood poured out of his wounds, spreading into a dark red pool that glistened in the mud.

'Help me, someone, get a doctor, please,' James cried out faintly, struggling to stay conscious.

'*Salla behan chode,*' swore the man with the knife. He dropped it by James and slipped into the crowd.

The chanting abated; the crowd fell silent and began to disperse quickly. Anil had seen the whole spectacle unfold and went to James's side. He noticed immediately that the knife was his and instinctively picked it up to examine it closely, not believing what he saw. James's eyes were now closing. Then his body went into the final death shake and soon it was still. Suddenly no one wanted to be around. Anil dropped the knife and decided it was time for him to go. Dutta had already disappeared.

A police truck with around twenty constables appeared around the corner of the factory walls. Soon khaki-clad policemen were *lathi*-charging the remaining crowd of about fifty young men with menacing bamboo poles, similar to the ones they used for killing mad dogs.

Anil ran as fast as he could to keep up with the retreating crowd. Men were being bludgeoned to the ground one by one as the constables lashed out.

Anil knew that while he was with this group his fate was at best arrest, or worse, a cracked skull. He had to make a break for it somewhere. There was a narrow passage to the left of his vision, which was probably used as a shortcut through to the railway station at the back of the factory. He knew he had to run for the passage.

He'd won the hundred-metre sprint three years in a row at school sports day but college had ended all that. Too many hours spent in the Coffee House and a lack of exercise made him wish he had been more athletic at college. But this was his only chance, so he heaved himself out of the slow-moving scrum; then he ran as fast as he could.

In seconds he had separated himself from the group and was in the narrow alley. It twisted and turned right and left for a few seconds and Anil blindly followed it, assuming it would lead him to freedom. But it didn't. A corrugated tin gate blocked the path and there was Dutta, trying to kick it down in his own bid to escape.

'Come on, help me smash this thing down, now!' yelled Dutta, giving an angry command, and Anil joined him in driving the ball of his right foot as hard as he could into the tin structure, which bent under the persistent hammer blows of the two men.

'Do you know where to go from here?' shouted Anil.

'Yes, but do not follow me. Is that clear?'

Anil nodded and they kept kicking the door until the bolt began to shake free of its fixings. 'Who stabbed the manager? He looked dead,' he asked.

'Bah! Just a gesture to show that we mean business. They will have to take us seriously now,' replied Dutta with another blow, which finally freed the bolt. The door flew open to reveal an open compound with storage drums and bits of scrap iron. 'Remember, don't follow,' he said, running off towards the right of the compound.

Anil followed the order and ran in the opposite direction, trying to find somewhere he might be able to climb over the fence. He had no idea what was on the other side but thought he was better outside than in. The police would almost certainly have seen him run down the passage and would come looking for him soon.

He looked around the compound for a low wall or some means of scaling the fencing that made up the perimeter of the enclosure. His eyes darted to and fro like an animal trapped by predators. Perspiration soaked his white cotton shirt.

He noticed a low point in the wall. A pile of discarded tin drums were stacked against it and a bluish pungent liquid, some sort of chemical waste, seeped out of the bottom of the pile. He saw this as his chance. He could hear men shouting down the passageway now, so Anil clambered up the tin drums and up to the top of the wall; he heaved himself over and jumped at least ten feet down to the ground.

He was clear. He gasped for breath. Then the *lathi* hit him and soon a rain of blows blocked out the pain.

ACCUSED

Anil had been badly beaten up in the van by one particular constable who seemed to take delight in ramming the end of his *lathi* into his groin. Anil yelled in pain each time and someone in the blacked-out van told his sadistic colleague that he couldn't stand the noise. By the time Anil arrived at the *thana* he could hardly stand because of the pain in lower parts of his body. His gaunt frame had suffered badly from each blow.

Together with the other protesters he was led into a windowless room without any seating. When the door was slammed shut there remained just a sliver of light from the gap in the heavy door, piercing through the dark. Anil couldn't stand up any longer, and he slumped down on what felt like a concrete floor. Some of the others sat down too and one of them said, 'Anil, *bhai*, you seem to be taking the most beating. They don't like your face or something.'

A couple of the other men had received the heavy end of a policeman's *lathi*, but none had been treated as harshly as Anil. He felt dizzy with pain and kept asking for water. But no one had been offered anything to drink. He began to slip into unconsciousness after a few minutes of lying on the hard floor.

He was not sure how long he had lain there but he awoke with a start as something crawled over his face. He felt the claws dig into his cheeks. Instinct took over from tiredness and he jumped up in a flash, scared that the room might be infested with more of the creatures. Anil's heart beat rapidly and his head still throbbed. He'd heard of a newborn child having its eyes gouged out by rats while it slept and Anil didn't want to fall victim to the vermin. But tiredness overcame him again; the next thing he knew a man was hauling him up onto a wooden chair and holding his head back by grabbing a clump of his hair, now matted with congealed blood and sweat. Through his blurred vision all Anil could make out was a short, fat, scruffy, unshaven man in a tee shirt and a *dhoti*, looking into his eyes to make sure he was awake.

'*Salla*,' the man swore, 'hope you're feeling really bad now after that kicking. But that's going to be nothing, you sister-fucking *behan chode,* by the time we've finished with you.'

'Water, I need water. I'm dying of thirst,' pleaded Anil.

'You'll get a *danda* up your arse, you fucker,' the man said, pulling Anil's head up by the hair again as it slumped over his chest. The man's breath smelled of alcohol and stale onions.

'Please can I see my father or a lawyer? I'm innocent.'

Back came another painful blow in response, delivered somewhere around his left ear.

114

'You're not seeing anyone until you've confessed to sticking a knife in that factory manager, you fucking criminal. Do you know you killed him?'

'I didn't kill anyone, really didn't, believe me.'

'Look I haven't even started on you. We'll fry your scrotum with electrodes, pull your nails out and then fuck you senseless with a *danda* until you confess, you scum of the earth. I'll be back soon.' The man kicked Anil in the shins and walked out of the room, shutting the door and leaving him sitting on the chair in the dark.

Anil shivered with a mixture of fever and fear. The physical abuse was taking its toll and his body's defence systems were beginning to react. He had begun to fear for his life, and the trembling grew into uncontrolled spasms.

The door opened again, and this time a tall Anglo-Indian man came into the room wearing grey trousers and a cream shirt. He had short, crew-cut hair and a scar over his fair-skinned right cheek; he was holding a plastic glass of water. '*Hai, hai, hai!*' he said in dismay. 'They've knocked you about a bit, *hah*?' He looked over for a few seconds at Anil, tut-tutting as he stared. 'My name is Mr Riley, CID. That factory manager James went to my church, you know. His wife would be pleased if someone owned up to being his killer. I would certainly be pleased. Look, take this glass of water and I'll try to help you.'

Anil held the plastic glass with both his hands and quivered as he swallowed down its entire contents in one go. 'Ahhh...' he sighed with relief, 'could I have some more please?'

'There's plenty more in the next room, but I'm going to have to ask you nicely to confess to the murder of Thomas

James, or that other horrible fellow will come looking for you as sport in a couple of minutes. I won't be able to stop him, you know.'

'I didn't... it wasn't me, please believe me. You're a Christian, please show me some compassion.'

'I know you went to Don Bosco's, so you've probably heard of an eye for an eye and a tooth for a tooth. Well, they'll be taking more than your eyes if we don't have a confession,' said the tall man, pulling out two sheets of paper with a statement typed on both sheets.

The thought of another meeting with the animal who had pulled his hair was something Anil couldn't face, and he desperately needed another glass of water. He reached for the pen being held out by Riley and signed the box on both pages as instructed.

The next morning's *Statesman* carried the headline 'GKW Murder'. A special report by top journalist Raj Chopra covered the tragic events of the day.

The company of Guest Keith Williams (GKW) was in shock last night when it was learned that its factory manager had been murdered outside the workshop gates by a mob calling themselves the Workers' Revolutionary Movement (WRM).

At eight o'clock yesterday morning, one single thrust of a kookri to the back of Mr Thomas James dealt a deadly blow to the forty-five-year-old man, who leaves behind a wife and two young children. The Calcutta Anglo-Indian community is in mourning at the news, and friends and family have been visiting his bereaved wife.

Not much is known of the WRM but sources close to

116

the Calcutta College, where the group was formed, say they are the Maoist faction of the Soviet-dominated Communist Party of Bengal. The group's leader, Sri Dutta, calls for a violent revolution in keeping with what we are currently witnessing in China.

Ten people were apprehended immediately after the stabbing by police, who were quickly on the scene. They are being held in Howrah thana *pending charges for murder. Speaking to reporters outside the* thana, *District Inspector Basu said, 'This murder represents a dangerous escalation of the union activism we have seen in Calcutta. We have the key perpetrators in custody and hope to make charges soon.'*

That evening Joan and Phillip made up a couple for canasta at the De Langes' house in the railway colony. The mood was sombre as Mr De Lange shuffled the pack of cards and dealt them out for the first round. Their minds were more on Thomas James than the game in hand. Nobody said it out loud but they shared a common fear that the death of James was symbolic of the knife-edge vulnerability of their community.

'Goddamn heathens. I'd line all ten of those buggers up against a wall and shoot them one by one, and get them to watch each other die. That would stop anything like this happening again,' said De Lange, intent on meting out the sort of justice that the British would have carried out to deter mutinous *sepoys* a century earlier.

'The funeral is tomorrow at St John's,' said Joan. 'Phillip and I are going. We've told Father Rector that he may have to close the school early. There won't be many teachers around to cover for all those who want to be at the funeral.'

117

The next morning Joan looked in disbelief at *The Statesman*. Anil's prison photograph was on the front page under the caption 'Profile of a Revolutionary'. He looked much older and very far from the boy she once knew at Don Bosco's.

This is Anil Sen, twenty years old and one of the prime suspects in the murder of Thomas James. Educated at the Catholic Don Bosco's School, he is now a B.Com student at Calcutta College, which is currently a hotbed of Communist Party activism and apparently the birthplace of the Workers' Revolutionary Movement, the organisation behind the violent protests.

The Chief Minister last night called on the new principal of the college to launch an immediate investigation into the use of the college premises for these political activities.

'Father, we have to do something about Anil Sen, he is being held in the *thana*,' she said to the rector after morning assembly. 'You'll have to speak to the authorities, maybe offer a character reference from the school? Anil was an exemplary student.'

'Mrs D'Silva,' said the elderly rector, 'we must let the authorities make their investigations in the normal way before we get involved, don't you think?'

'My worry is, Father, that the police are so ham-fisted you know. Heaven knows what they will get that poor boy to confess to.'

'But his father is very well connected, so I'm sure there are people working on his behalf already. But let's wait a couple of days, yes?' said the rector, tilting his head slightly to one side, urging Joan to agree with his suggestion. She nodded, knowing that the Salesian was not in the habit of interfering with the course of the law, preferring to render unto Caesar.

Much of the success of the order was down to a strict separation between the matters they controlled within the confines of the school and the church, and the world outside. No one from the religious order commented publicly on politics or any matter of civil concern and, in return, the state left them largely to their own devices.

The school bus was commandeered by many of the Anglo-Indian teachers, who had decided to attend the funeral at St John's church, a large place of worship built in the eighteenth century. The church housed an obelisk commemorating the Black Hole of Calcutta at which, two hundred years earlier, some hundred or more British and Anglo-Indian soldiers had perished from suffocation at the instigation of the *Nawab* of Bengal. The irony of the location for Thomas James's funeral was not lost on the people attending.

Christianity came to Calcutta in the fourteenth century, when the Portuguese traders set up a church by the Hooghly river. With intermarriage and a host of conversions, there was soon an active Christian community that survived the conquests of the Mogul invaders and various other phases as the centuries passed. As a result many who came to church could trace their Christian heritage back several hundred years.

The church was already full when Joan and her colleagues got there. The garden and cemetery outside were also filling up with people and, while the mood was sombre, people seemed to be conversing in lowered voices as though everybody knew each other.

Joan caught sight of the Smiths, who had arrived with a police escort; Mr Smith acknowledged her.

'Ah Joan, a sad occasion for us! Would you come in with us? I'm sure there will be a VIP section for the company.'

Joan looked at Phillip who indicated that he would wait outside for her after the proceedings were over. She was pleased to be inside the church as it was much cooler there.

'You must be very concerned for your own safety,' she said to Edwina Smith.

'Oh, well, dear, when you have to go there's very little you can do,' she replied philosophically, perhaps feeling that her status as an Englishwoman made her somehow immune to danger in Calcutta.

The coffin was laid out by the altar and the congregation had been filing past the lily and orchid-laden arrangement since its arrival. Thomas James had been popular with his workers and they appeared to have turned out in large numbers to pay their respects, filing past with their hands joined in a *namaskar*.

The vicar of St John's appeared at the altar and the service began. In his short sermon the vicar said that he spoke for the congregation in expressing the deep shock at the death of one of their own, and he paid tribute to Mr James's Christian qualities of service to his neighbour. Mrs James, dressed in black veil, sobbed throughout, comforted by relatives.

Then there was the final hymn 'Abide with Me', which didn't leave a dry eye in the congregation. It was said to be Mahatma Gandhi's favourite and, given that he too died at the hands of an assassin, its choice seemed particularly poignant.

Outside in the bright spring sunshine, the mourners wiped the beads of sweat from their foreheads as the coffin was carried to the open grave. Joan saw Inspector Basu following a few yards behind the coffin. She desperately wanted to speak to him. He noticed her and nodded in acknowledgement.

By the time the final prayers had been said and the few clumps of earth dropped on the coffin, Joan had detached herself from the Smith group and worked her way to Basu's side.

'You're holding one of our ex-boys, I hear,' she said, without any of the usual pleasantries associated with such a serious occasion.

'Yes, is Father worrying about the reputation of the school?'

'No, not particularly, more that an innocent bystander may have been caught up in this awful business.'

'Miss Joan, you aren't understanding how this *badmash* element is working to pollute the young people of our country,' said Basu, still looking towards the grave in his black sunglasses at the people dropping in yellow *gainda* flowers.

'But Anil comes from a perfectly respectable family, inspector. I know them. His father has brought him up in a strict Bengali tradition.'

'Maybe, miss,' said Basu, now looking around at her, 'but I'm respectfully suggesting that many of these activists come from quite good, well-off families. We are only just forming a view of these people's fathers. They are lawyers, businessmen, accountants and such like.'

'I would like to see him, however. I know the boy,' Joan persisted.

'Miss Joan, you are wasting your precious time. The fellow is already confessing to having the knife, and I'm having much difficulty with your request as the case is being handled by a special CID unit.'

'Inspector, we've all heard about the torture and the extraction of false confessions, really.'

'Miss Joan, we don't apply torture in these cases; usually the perpetrators are proud to boast of their actions. They are most ruthless, these "young blades" I think you call them in English. At least one eminent person who stood up to them, the principal of the Calcutta College, has disappeared without any trace. He just was never coming back home one night. Now we have to put a guard on the new principal's house and office. These people are getting their training from Mao. From India's enemies, can you believe?'

'Inspector, you're a good man. I can tell from your boy Beelu that he comes from a good home. Just imagine if your son was Anil, now in jail, probably innocent, caught up in some unfortunate incident and his Don Bosco's teacher wanted to see him and offer words of comfort, would you help me?'

'Miss D'Silva, that is a completely different question you are posing. I would not be permitting my son to do these things,' said Basu, feeling a little uncomfortable with the hypothetical dilemma.

'Inspector, you're missing the point. I'm just appealing

to the good, ethical man in you. I'm off to Lucknow in a few days for the New Year celebrations. The school knows my address there. Please let me know if you can get me into the *thana* to see Anil.' The directness of Joan's appeal seemed to have had some effect; Basu shrugged his shoulders a little and leaned his head to one side in a Bengali gesture that signalled a hint of agreement with Joan's request.

The Smiths finally caught up with Joan. 'Joanie,' said Edwina, 'we're going for the post-funeral tea at the James's home. Will you join us?'

'I'll have to ask Phillip, if that's OK,' said Joan, remembering that he would be waiting for her.

'Bring him along. He's the maths and PE teacher, isn't he? Interesting eyes, I'd say,' said Edwina in a jolly sort of way.

Thomas James had lived in a bungalow provided for him by GKW. The house in Tollygunge was a little more modest than the Smiths' own home but nevertheless palatial for most Anglo-Indians, with its well-kept gardens and seven bedrooms.

Refreshments had been arranged on the lawn outside, and professional caterers had been hired by the company to provide tea for what would be a few hundred people invited there after the funeral.

Twice that number came to offer their condolences. The James murder was for them not just another murder in the day-to-day violence of the city, but a milestone signalling a disregard for position and authority. Anglo-Indians came in solidarity with their community, and so did other minorities such as Muslims, Marwari and Parsi businessmen. Mrs James continued to wear a dark veil, her sons by her side, as mourners filed by to offer words of comfort.

Joan caught sight of Philomena. She was on her own, wearing a long, dark brown frock, her head covered with a white shawl to shield her face from the sun. Philomena caught Joan's eye and walked away from her into the gardens. Joan followed her.

'Philomena, Philomena,' shouted Joan in increasing volume, and a few people in the vicinity looked round at her. The head in the white shawl finally stopped to turn around too.

'Philomena, it's me, Joan D'Silva,' she said, giving the girl the benefit of the doubt.

'Oh hello, miss. Good afternoon,' said Philomena sheepishly.

'Philomena, I think we'd better talk about Anil and this nasty incident, don't you?'

'Miss, I wasn't there, I don't know what happened but I'm sure Anil did not kill Mr James. He's just not that type of person,' said the young woman, with an anxious sincerity to her voice.

'You may have to tell that to a judge in his defence.'

'Miss, I cannot get involved. My job, you know? The Smiths would almost certainly sack me if they found out I was close to Anil.'

Joan found herself promising to keep Philomena's secret.

'Then you must help me in every way you can to build a solid defence for Anil. We have to make sure he is not convicted of a crime he did not commit.'

Philomena looked up at Joan; there was a question, something she wanted to say. Joan considered pushing her

124

further but, not knowing what else to say, she let Philomena hurry away.

Joan found Phillip talking to someone he had met during the funeral. 'Hello, I'm Joan,' she said, putting out her hand in greeting. The man shook her hand and looked uncomfortably at Phillip. He immediately sensed the need for a more lengthy explanation of their relationship.

'Joan's a fellow teacher at Don Bosco's where I now work,' he explained. The atmosphere of discomfort lifted and they all smiled at each other in acknowledgement.

'What a terrible Christmas present for Mrs James,' said the man.

'True. Just think of the children without their daddy on Christmas Day,' said Phillip with due sobriety. They observed a few seconds of respectful silence. It was time to let the funeral rest.

'Phillip, that reminds me, I need to get some Christmas presents. I can't believe we've only got a day to go before Christmas Eve,' said Joan.

'Would you like me to come with you? Can't say I've got much to get,' said Phillip.

They were at the New Market in an hour, wandering around the shops. Paper lanterns and baubles hung in the air, making the place look festive. 'I've no idea what to get Errol,' said Joan in the hope that Phillip's many hours with her son had yielded deeper insights into what he might like than she seemed to have.

'I think I might just have the answer,' said Phillip, quite excited at the prospect of choosing a present for Errol.

He led Joan to a toyshop with rows of brightly coloured

Japanese tin toys. The owner was demonstrating to a woman a locomotive that threw out sparks from its funnel as he rolled it along the ground. There were dozens of military tanks, Jeeps, tankers and other transport paraphernalia. On the top shelf, right there in the centre, was a wooden, scale model of a Winnipeg express locomotive with the number WP7700. Phillip pointed to it and asked the man to take it down.

'Ah, sir, this is very special model made by my cousin brother doing apprenticeship at the Carriage and Wagon works of Indian Railway in Liluah. You see the front searchlight works and the side piston rods are all connected and go around when I'm pushing the engine,' said the shopkeeper, most proud of his relative's creation.

Phillip had been looking at the model in the window for a few weeks and had yearned for an excuse to handle the locomotive and see it up close. Now he had his chance. He was brimming with excitement but didn't want to show it and risk the shopkeeper quoting an unspeakable price for its purchase. Joan was not an expert in these things and blankly asked, 'Do you think he'd like it?'

Phillip knew it was just the thing that Errol would do any amount of homework for. He could talk for hours about the power and the versatility of the WP engines; he had pictures, postcards and all manner of memorabilia connected with these steam juggernauts.

'How much is it?' asked Joan.

'Only one hundred rupees, madam.'

'*Bah!* What is it made of? Gold?' Joan's surprise was genuine and not just a natural response to bargaining the price down. A hundred rupees was a lot of money and she could by no means afford anything so expensive for Errol.

The shopkeeper didn't offer a response; he lifted the model back up onto its perch on the top shelf and continued his demonstration of the cheap Japanese toys with sparks and horns and other strange gimmicks.

'Joan,' said Phillip as they walked away, 'I'd like to help out with that present. Errol and I are good friends now and I'd be buying him something anyway.'

'Phillip, I couldn't take money from you for a present for *my* son. How would that look to my *beta*?'

'He doesn't have to know, I'd just like to see his face when he opens it on Christmas Eve.'

It took a good deal of persuasion, but in the end Joan did agree to buy the locomotive as a joint present. If that was exactly what her son would like for Christmas, then so be it.

And so on Christmas Eve, after midnight mass, Phillip was invited back to Joan's for a glass of sherry and cake and Errol unwrapped his present. It couldn't have been a better purchase. The boy was full of questions immediately and reeled off a string of facts about the pressure in the boilers, pulling power and the tons of coal carried in the tender. He checked out the minutest details in the model with his pictures and photographs and found everything in place, just the way it should be.

'Ma, this is the happiest day of my life,' he said before he was sent off to bed, and Phillip smiled at Joan.

THE DOON
EXPRESS

Dehradun lies among the foothills of the Himalayas, about fifteen hundred miles northwest of Calcutta's buzzing main railway terminus, Howrah station. The Doon Express, as it was commonly called by Anglo-Indians, officially left at 8.32 every evening, but most nights it was gone nine o'clock by the time it managed to pull away from the sea of red-turbaned coolies, *chat* wallahs, families and well-wishers who came to say their goodbyes.

Travelling by train in India was more of an expedition than a mere trip somewhere. Coolies could be seen carrying huge boxes on their heads with giant rolls of bedding perched on top. This was in effect a mattress, complete with pillows and sheets to ensure a comfortable sleep for the journey.

Such a journey could not be undertaken without ample supplies of tiffin. The *chat* wallahs and the other pedlars of the snacks that seemed to be available at every stop along the way could not be relied upon for cleanliness.

The first-class compartment would soon be filled with

the aroma of food, for the two travellers sharing the accommodation with Joan and Errol, a middle-aged Marwari couple, would also have packed enough to feed a garrison, with the full intention of showing off their culinary prowess. Quality and quantity were important bedfellows to connoisseurs of good food and hospitality. The array of their shiny aluminium tiffin cans was testament to a feast in store.

Errol and Joan were taking the Doon to celebrate the New Year at the railway colony in Lucknow with Joan's sister Irene and brother-in-law Gerry. The sisters were friends but had never been close. They led very different lives, with Joan more fiercely independent than ever after her husband's death. But now she was looking forward to her visit to Lucknow where Gerry was the senior Permanent Way Inspector. Gerry oversaw a hundred miles of track with pride and perfectionism, and Errol would always notice how the train seemed to glide along the track without a jolt or a bump as soon as Uncle Gerry's attention to engineering detail took over. He had ridden this section numerous times on the inspection trolley, with his uncle pointing out the little details that made sure the camber of the track was perfect and the small adjustments to the expansion joints over bridges and viaducts that allowed the wheels to glide over the rails without the clickety-clack of the older permanent way.

Gerry was entitled to free railway passes that allowed him and his family to make journeys anywhere on the Indian railways three times a year. Gerry was a bit of a stay-at-home and preferred the comfort of his domain: the hundred miles of track he controlled, the loyal trolley men under his command and the Lucknow railway colony where he was a bit of a *burra* sahib.

'*Areh*, why would I want to go anywhere at the moment?' he would always say. 'Joan, just use my pass and come to visit us for the New Year.'

So Joan and Errol travelled as Mrs and Master Shaw to take advantage of the free travel and were immensely grateful for the privilege of the first-class accommodation, a luxury that they would never have been able to afford otherwise.

This of course was not strictly legal, and Indian Railways had rules about the abuse of free passes, as the company did not want its officers and employees selling them on the open market. As a result, Joan reminded Errol that if any official asked him his name, it was not D'Silva but Shaw.

This was quite confusing for the young boy as he had been told never to tell lies and yet here was his mum officially sanctioning one. 'But, Ma, why am I Errol Shaw when I travel on the train?'

'*Beta*, sometimes you just do as I say and don't ask why. I'm your ma, I wouldn't ask you to do anything wrong,' she said.

'But, Ma, will I have to confess this to Father on Sunday,' he said, digging deeper into the quagmire of Joan's simple deception.

'No, Errol, no,' she replied, losing her patience a little, 'it's your ma telling you. You don't have to confess that. It's OK. Look, Uncle Gerry is giving us his pass and we have to pretend for just one day that you're one of his sons and I'm Aunty Irene.'

This confused Errol even further and it took a good deal to make him promise to answer to Shaw if asked by the ticket conductor. The bit that clinched it finally was that they would not be able to go to Lucknow any other way as the trip was unaffordable.

A berth on the Doon Express was a coveted prize only available to those who queued for long hours at the central reservations office in Calcutta or, more accurately, had got their peons to do so. Those deciding to travel at the short notice of less than a month hadn't a chance of getting a berth on the night train.

For those who were legally occupying the four berths, this was the perfect time to make acquaintances and form a united front to ward off any unwelcome intrusion. Train robberies were quite common and dacoits preyed on people travelling on their own while they slept in their compartments.

'Where would you be going?' said the man opposite Joan, kicking off his *chappals* and sitting down next to a lady whom Joan assumed was his wife.

It appeared that Mr and Mrs Agarwal were travelling to Delhi to see some relatives, so Joan and Errol would have them as company for the whole trip to Lucknow. That was comforting to her, as you never knew who your cabin companion might be these days, she thought. Last year an entire family of eight Sikhs, two adults and six children, shared the cabin with her and Errol. The man snored for the entire sub-continent, sending tremors through Joan every few seconds when he inhaled.

The guard was blowing his whistle somewhere on the

platform. No one seemed to take any notice. Then the train jerked a little and began to move very slowly. People left behind merely began to walk along beside the train, talking to those in the compartments through the windows, apparently oblivious to the fact that in less than a minute their conversation would be terminated.

Elders stroked children's faces through the window grill. Men and women never touched, yet their eyes said it all as they made a yearning *namaste*. The din of final haggling with the *chat* wallahs, sweet vendors and anyone else who had something to sell reached its climax as the quarter-of-a-mile-long train gradually built up speed until no one could walk alongside any longer, and soon the train left the platform behind.

'Errol *beta*, come and have something to eat,' Errol heard his mother say as she began to open the tiffin box and lay out the results of her day's labour in preparation for the journey. Her food tonight was simple by comparison with previous attempts. She heaped a few spoons of yellow rice onto a white plate, her best china, then undid the upper catch of the second tiffin canister to reveal the *koftas*, a cluster of spheres of meat, about the size of golf balls in gravy.

Mrs Agarwal in the meantime was putting out the contents of her own tiffin cans, more numerous in the expectation of a flood of last-minute visitors. In the Hindu tradition all her food was strictly vegetarian; it was stored in various compartments containing cooked vegetables, a pile of neatly folded, wafer-thin chapattis, an assortment of pickles and chutneys and probably the best sweet milk curds in the world from a shop on the corner of Chowringhee in Calcutta.

'Please take,' she said in her faltering English, pointing to the rich array of delicacies laid out on the carriage's fold-up table.

'Oh no, we couldn't, you won't have enough for yourself. It's a long journey,' said Joan politely, being cautious not to offer her meaty *koftas* lest she give offence to her vegetarian travel companions.

But accepting food is a ritual in India and the early polite refusals are all part of the process. Some cultures may smoke peace pipes, others share a cup of intoxicating liquor, but here on this train journey in India, chutneys, chapattis and curds seemed to be the common currency of friendship.

Mrs Agarwal was scooping up dollops of *misty dohi*, the smoky-white sweet curd, and offering it to her new friends. The soothing curds were the perfect dessert to cool the taste buds and to help digest the richest of meals.

The *misty dohi* was exquisite and over the next hour the Agarwals told Joan their entire life stories and family history and, of course, they wanted to know how Joan was travelling with her son without her husband.

'My husband was killed in the 1955 train crash in Bihar,' she explained. 'Errol was only six. I never got to see his body: there were so many casualties and they had to cremate the hundred or so corpses because of the intense heat that summer. I only identified him through photographs of his body lying in the wreckage, taken by a railway photographer.'

The Agarwals expressed their regret at this revelation and, as if in sympathy, offered Joan more curds and sweet tea. What an awful fate to befall a woman with a young son.

'Mrs Shaw, I'm being very sorry to hear this,' Mr Agarwal said with a sad shake of his head, and his wife nodded in sympathy.

'But life has to carry on, Mr Agarwal. I got a job as a teacher in Don Bosco's. Have you heard of it?' she said.

'Oh yes certainly. Many of my brothers and sisters are wanting to send their children there,' he replied, smiling in acknowledgement.

The Agarwals had performed their ablutions and were getting ready for bed when there was a knock on the door of the compartment. An official-sounding, firm knock made by the edge of a metallic object. Errol knew this was the conductor guard as he had heard a previous knock further down the corridor, followed by a muffled conversation in Bengali. This was undoubtedly a ticket check before everyone retired for the night.

It was the moment he had been dreading, when he would have to lie about his name. What would he do if the conductor suspected he was an impostor? He had heard that ticket collectors and guards were well tuned to spotting fare dodgers and cheats.

One of the boys in his class at school had a brother who had been caught travelling without a ticket and the boy had been given a public beating in Howrah station by the railway police. He'd even had his head shaved to warn any other would-be fare dodgers of the dangers of cheating on Indian Railways.

This was Indian justice at its harshest and arguably its most ineffective, as thousands of people defrauded the system daily. The risk of public humiliation and the pain of a beating were insignificant compared to the personal economic cost of paying for your ticket.

But as an Anglo-Indian this was a different matter. Now, more than a decade after independence, Indians were shedding the shackles of their British rulers. Anglos had previously enjoyed the protection of the British. Now they were just another minority in the complex racial mix that makes up the Indian sub-continent. The public humiliation of an Anglo would have special poignancy for the Railway Police. They would be showing all those who passed by that no one was immune to the long arm of railway justice. Not even these people, products of the once mighty British Empire.

For one scary moment Errol saw himself being publicly flogged and disgraced for the rest of his life. He could never show his face at school again. What would Father Rector say at confession on Sunday? 'Never mind, my son, just ask God for forgiveness and say twenty Hail Marys' might do it for Father Rector, but the stain on his reputation would be indelible.

Mr Agarwal was the first to go to the door and unlock the heavy safety latches at the top and bottom that secured the compartment from the most persistent intruder. The door slid open, revealing a short podgy man in an official-looking cap, dressed in a dark blue uniform with half-moon spectacles on the edge of his nose and a scar on his face.

'Conductor guard, tickets please,' said the guard in an official, repetitive tone of voice which set Joan and Mr Agarwal shuffling around for their wallets. They both managed to extricate the necessary documentary evidence proving their legitimate right to travel in the first-class carriage of the Doon Express.

'Mr and Mrs A N Agarwal, and Mrs J Shaw and Master E Shaw,' he said, reading off the inventory of passengers. Mr Agarwal was the first to produce the tickets and the reservation documents which seemed to pass the cursory scrutiny of the conductor guard. He gave the documents back with a comment, 'Travelling to Delhi,' as if in agreement that everything seemed to be in order. Now it was Errol's turn; the official showed no emotion, as if he could turn into an ogre at the slightest hint of skulduggery.

'Ah, Mrs Shaw. Your husband is the PWI of the Lucknow sector,' he said looking at the pass and Joan was for a moment stunned into silence, not knowing whether she should agree or say that she was a relative. 'Mr Shaw, best PWI on this route. All train crew are speaking highly of Mr Gerry's fine track on the LKO sector.'

Errol shuddered at this, and Joan wondered what on earth the Agarwals must be thinking. But they appeared to be deep in discussion with each other and she thought that either they were not following the guard's conversation or they had decided that, as with so many of the passengers on the Doon Express, Joan's ticketing and family arrangements were her own business.

The guard turned to Errol with a smile, reaching out and holding his cheeks with the palm of his right hand. 'Hope you will be famous man like Mr Gerry, *hah*?'

Errol gawped. Mrs Shaw smiled demurely. The man looked again at Mrs Shaw. 'Thank you, goodnight. Please don't forget the security latch,' he said and he was gone, sliding the door behind him.

Errol didn't sleep during the night; he was filled with dread every time the train stopped, and he waited in terror for footsteps and the final knock on the door. He imagined being dragged off the train in the middle of the night. Would it be Patna in the middle of Bihar, bandit country, or some time in the morning in Benares?

When morning did come he fell asleep at last, exhausted, until he was woken by his mother shaking him, telling him to get up and have some breakfast and a cup of sweet tea.

When the train stopped at a station, Mr Agarwal bought the day's *Hindustan Times* to catch up on any news he might have missed in the night. During the thirty-minute stop, the Doon Express had the benefit of a new locomotive, fresh driver and crew. The train was soon moving off on its northerly journey towards Benares.

As Mr Agarwal opened up his newspaper, Joan saw something on the front page in front of her that immediately attracted her attention. 'Bengal in Communist Grip' screamed the headline, alongside a picture of Thomas James. But Joan could not read the fine print, much as she strained to decipher the content of the article.

The train had now passed the Dilkusha bridge and Errol shouted, 'It's Uncle Gerry's section of track, Ma!'

As if by magic the train instantly stopped jolting from side to side and seemed to glide over the track effortlessly. They were nearing Lucknow station now and much as Joan wanted to prize the paper from Mr Agarwal she knew there was no way of doing so.

The train slowed as the station came in sight and the brakes brought the carriages to a firm halt. Red-turbaned coolies swarmed around, hoping to be assigned to carry Joan's baggage off the train. She was saying goodbye to the Agarwals, dying to ask if she could have the front page of the *Hindustan Times*. Then a coolie came in and whisked away their bags and Joan had to follow to keep the man in sight.

As they got off the train the conductor guard spotted them and waved goodbye. Errol breathed a sigh of relief.

Lucknow sat decorously in the great Gangetic plain, soaking in centuries of peoples and beliefs, stretching back to the *Nawabs* of Awadh who brought courtly manners, gardens ablaze with colour, such fine poetry and music and, of course, a cuisine that redefined the meaning of food.

Known variously as the City of *Nawabs*, The Golden City of the East and Shiraz-i-Hind, it lived up to its name for centuries, giving the British good cause to establish a garrison and place it as the capital city of the state of Awadh.

For Joan, New Year's Eve was the highlight of the holiday. All the Anglo-Indians from the railway colony at Lucknow, the apartments by the Gunge, the cantonments and places much further afield would travel down for a *tamasha* at the Institute, a brick building which resembled a large church hall, complete with stage. The New Year was always celebrated with a party, a dance with obligatory fancy dress.

Joan had decided to go as a hula girl accompanied by her hoop, which was all the rage at the time. She'd spent all day cutting up strips of silver-coloured wrapping paper and fixing them to a rebelliously short skirt to make a rather homespun but exotic version of the Polynesian garment. The *khansamin* had lent her a red *choli* sari top, and the combination was little short of jaw dropping to the rickshaw wallahs, and to Mr Macleod, the chairman of the Institute.

The immaculately tailored Mr Macleod, a fit septuagenarian, was so taken aback by Joan's outfit that he stopped in mid conversation with the head bearer and just stared at her as she ascended the steps, hips swaying in time with her tinsel grass skirt. 'Ah good evening, my dear,' he half mumbled as he regained his composure. 'I don't believe we've seen you before.'

'Oh I'm Joan, Joan D'Silva. I'm Gerry Shaw's sister-in-law, and this is my son Errol,' said Joan, shaking the man's hand. He turned with some effort to Errol.

'Well, young man, a train driver eh!' he said with a forced smile, though his eyes kept cutting back to Joan, and were now transfixed on her exposed navel. 'Hope you'll be keeping those *chokras* feeding the firebox as we go up the Dilkusha incline, eh boy?'

With his infatuation for trains, it had not been a problem persuading Errol to dress up too. He was an engine driver with check shirt, blue denim trousers and a cap turned around backwards. He would stay for a couple of hours and then be sent home with his cousins as the adults began to get engrossed in their all-night partying.

Macleod had been one of the elite category of mail train drivers, respected and revered by status-conscious Anglo-Indians. Firemen, signalmen, foremen and the myriad other employees entrusted with operating the railways were all subservient to mail drivers, who commanded the best salaries, lived in the best quarters and were given the respect due to an elite cadre.

Logically, wives, girlfriends, children and relatives of these superior beings all assumed an appropriate air of superiority in their dealings with anyone connected with underlings. Fortunately for Joan, Gerry Shaw was above all of this as an officer of the Indian Railways, and the Shaw family was allocated a table in an appropriate corner of the room, away from the hoi polloi.

The trail of rickshaws wound their way towards the Institute in the failing light of the early evening. Their occupants looked an odd sight to most of the onlookers, even though they were quite used to the rather strange and eccentric behaviour of the *engrajee* sahibs, now dressed as Arabs, Roman soldiers and Mexican bandits. The partygoers resembled a weird assortment of extras who had wandered out of MGM's Hollywood studios for a night out.

Joan could sense that her hula skirt was having a profound effect upon the early arrivals. She noticed a momentary silence as she entered the hall with Errol, and all eyes seemed to turn towards her. Men gawped, women looked daggers and Joan averted her eyes to Errol, saying, 'Come on, *beta*, let's find our seats.'

Joan had only just settled into her seat when Macleod presented himself at her table.

'Miss Joan, I was a good friend of your mother,' he smiled at her confidently.

'Ah, Mr Macleod, would you join us for a drink? Gerry and Irene have not arrived but please sit down.'

'Oh I shouldn't really, on duty you see, got to keep out

the riffraff tonight. But why not, just a quick *chota* eh!'
he said, winking to one of the bearers, who appeared
miraculously not more than a minute later with a whisky,
diluted with warm water.

'So you knew my mum?' said Joan, curious to know
the connection.

'Yes, she was such a fine dancer. All the men were
always trying to get a dance with her. Such a graceful lady
and so fashionably dressed. Your father was a lucky man
to have her,' said Macleod, his expression sad as he sipped
his whisky.

'I would like to hear more about her, Mr Macleod. I was
only seven when she died of pneumonia, and all I have is
a faded photo of her and my dad on their wedding day.'

'I'd love to tell you all about her,' said Macleod,
encouraged by the sudden warming in the tone of the
conversation. 'You reminded me so much of Dilys when I
saw you come up the stairs this evening. I was quite taken
back; they were good times.'

'Hey, you old *badmash,* chatting up the young ladies,
hah!' said Gerry as he and Irene strolled up to their table.
Macleod stood up immediately, ever the perfect gentleman,
and pulled aside a chair for Irene. But he looked slightly
embarrassed as if he'd been caught in an illicit act.

'I must disappear now and greet some of the other
members,' he said hastily.

'You must tell me about my mum sometime, Mr
Macleod,' said Joan, wanting to hear more but sensing that
the old man felt ill at ease at the arrival of Gerry and Irene.

'Oh yes, certainly.' He regained his composure. 'If
you're not doing anything tomorrow why don't I come and

pick you and your son up around lunchtime?'

Joan was cautious but her brother-in-law said nothing and she wanted to know more about her mother.

'Yes, I would like that.'

Macleod nodded and then retreated into the crowd of dancers already beginning to fill the floor. Joan's brother-in-law turned to her.

'What did that old *bhageera* want then?'

'Oh he was just being friendly. Said he knew Mum,' replied Joan, looking at Irene, who smiled and nodded, but showed no real interest. Joan thought she must know all this already.

'Watch him. Despite his age he has a bit of a reputation with the *larkies*. Keeps a bit of a harem back at the Gunge from what I hear.'

Joan smiled at Gerry. 'I'll be careful,' she said.

A man came down to the table and began to talk to Irene; he was soon followed by another. There was clearly a lot of interest in Joan, although they all came on the pretext of passing the time of day with Gerry and Irene.

As one of the most senior members in the railway colony, Gerry attracted a string of visitors, all wanting to greet him. Their house at Number One, Cantonment Drive, was like Howrah station, with people turning up to be seen by the PWI, the senior officer of the railway, sometimes on the pretext of business, sometimes just to pass on a bit of gossip that might curry favour with the boss.

Gerry saw most of these people in his pyjamas in an effort to reduce the impact of his high position in their eyes. He also hated the idea of wearing what he called his 'working clothes' when at home. The pyjamas, however, didn't do much to stem the steady flow of visitors and well-wishers and, if anything, made them feel more at home at Number One.

But Joan was the attraction at Gerry's table that night and most of the members wished to be introduced, many commenting favourably on her choice of costume. For the men it was a licence to flirt with a young lady fully chaperoned by her family. And Joan enjoyed the attention, which she didn't get back in Calcutta. For now, the unpleasant business of the Bandle Girl, the murder of Thomas James and the imprisonment of an innocent young man were almost forgotten.

Then the music stopped and Macleod took his place by the microphone. 'Ladies and gentlemen,' he said, 'now for the refreshment break. The *Biryani* is served.'

There was nowhere in the world where this dish of the *Nawabs* of Awadh was better prepared. And tonight was to be no exception as the smell of the heavily perfumed rice permeated the hall. Five centuries earlier the invading Persian princes had brought a rich cuisine to northern India, using dried fruits and spices to infuse excitement and vigour into what had previously been a rather dull peasant cuisine.

Tonight's *Biryani* had been prepared by Muzaffar Khan, the head cook of the Institute for the last twenty years. This was his signature dish and every year he recalibrated everyone's idea of the perfect meal. 'This is, by anyone's measure, the best we've tasted,' people would exclaim. And again and again Muzaffar would surprise the guests with another subtle change in the combination of dried fruits, cloves, cinnamon, cardamom or some other humble ingredient that seemed to make monumental shifts in the flavours and textures of the dish.

Muzaffar's arduous task would have begun by picking the *bakri* from the herd and haggling for the animal. He would have led it back to the Institute as though it was a family pet and tied it up under the *peepal* tree in the backyard, where he would have slit its throat and allowed it to bleed to death painfully, strung upside down.

Hours later he would have skinned it and cleared out its entrails, passing these valuable body parts to a brother-in-law who would extract a few *annas* by selling them further down the food chain.

Biryani Lucknowi style requires long labours, starting with the preparation of the meat stock, which Muzaffar had boiled for hours to allow the tough goat meat to fall away from the bones. He then used the stock to cook the rice, giving it its rich meaty texture. Later, raisins, almonds and fried onions, and an array of various spices in their stick and seed form, all helped to make the *Biryani* a complete meal rather than a mere accompaniment.

All dancing stopped for the *Biryani* as the New Year revellers tucked into the piles of rice heaped on their plates. Knives and forks rattled, adding to the din as conversations became louder to compensate for the extra noise of cutlery on china.

The wall of sound eventually abated as the *Biryani* ran out. Then a female singer in a pink two-piece began singing the Doris Day hit 'Please Don't Pick the Daisies' and Joan got her first request for a dance that evening.

144

Gerry gave the fellow a sideways glance like a watchful father as they slid away down the dance floor into the crush of dancers.

And so the night rolled on, the men got drunk on their whiskies, the dancing continued and the band played without pause. Then at midnight, as the make-believe Big Ben struck twelve, the crowd linked hands for 'Auld Lang Syne'. Astonishingly most of them knew the words and the singing ended in a flood of kisses and greetings to welcome in the year 1961.

The scene could have been anywhere in a church or village hall in provincial England on New Year's Eve. Except the faces here were different shades of white, black and brown and the accents an odd mix of Indo Welsh, inherited a century earlier during the construction of the railways, when workers from West Wales, brought to India, intermarried with Indian women.

And as they hugged and kissed, many of them knew that these celebrations were already marking the beginning of the end of an age when this community, which felt abandoned by its British half and marginalised by its Indian home, would find it increasingly hard to hold on to its unique mixture of two worlds.

When Joan got back to her bedroom in the early hours of the morning Errol was fast asleep with his mouth wide open. She gently closed his mouth shut and stroked his cheek saying softly, 'Happy New Year, *beta*.'

She passed by the long mirror on the way to the bathroom and paused to take a look at herself, posing as if someone were taking her photograph. She passed her hands on either side of her upper body as if to get a fuller appreciation of how attractive she had looked that evening.

Yes, she had dazzled everybody in her hula outfit and yes she had turned heads, but Joan felt unexcited by any of the men she had talked to or danced with. Suddenly the New Year celebrations seemed very far away.

She undressed and went to bed naked, tucking herself deep into the quilt that had benefited from a couple of hours warming by a hot water bottle thankfully supplied by one of the servants.

She lay awake thinking of her husband George whom she had met over a decade ago at the New Year's dance of 1949. Now all she had of him were a few photographs, memories of good times now gone.

THE RESIDENCY

The next morning a snorting horse outside Number One Cantonment signalled the arrival of Macleod's *tonga*. Mother and son mounted the two-wheeled carriage with Errol taking his seat beside the *tonga* wallah and Joan in the rear seat, facing backward. With a further snort from the horse and a '*hut, hut*' from the *tonga* wallah, they were off to pick up Macleod who lived down the Gunge, in an Anglo-Indian enclave with other retired railway families.

The *tonga* pulled up at an apartment building, Number 107, Hazreth Gunge. Surrounded by a burgeoning group of young and old, Macleod lived by himself with a comfortable pension to cover a relatively garrulous lifestyle. His was a ground-floor apartment which, together with his old *tonga* wallah, he maintained in perfect order, despite having retired more than two decades earlier.

He appeared on the pavement outside, again immaculately dressed, emerging from the drab building in a blazer replete with red carnation, grey trousers and a purple silk cravat.

'Joan, good morning, lovely to see you. Errol my boy; how is our train driver today?'

'*Challo*,' he said to the *tonga* wallah as he took the seat next to Joan, and they were off.

'Where are we going, Mr Macleod?' asked Joan, quite surprised that this was not the end of the journey.

'Oh please call me Jonty, it's much easier,' he responded with a definite sparkle in his eyes.

'Well, Jonty, where?' She insisted on knowing.

'Ah it's somewhere you will find very interesting.'

'But weren't you going to tell me about my mother?'

'Ah yes, of course, and I will keep my promise,' Macleod said reassuringly.

'Mummy, where are we going?' chimed in Errol.

'*Beta*, uncle is taking us for a ride and a nice surprise.'

The *tonga* clattered along the cratered streets, being overtaken by the occasional rickshaw or bicycle and now and then swerving to avoid an abandoned cow that had decided to rest in the middle of the road. Joan wondered if this was such a good idea after all, trusting a man she had only met once and his *tonga* wallah to take them out to some undisclosed destination. But Lucknow seemed so much safer than Calcutta, the place where people went missing, keeping Inspector Basu and his hungry constables busy.

It took about twenty minutes for the *tonga* to pull up at the entrance to what looked like a park with a grand arch built some centuries earlier.

'Well Joan, Errol *beta*, this is the Residency,' proclaimed Macleod as if they had travelled some considerable distance and overcome much adversity to get there.

'Oh I've heard Gerry talk about it, Jonty, but never been here,' said Joan, beginning to look interested.

'Mum, what's the Residency?' said Errol in a tone that meant he was yet to be convinced.

'You'll see. Uncle Jonty will tell us all about it in a moment.'

The area looked well kept. There were people tending the gardens in a slow, disengaged sort of way. Broad grassed areas had been recently cut and the borders had been planted with chrysanthemums, cannas and bright yellow marigolds. Jasmine trees were laden with white flowers, soaking in the sun's rays and pouring out their heavily scented perfume.

'This is where the Britishers defied a siege by their Indian *sepoys* back in 1857. We're going to see the big house where they held out until they were rescued,' Macleod began to explain.

An enamel sign gave a brief historical perspective in white-painted English and Hindi writing:

This is the site of the historic sepoy *mutiny of 1857 when two thousand brave Indian soldiers gave their lives for the freedom of India. Thus began the first war of independence and the long process of breaking down the notion that the great colonisers were perhaps not as invincible as had previously been thought.*

The British commissioner at the time, Sir Henry Lawrence, and over two thousand European residents were besieged by the rebellious Indian *sepoys* for eighty-three days until they were released by Sir Henry Havelock and his troops, loyal to the British crown. A thousand of the British inhabitants perished as a result of the siege, as did thousands of the Indian soldiers at the centre of the rebellion.

The Residency was an area surrounded by a mile of heavy perimeter wall. The building itself had been constructed in 1780 in a grand style that was consistent with the seat of power for this capital city of the state of Awadh. Grand verandas and tall colonnades marked the entrance. Inside, ballrooms and staterooms were large and spacious and the Europeans who were besieged must have valued the space to take shelter from the elements and the seemingly endless weeks of intermittent fire from the *sepoys* amassed outside the perimeter walls.

Jonty Macleod led his small touring party inside the building, which was relatively free of visitors. It was New Year's Day and a local holiday. He knew the Residency well and strode in with confidence. Errol slouched behind, more interested in sitting on the marble lions at the entrance.

They were walking into the main hall when Macleod declared, 'We used to come here a lot in our courting days, your mum and I.'

Joan cut her step and looked at Macleod.

'My mum and you?'

'Ah yes. Does that surprise you?'

'Well no, it's just that I never thought of her courting anyone other than my dad.' She turned away, looking deeper into the Residency to hide her surprise.

'Her father did not approve, you see. I had a few things against me. I was a poor, uneducated Anglo-Indian for a start, and life with a man earning just a few rupees a month on a fireman's pay was not the sort of future he saw for her.'

'So why did you choose to come here?' said Joan, full of questions.

'Well, look around you. Isn't it beautiful and calm? Doesn't it transport you to another world?'

Joan did look around and her eye was immediately caught by a portrait of an English lady in a lacy, high-necked blouse with her hair up in a bun. She sat across an armless chair, her upper body and face turned towards the viewer and her right arm folded over the back of the chair. Joan was mesmerised.

Macleod remained silent, as if he knew why Joan's stare was fixed on the painting. 'Jonty, there is something strange about this painting.'

'Yes, isn't she beautiful?'

'Yes, but it's more than that. It's as if I can't take my eyes off her. There are all these portraits of these European men and women in their finery but I seem to be shivering just looking at her.'

'Have you got a small mirror on you, Joan? You know, like the one you women use for make-up,' he said, deepening the mystery.

'Well, yes.' She fidgeted in her bag and pulled out a small, round mirror case and flicked it open.

Macleod took it from her and held it by the painting, facing towards her. 'Look at your face in the mirror and then look at the painting, Joan.'

She did so, her eyes widening suddenly.

'It's amazing. I've never seen anything like it,' she stammered.

151

The sharpness of her high cheekbones, a slightly twisted nose, large brown eyes that stared out with interest, a half smile that showed contentment with life, even the long eyelashes. Had Joan been a few shades lighter in complexion with her hair tied up in a bun, the portrait could have been of her.

'That, Joan, is your great-grandmother and the main reason your mum and I came here every Sunday.'

Joan stared at the portrait in silence, drawn irresistibly into a lost world, one which she found strangely comforting and reassuring. Macleod gently held her hand.

'Tell me more about my family,' she said, happy to keep the physical contact with him.

Errol had ended his fascination with the marble lions and was engrossed in a big glass case that showed a re-enactment of the siege. Small clay figures represented the *sepoys* massed on the outside, some with cannons and others digging underground mines in an attempt to breach the walls. The British and their loyal Sikh soldiers on the inside defended the sporadic attacks with musket and sword.

'Your great-grandmother Ellen was married to an English officer, Captain Fulton, who was killed when a mine exploded and a fragment shattered his skull. The conditions in the camp were deplorable for a lady of her sophistication. She was one of the few memsahibs who had come out to India with her husband in 1850 to escape the female drudgery of life in the Shires.'

'She looks as though she came from quite a well-off family,' said Joan.

'Middle class, the Britishers might have called her. She was a bit of a rebel by the sound of things: during the siege she struck up a friendship with the Raja of Tulispur who was a prisoner at Her Majesty's orders. The Raja was suspected of inciting a rebellion against the British and had been incarcerated before the mutiny took root. The Raja was mesmerised by her beauty and took to singing her ancient Sanskrit songs in the evenings. This liaison would normally have been discouraged, but the Raja was an extremely important political prisoner. Fulton would appear to have approved of the contact; maybe he saw his wife working to convert the Raja to the liberal ways of the British.'

'So obviously my great-grandmother survived the siege,' said Joan.

'Very much so, but only thanks to Tully, which was her name for Raja Tulispur. People were dying of chronic dysentery brought on by contaminated water supplies and poor food supplies. Fulton was dead. Tully's affection for Ellen had strengthened and she was fascinated with him. The camp had a fixer, a man called Tewari, who seemed to be able to cross freely outside the walls and bring news to both sides. Tewari, bribed by Tully, told him of a secret passageway from the Residency to the world outside. Let's go down to the end of the mango grove and I'll show it to you.'

They walked out to the gathering of trees while Errol stayed behind, studying the model layout. The entrance to the passage was at ground level and was partially covered over with grass. A small sign at the site said 'We regret due to safety considerations this exhibit is not open to the public'.

'What a shame,' said Macleod, 'this was where they escaped one night to the world outside. Ellen blacked her face with a walnut dye and wore a *chuddar* around her as if she were one of the Indian women. Tewari had arranged for a bullock cart to take the two to a safe village, fifteen miles south of Lucknow. From there they made their way to Allahabad where Tully knew a *Nawab* who would offer them shelter.'

'Gosh, what an amazing story,' said Joan, in disbelief at the fairytale ending.

But Jonty continued, 'Of course that wasn't all. Tully continued to be in danger with the British and Ellen felt that she wanted to spend the rest of her life with him. Your grandmother, Margaret, was born as result of their union. But their happiness was brief. Tully was betrayed by one of the *Nawab*'s servants: he was taken away one night by soldiers and never seen again. Ellen died of a broken heart soon afterwards. Your grandmother was taken in by the nuns of the convent at Allahabad.'

Joan looked solemn. 'Jonty, I feel like someone new has entered my life. It's hard to describe but I can feel her spirit right here in the grounds.' Macleod now put a cautious but supportive arm around her.

'That's exactly how your mother, Dilys, felt, Joan. We were drawn together by the spirit of your great-grandmother. Every Sunday we came here, like today, and bathed in the spirit of Ellen Fulton. It drew us very close. And then it all stopped when Dilys's father decided I was unsuitable to marry his daughter.'

They walked slowly and in silence back to the main building. Errol had begun to get impatient and ran out to meet them when he saw them returning.

'Mum, have you been crying?' he said when he looked at her red eyes. He never saw his mother cry. He looked suspiciously at Macleod.

'*Beta*, I was just feeling happy. Sometimes people cry when they're happy,' she said to reassure her son.

The next morning was a normal workday again and Gerry went off with his trolley men to do a twenty-mile track inspection. Errol went with him to learn all he could about camber and continuous track. He rode up front with Gerry, loving every inch of the journey.

After a late breakfast Joan was sitting out on the veranda reading the *Hindustan Times*, delivered that morning, when she noticed one of the pariah dogs in the grounds barking. This usually signalled the arrival of a stranger and brought the *chowkeedar* to his feet.

A uniformed man on a red bike approached and the barking got more intense. The arrival of the telegram man only ever signalled two things: a note of congratulations or the death of someone near and dear.

Joan had to sign for the sealed envelope. It was addressed to her. She opened it with great curiosity, as all those near and dear to her were present and accounted for. She read the terse, ticker-tape message. *Please come to Howrah* thana *by return. I can get you meeting with Anil Sen. Chief Inspector of Police.*

BACK TO SCHOOL

When Joan and Errol returned to Calcutta a day later, there was a further letter waiting for Joan from Basu, suggesting that she attend the Howrah police station in three days' time for her meeting with Anil. The school term was due to start the next day, so she used her last day of the holiday to prepare Errol for his new term by making sure he had completed his holiday homework. Errol had to spend a few hours that afternoon finishing off his arithmetic, which had to do with calculating the number of square carpet tiles needed for a house of given dimensions. He found the task perplexing for he had never seen carpet tiles in his life and wondered how they, or the task, could ever be of any use to him.

When Joan entered her class the first day back after the Christmas and New Year break there was a scuffle going on, with a couple of boys pinning Lee Young, a small Chinese boy, to the ground. 'Stop that right now!' she exploded, raising her voice to a level that the pupils didn't hear from her too often. Jonty's revelation and her intended visit to the *thana* were playing on her mind and Joan's normally pleasant, relaxed manner had given way to a feeling of anxiety. The boys in her class were on the receiving end.

The affray broke up abruptly, with Lee Young looking shaken. 'They were beating me, miss,' he said.

'The three of you, now, up here in front of the class,' commanded Joan.

The three boys approached. 'They're always telling me I'm a spy, miss, just because my parents are from China. I say they from Hong Kong, miss, but they don't understand.'

'He called us names, miss,' said one of the other boys.

'Now look, and this applies to all of you: in this class and in this school it doesn't matter where you or your parents come from, you're here to learn to respect each other for what you are. I don't care if you're a Christian, Hindu, Chinese, Sikh or Mohammedan, we all have to get along and respect each other. Just because China is an enemy of India, doesn't mean that all the Chinese people who have been living here for generations support them. If I see or hear of any bullying like this again I shall report it to Father Rector, and you know the consequences of that, don't you?'

The class was silent. The threesome shuffled back to their desks and Joan began her roll call.

In the common room at teatime she raised the subject with the other teachers. 'Has anyone seen any bullying of the Chinese children lately?'

'Yes, I've been picking up a bit of pushing and shoving at PE time,' said Phillip.

'I had to give my lot a telling-off this morning when little Lee Young seemed to be getting a pounding,' said Joan.

'Ah Young, his family is running the famous restaurant in China Town,' said Punditji.

'And the shoe shop at the New Market. I've had several pairs made there. Very good they are too,' said Phillip. 'The Chinese community is having a few difficulties at the moment. The CID has locked some of them up on suspicion of spying for the enemy. There are allegations that Mao Tse-Tung has sent a few of his people here to infiltrate our colleges and create disturbances.'

'Yes, I'm reading that the Communist Party is breaking up into two splits. One split is supporting the Russians and the other the Chinese. I'm a Brahmin, so you can imagine what I'm thinking of these people. How can they call themselves Indians and support any of these splits, especially when the Chinese are killing our own *javans* on the border?' said Punditji, clearly not a supporter of the communists.

The thriving Chinese community in Calcutta came from Cantonese-speaking Hong Kong, which was still a British colony, and Shanghai, a Mandarin-speaking area. The two kept apart from each other and from their host country, unsure of how to engage with them. They definitely did not wish to be associated with the Workers' Revolutionary Movement, as many had fled the home country to escape the Maoist persecution of their families.

Many were hugely industrious and made a strong contribution to the commercial life of Calcutta. One of their remarkable gifts to the city was their food. Generations of Chinese in India had blended and adapted their traditional cuisine with the Indian love for spices and herbs. The result was a unique Sino-Indian blend of cooking that could only be obtained in Calcutta. And

Young's was perhaps the best exponent of this culinary multiculturalism. Residents of Calcutta would travel miles to eat at Young's, not the cleanest place to dine but certainly with the best food.

Eating out was a special treat for most middle-class people, so when Phillip suggested to Joan that on Friday night they go to Young's for a meal and take Errol with them, she was not only delighted but surprised at this sudden fit of generosity.

'I'm just getting over Audrey, you know. So I thought I would get out and celebrate. What better way to do that than with you and Errol, my closest friends,' he said.

Joan was silently pleased that he felt like this about her little family and was also glad at the chance to take her mind off her current preoccupation with Anil.

Young's was its usual bristling self on a Friday night with every table taken, mainly by Anglo-Indian couples and some large Chinese families. Little Lee Young was at the far end by the kitchen on a small table of his own, apparently doing his homework.

He noticed Joan and nipped into the kitchen to tell his mother and soon Mr Young emerged in an apron, with a beaming sweaty face. 'Ah, Miss Joan, good evening. Welcome. We will have table ready for you soon,' he said, then turned to Lee and gave him a more elaborate instruction that came out like rapid gunfire.

'Miss, my father says that there are a few people ready to go quite soon. So could you wait for a few minutes?' explained the boy helpfully.

So they waited while a few couples continued to linger,

clearly having finished their meal but probably with no intention of leaving just yet. Mr Young asked one table if there was anything else but still no joy. Finally one of the large Chinese families began to stand up to leave and the trio had their table.

Joan's favourite was the signature dish of the establishment: butterfly prawns. These were freshwater prawns, caught in the paddy fields of Bengal. They were nearly as large as lobsters and just one provided enough protein for an entire meal.

The prawns were shelled, half cut down the centre and spread out to look like giant butterflies, then gently breaded with crumbs and fried crisp and golden brown; food to die for. Phillip went for the safety of noodles and Errol just ordered plain old fried chicken.

The steaming food arrived, glistening with the promise of Young's kitchen. Lee hovered around their table until he plucked up the courage to ask Errol if he would like to see the goldfish. The two boys disappeared behind the goldfish tank, leaving Joan and Phillip alone.

'You seem a bit on edge this evening, Joan?' said Phillip.

'There's lots going on in my head right now,' sighed Joan. 'To begin with, there's this visit to the Howrah *thana* tomorrow. I feel like I'm longing to do something to help but I'm also scared by the whole thing. I've never done anything like this before.'

'You're very brave, far more so than me,' answered Phillip. 'The way you've got involved in this whole business, just to try to find out the truth, is courageous, putting it mildly.'

'I just can't help thinking what it must be like for Anil

right now, lonely and desperate to know someone is out there trying to help him. He feels like one of my own. I've seen him as a youngster in my class struggling with his grammar. But I know I'm going to hate the dirt, the smell and the way people in there will look at me.'

'I'll come with you.'

'No. There is a lot more I can do by playing the vulnerable memsahib, Phillip. You'll just get in the way.'

Phillip was slightly hurt that his offer had been turned down so abruptly, but Joan failed to notice. 'So what else is getting you down?' he asked, passing it off.

'Oh, I had this strange experience in Lucknow which has made me begin to think about my past in a new way. This old gentleman called Jonty took me to a place where there was a picture of a woman that he said was my great-grandmother. And I believe him because there was such a striking likeness between myself and the portrait. So now I've begun to think about myself; why I'm the way I am. She appeared to have been quite a brave sort of woman and so apparently was my great-grandfather, the *Nawab*, who was imprisoned by the British. I feel like I need to know more about them to understand more about myself.'

'Incredible, all this going on in Lucknow while you were away,' smiled Phillip. 'Mind you, the latest research shows that we are more influenced by our environment and how we were brought up than who we were born to.'

'I don't believe that. How could that be? Look at all the musical geniuses that have come from talented families and the same goes for criminals and *goondas* and the like who've come from bad families.'

'Well then, it must be debatable whether their talents

161

are down to their inheritance or the conditioning from their families.'

'I think that's the problem with us Anglo-Indians, we don't want to look at the past and see where we came from. It's all in the present. Enjoy the now,' said Joan, sticking to her 'nature' over 'nurture' argument.

'Thing is, Joan, many of us wouldn't know. We're just a sort of mishmash of people from different races who only have two things in common: English is our first language and we draw more heavily from British culture than we do from our Indian roots.'

'*Hah, hah*, but really this discovery about my past seems to have had a real effect on me; it's made me think a lot more about who I am.'

'In what way?'

'It's made me feel I'm doing the right thing with this Agnes affair and going to see Anil. You know, being a bit braver about wanting to see justice done.'

'Joan, you'll need all the strength you can get, wherever it comes from,' said Phillip, putting his hand on her arm. She reached out and touched it, smiling in acknowledgement.

REVELATION

The next morning the post arrived with a single letter in a white envelope addressed to Joan. The writing was in a clear, old-fashioned hand. It bore a Lucknow postmark and Joan was too intrigued to leave it unopened. She was late for her appointment at the *thana* and reading the letter would delay her further. But curiosity got the better of her and she began to read:

My dearest Joan,

I do hope this letter finds you well and enjoying the travails of modern living in Calcutta, a city I have never visited and probably won't in this life.

You may find this letter rather odd coming out of the blue but I hope once you have read it you will consider its contents very carefully.

Since our day out at the Residency I have had you in my thoughts nearly every day. I think it was the memory of your dear mother that came back to

163

remind me of the wonderful days we had together so many years ago. Oh what it was to be young!

Today I came back from the doctor after a check-up to investigate a general deterioration of my health. He told me that my diabetes has got to a point of no return and that the prognosis is not good. I may have no more than a year to live on this earth, maybe just a few months if the good Lord sees fit to take me away earlier.

I have given this impending termination of my life much thought and have come to the conclusion that the happiest thing that I could do is to spend my last days as your husband. Please Joan, will you marry me?

There would be significant benefits for you and your dear son Errol whom I much enjoyed being with. I have a good pension from the Indian Railways, which will be lost to the government once I die. This is not a trivial amount and you would very much improve your standard of living and be able to provide for the boy's further education.

Please take your time to consider my proposal and let me know your answer. Although it would give me the greatest pleasure if you were to accept, I would completely understand your refusal.

In great anticipation of your response,

Jonty

Joan quickly read the letter again to see if it was a hoax. The letter was written in one person's hand and therefore looked genuine. The formal, stilted tone did also sound like the work of Macleod, which sent an uncomfortable, cold shiver through her. A dozen thoughts raced through her mind.

She had not the faintest glimmer of love for Jonty and yet was it wrong to provide a bit of companionship to someone for a few months before he died? What would Errol think if she had given up the opportunity for his financial independence? What would her relatives in Lucknow think of her? What if Jonty was lying?

She hastily pushed the letter into her bag and left the house.

Once she was on the number 54 bus heading for the *thana* her mind moved to the prospect of seeing Anil again. She wondered why Basu had agreed to a meeting with the young man's ex-schoolteacher but not with his parents or other well-wishers.

The room in the *thana* stank of stale *bidi* smoke. Partially used butt ends littered the floor, which hadn't seen a broom for decades. Red splodges and stains of betel nut, spat out by previous occupants, covered the indifferent colour of the peeling wall paint, like a disturbing impressionist painting. A chipped Formica table and two wooden chairs were the only furniture in the room. The only light was provided by a small, bare, low-watt light bulb, which hung from a twisted black length of wire.

The door clanged shut with a cold echo and Joan found herself looking at Anil. His once-white shirt was grimy with sweat, a deep shade of dirty brown. His blue jeans were covered with crimson-red blotches around the knees. They looked as though they had been worn and slept in continuously for weeks. With his hair hanging over his heavily unshaven face and his head drooping down, he shuffled towards the table to sit on the wooden chair. The chains connecting his feet dragged, jingling, on the stone floor and a pair of rusty handcuffs held his arms forward. His eyelids, almost closed, showed dark purple, the whites nearly gone.

'Anil, what has happened to you?' said Joan, horrified.

Anil sat down on the chair. Putting his elbows on the table, he bent his head to his chest and began to sob, first quietly and then in fits of heavy sighing. Joan saw his back heave, the tips of his shoulder blades moving intermittently as the uncontrolled spasms of crying shook his now-frail body. It was several minutes before he was able to control his breathing again. She kept silent through all of this, merely holding his arm in an effort to connect with his sorrow.

'Aunty,' he said eventually, 'it was not me, I didn't do it.'

'Do what Anil? Who is accusing you and of what?' she responded softly.

'Killing, Aunty, killing, the factory manager, it wasn't me.'

'But no one has accused you, have they?'

'Yes, the CID. They made me confess, Aunty. I was beaten with a *lathi*, here and here,' he said, pointing to his knees and his back. 'And there was an Anglo man who I knew hated me for supposedly killing one of his people. He made me sign a confession to stop the torture. I couldn't take it any more. All my strength was gone.'

'Can I look?' She gently pulled up the back of his shirt. There were marks of severe bruising across his left side. 'Anil, have your parents been to see you?'

'No, Aunty, I asked to see them, and a lawyer or

166

solicitor, but they refused, saying that I was a criminal and needed to be punished like other criminals.'

'But that's against the law. Has no one seen you other than the CID?'

'No, Aunty, I've been kept in confinement in a dark cell, sleeping on a hard floor. This is the first light I have seen for two days.'

'Tell me what happened. Why were you picked up?'

Anil lifted himself to try and sit up as straight as he could. The sobbing had stopped and he gazed up at the light bulb as if he might see something in it to give him an answer to Joan's question.

'I was there at the factory with the others, the other brothers and sisters from the Movement. We were all going to be in this together. Solidarity to stop the factory from working.' He paused, looking at the light bulb again. Silence. 'Dutta had told me to carry a knife to defend myself or any one of us who might come under attack from the *goonda* security used by the capitalist owners.'

'*Bus, bus*, hold on, Anil, I'm losing you. Where is all this stuff about capitalists and knives and Dutta coming from? You're Anil Sen, educated at Don Bosco's; do you know who you are? Are you in this world, Anil?' said Joan, not quite believing she was speaking to the boy she once knew.

'Aunty, we need to fight a new revolution to give our country back to the people. We have to throw out the capitalists and all their supporters, the Marwari landowners, the reactionary professors, people like that. But I didn't kill. Aunty, I didn't kill....' He began to sob again. He looked away from her, ashamed.

Joan waited while Anil composed himself before

167

continuing with his story.

'We met the night before and agreed our plan. Philomena was there too, the only woman in the group.'

'Philomena?' Joan was stunned. 'Is she involved in all this too? Was she there on the morning of the stabbing?'

'Yes, she was at first and then she went to tend to a man who had been injured in the protest. I didn't see her after that. Dutta had always said that it was not appropriate for women to be there, but Philomena is a strong person. We needed to hold the barricade; women would be the weak link in the chain, he said.'

'Tell me about this Dutta,' said Joan indignantly.

'He's our leader, Aunty, of the Workers' Revolutionary Movement. We follow his teaching. It's the only way for our country; to bring down the corrupt system.'

'You're talking like a communist, Anil. That's not what we taught you at school. What about tolerance, forgiveness and all those things?'

'Ah!' Anil winced as he moved his body to relieve the pain in his back. 'Those are your ways, miss, OK for England maybe. We're a new country starting from the beginning. We need our way.'

'But you don't go around killing people, Anil. That's just wrong,' said Joan, amazed that Anil seemed to be condoning death to achieve his ends.

'I didn't kill him, miss....'

'But somebody did. The man is dead. You were there. You said that you were carrying the knife. What did happen, Anil?' Her tone had hardened and she was losing her patience.

There was silence for a while as Anil looked up at the

glowing red filament in the light bulb. 'Miss, I... I can't remember. The *kukri* was in my back pocket. It was only a protection. There was a lot of shouting when the manager got out of his car. An argument broke out. We were all shouting and chanting "*jao, jao, jao!*" Then the next thing I saw was him falling, and I heard the police coming, then we were running. I tried to escape but was cornered. Then I was hit on the head and that was it, Aunty. I remember being beaten and kicked by these men in the police van. There were some of our other brothers with us. They were all being beaten too.'

'Anil, Anil, what a state to be in!' Joan touched his arm again. He didn't move.

They both sat in silence for a few moments. The usually noisy *thana* was quiet this afternoon. 'Where was Dutta when all this was happening?' asked Joan.

Anil kept silent for a full minute. 'I don't know, miss. He is our leader; he needs to be free to continue the struggle. He was the person closest to me at the time. I keep seeing his shouting face in flashes.' Again there was silence, which Anil broke first. 'What will they do to me, miss, do you know, the authorities I mean? The government.'

'Well, a case will come to court and you will have to defend yourself with a lawyer to prove your innocence....'

'But the CID made me sign a confession to say that I thrust the knife and killed Mr James.'

'They forced that confession out of you. We'll have to get a lawyer to prove that you were put under pain and duress.'

'But what if he can't, will I be executed, miss?' The sobbing began again slowly.

'Anil, I'm sure you'll be OK,' comforted Joan.

'Miss, there is something more I have to confess to you.' Anil looked up at Joan, then down again, barely able to look her in the eyes to say what he was about to say.

'What is it?'

'I lied about Agnes. I tried to tell you she may have taken her life because her husband asked her to sell her body. There were other bad things that happened.' He stopped for another long minute. Joan could feel the *thana* surround them.

'Agnes was also an early follower of the movement. Dutta asked us to prove ourselves with a test of our devotion to the revolutionary cause. The plan was to expose a member of the establishment whom Dutta said needed to be taught a lesson; Agnes would be the bait.' He looked unsurely at Joan.

'Go on, Anil, I think I know what you mean,' urged Joan, trying to hide her surprise.

'I loved Agnes very much and didn't want her to get hurt, but more than anything I hated the idea of her giving herself to another man, even if it was for a great cause. Dutta said that it would only be to lure the man into a house where there were abductors waiting. The man was always taking sex from prostitutes and young Anglo-Indian girls who had fallen on hard times. Agnes posed as one of these young women and lured him into a house in Lindsay Street. But the plan went wrong. Dutta never said exactly what happened. The next thing we heard was that her body had been identified after it was found by the river. Aunty, I was heartbroken. It was my fault. I got her involved with Dutta and the Movement. And now this murder. Miss, I'm getting blood on my hands. Do I deserve to live?' He broke down and sobbed again.

'How do you mean things went wrong with Agnes? Did nobody even ask *what* exactly went wrong?' Joan suddenly began to see a weave of sadistic exploitation by a man bent on achieving his political ideals. How was it that a young life could have been used in this way? Dutta seemed to be the source of the evil.

'I want to meet this Dutta, Anil. If only because he could provide you with the evidence you need to prove your innocence. If you're sure you did not do the murder, then someone else must have taken the knife from you.'

'Probably, but I cannot be absolutely sure. I remember taking the knife with me and then actually holding the knife in my hands with the man lying on the ground in a pool of blood. Anyway, Aunty, the entire Anglo-Indian community will be out to kill me if I'm set free. This is our crude Indian justice, "guilty until proved innocent".' Anil looked down to the floor. He was losing himself in the guilt.

'So we have to identify the real culprit. We've talked about Dutta. What about the others in custody, have you spoken to them? They must have seen what happened.'

Anil's head sank. 'There has been no contact. I've been kept apart, in the dark most of the time. It's horrible, miss, I'm going mad. I need this to end. Please, miss, get me out of here.' His eyes pleaded with her, even in the gloom of the cell.

'I am going to help you, Anil, trust me,' said Joan, worried by the desperation in the young man's tone. 'I need you to stay strong to help Agnes. How did she get mixed up in all this? Much the same way as you did I suppose?'

'When Agnes came to the college she was very shy, unlike her friend Philomena who was quite confident. Agnes felt she had been betrayed by the nuns; offloaded onto Xavier who had married her only for the sake of his social acceptance in the Christian community. Philomena and I brought her to one of Dutta's meetings and he had an instant, magical effect on her. He did with most of his followers. I think from that moment on her sense of betrayal by the nuns became more intense and, like us, she wanted to take part in a new revolution, Dutta's revolution. The Movement...'

'And what became of her in Lindsay Street? You really don't know, even now?'

'No, Dutta would not say. He said that one of our sisters had given her life to the cause. We know there are many *goondas* in this city who are keen to put an end to Dutta. She was a girl and her life was worthless to many in this city.'

'May her soul rest in peace,' recited Joan with her eyes closed. There was silence.

'Your parents, Anil, shouldn't they be coming to see you? They can help?' said Joan, wanting to sound hopeful.

'Please no, I don't want them to see me like this. My mother will cry and my father will feel disgraced. I have let them down so badly.'

The door was opening. The favour she had called in was now running out. 'Madam, my superior is now coming to the *thana*, I have to return the prisoner to the cell, *jaldi, jaldi* memsahib.'

There were still questions Joan wanted to ask but Anil was carried away, chains dragging along the ground as he went.

He looked back at Joan. She ran up instinctively and hugged him for a moment in a sudden uncharacteristic burst of emotional empathy. The handcuffs stopped Anil from reciprocating and he broke down and cried again, uncontrollably. Joan had to fight back her own tears.

How frustrated she was to have so very little at her disposal to help Anil. Here was a state in the young Republic of India, dangerously close to becoming a lawless region and she, a single parent on a meagre salary, without power or influence.

The end of Agnes's life, the villain Dutta, the way Anil appeared to have been framed and the mysterious life of Philomena were all thoughts that swirled around in Joan's mind. She would be caught up in the eddy of one idea and dragged down deep in thought; then, moments later, another thought, another idea would push out the first. She walked slowly away from the cells.

Phillip had been waiting patiently at the entrance to the *thana*, ignoring Joan's wish to go through with the visit on her own. He had bought a copy of the day's *Statesman*, a paper he did not read regularly. There was a special feature on the latest intrigue in the GKW stabbing, by the paper's special reporter, Raj Chopra.

'There's more in here than you found out in there I bet,' said Phillip as Joan appeared looking quite glum, but secretly pleased to see him. 'Are you OK? You look like you've been to a funeral.'

'I didn't think people could be so bad. What's happening to this world?' said Joan, vaguely attempting to explain her feelings.

'According to this article, it doesn't look too good for your ex-pupil. He's fallen in with this *goonda* political crowd who appear to want to overthrow the government and all that we might call the established order, and then gone and put a knife in the back of poor old James. It mentions him being an ex-pupil of Don Bosco's, which will be fine for our reputation.'

'He didn't commit murder, I'm sure. It was that man Dutta. Anil has been framed. In fact I'm sure he's been framed by this lot from the Workers' whatever they call themselves.'

'This Dutta fellow looks a bit like a troublemaker. He has a long record of being a *goonda*. Apparently he's Chinese-trained in all sorts of guerrilla warfare and skulduggery,' said Phillip. He read from the article by Raj Chopra aloud:

'For four months I monitored the Workers' Revolutionary Movement and can report that the state of Bengal needs to take note of this political party. It has no fear of established institutions and makes a mockery of them.

Their self-elected leader, Sunil Dutta, rules his domain with demagogic efficiency, tolerates no dissention and is ruthless in his pursuit of a workers' revolution. His disciples are trained in urban warfare, including poisoning, kidnapping and torturing. They have acquired their skills...'

'Wait,' said Joan, 'if this chap Chopra knows so much about Dutta, we should be talking to him to see if he can help free Anil and use the power of the press to get the *badmash* locked up.'

'I know a chap at *The Statesman* who can introduce you to Chopra,' said Phillip.

'Phillip, you have your uses,' Joan replied, breaking into a half smile.

She had not given the proposal letter from Jonty one moment's thought all day. Now, on her way home, she began to think about how she might respond. She was far too preoccupied to notice that Phillip was holding her hand all the way back on the bus. A man and woman holding hands in public was not considered normal accepted behaviour in Calcutta. And Father Rector would have thought that two work colleagues holding hands was completely out of order. But Phillip didn't care.

Journalistic
Endeavours

After breakfast the following Saturday morning Joan went
to see Father Rector.

'Father, I wouldn't mind a chat about something that
is troubling me,' she began.

Joan often used her superior as an advisor when things
of a moral or spiritual nature needed clarifying and,
although she knew what her answer to Jonty would be,
she thought she should solicit the priest's view. Just to
make sure, she thought. The rector, a Spanish priest
who'd been in India for at least thirty years and ordained
for more than twenty, was a pragmatic man of God,
certainly not one of the 'hell and damnation' variety.

'Mrs D'Silva, there would certainly be no impediment
in the eyes of God. Your ex-husband is deceased and Mr
Macleod has not been married before. But the answer to
your question of 'will you be doing the right thing?' is only
in your heart. You are a woman of good character and I'm
sure you won't make a decision on the basis of greed or

exploitation,' advised the rector.

'That's my problem, Father; I'm worried about making a decision on the basis of greed rather than compassion or indeed without any love for the man. Surely not marrying for love would be against the will of God? To love, cherish and obey I believe are the form of words we Catholics use.'

'Yes, but love and cherish are very unreliable words. If I were to make a rigorous check of all the marriages I have done in India, I'd say that most of them would not really pass the "love" or "cherish" criteria. They are done mainly for convenience and security and the loving and cherishing comes many months or years after. As for "obey", well we may be dropping that from the text altogether in a few years. Joan, I think you know the answer: it's in your heart. Follow it.'

And that was it. Joan had made up her mind. She left Errol with a group of boys in the school who were taking part in a cricket-coaching day and went off to keep the appointment she had nervously made with Raj Chopra of *The Statesman*.

Raj Chopra was a product of the English-medium education system. He was an avid Gilbert and Sullivan fan, loved reciting some of Shakespeare's greatest speeches and at six every evening he celebrated the end of his working day with a *burra* gin and tonic at the Calcutta Club, watching the sun go down. He had been a junior reporter on *The Statesman* just after the surrender of Rangoon and had made his name by covering the heart-rending stories of the refugees who made the long march by foot from that city into India.

Many of these families were Eurasian, of mixed British and Burmese descent, and had been given just a few hours to pack up their belongings and escape the fall of their capital to the invading Japanese army. Raj covered the arrival of these people into India. Only the fit and able survived the crossing, arriving thin and emaciated after days of walking without food or sustenance. The elderly had perished by the wayside; some had been attacked and killed by tribes friendly to the Japanese. Raj married one of the survivors, a strikingly beautiful woman called Kay, who brought some of the exotic ways of the Burmese people with her, such as bathing in a bath of coconut milk to keep her skin soft, and cooking wonderfully flavoured, aromatic *cow sway*.

He had been with the *javans* fighting the Chinese incursions into India, and his regular reports of the gallantry of the Indian soldiers defending the borders with First World War Lee-Enfield rifles were popular with readers. Chopra had come within a cat's whisker of death several times and he had now come to the conclusion that a halo of protection surrounded him. It made his investigations more daring and his reports therefore more insightful than anything else on offer, rendering articles by his peers rather dull and bland.

Raj had become aware of Dutta and his Workers' Revolutionary Movement after a friend at the military intelligence made it known that the same Dutta was linked with the Chinese communists. A fluent Bengali speaker, Raj infiltrated the organisation to gain insight into the training and indoctrination they received. To have been discovered would have meant certain death. But Raj was a risk-taker and enjoyed the pursuit of a good story.

Joan met Raj at the Calcutta Club just a day after she saw Anil. She had never set foot in this revered establishment as membership was solely for men; a decade earlier only Europeans had been allowed to join. The membership committee consisted of seven men and any one of them had the power to veto a new member.

The dress code included a jacket and tie even in the most excruciatingly hot weather, and after independence the Bengali *dhoti*, with one end tucked into a shirt pocket, had been included in the allowable attire. But elitism continued to thrive, with only the upper echelons of Calcutta society being admitted.

The guest room was lined with mahogany panels and the various trophies of hunting men who had, during the twentieth century, made their contribution to the impending extinction of the tiger and other members of the cat family worth shooting. Photographs of past presidents and dignitaries further indicated the *pukka* colonial credentials of this establishment.

'So, Mrs D'Silva, I hear you liked my piece in *The Statesman*?' said Raj, pouring himself a top-up of tonic water.

'Yes, I have some connections with this case which encouraged me to come and see you. May I say that the country needs people of courage like you at the moment: it feels like many of the reliable institutions are collapsing around us just now, either because of corruption or a lack of resources. The police are not equipped to deal with this. I'm just a humble teacher at Don Bosco's and have very little influence over anything. I've been drawn into events without meaning to be and now, maybe rashly, I feel I need to do something,' explained Joan.

'Do tell me more. What events?' said Raj very interested to see what direction the conversation would take.

'It was my son who discovered the Bandle Girl: the corpse of a girl called Agnes. I was with him on that day. I taught Anil Sen at school five years ago. Now it looks like they were both the victims of their association with Sunil Dutta.'

Chopra took a big gulp of gin. No one had made the connection with the Bandle Girl and Dutta before. The case was still open and unsolved like the many other murders in Calcutta. He smiled, inviting Joan to continue. Joan paused. She had never met this man before so she wanted to be careful about what she said and how much of her conversation with Anil she gave to Chopra. But she was at the Calcutta Club with Chopra of *The Statesman*. She had to continue.

'What Anil told me was in confidence to his mentor, but I have good reason to believe that someone took a knife from his person and stabbed James. Agnes too fell foul of one of Dutta's campaigns and paid with her life,' explained Joan.

Chopra reached for his gin, careful not to show his amazement. 'Dutta is running rings around the police, the Chief Minister and the Communist Party of Bengal at the moment,' he said. 'Their main recruiting ground is the Calcutta College. It's where they hold these clandestine meetings. I have a few people I know working for the newspaper who attend these meetings, so I receive reports of planned actions and the like. But the Dutta link to the

Bandle Girl is an interesting one and I shall have another dig around. I did hear about a vendetta against some of the members of the establishment, many of whom are members of this club.' Chopra drained his glass.

'I took a look at Lindsay Street; I even talked to a leading madame there: Jessica, she called herself. She said she had never seen Agnes there before.'

'Ah, Jessica, yes: a well-known name to some of the men here at the club. I must hasten to add, Mrs D'Silva, that I have no personal knowledge of her myself. But what made you look there?'

'Oh, I'd just heard one of Agnes's friends mention that she may have been going there to do a bit of reconnaissance for Dutta.'

'My God, you have been having a good old dig around, haven't you? *Shabash,* good for people like you who take some personal responsibility for finding out the truth.'

'Doesn't it seem odd to you that we should be trying to solve a crime when it's the job of the police?' puzzled Joan.

'I think we Indians are far too passive when it comes to wanting to take a role in righting the wrongs of society. And you are doing an excellent job as Miss Marple, only this is real life. The police are just as corrupt as the crooks, only not as competent,' said Chopra in an attempt to make light of the hopelessness of the situation.

'Yes, and the country is going to hell minutes after independence. People are saying they wish the British were back. Life was much better under them. What good is freedom when you starve?'

'Mrs D'Silva, these are the symptoms of early

childhood, if I may use the metaphor. We're still finding our feet. Consider how long it took England to establish a democratic system of government after the Magna Carta. What's that, seven hundred years?'

'But India isn't starting from scratch. It's had a system of civil governance for years,' said Joan.

'Yes, but the democratic institutions were offloaded onto us one night on the fifteenth of August 1947, and here we are, still coming to terms with making it work. It is definitely the best form of government that we could have inherited but it's going to take time. Ninety per cent of our citizens can barely read or write, let alone decide which party to vote for. The rupee determines all sorts of political favours and it will take education and a degree of economic well-being to get the people in the villages and cities alike to value their freedom.'

Chopra spoke the way he wrote, so eloquently in his editorials, of the opportunity facing India and how education needed to be the engine of growth for the economy and for the country. He had strong affiliations with the Congress Party and was frequently invited to New Delhi to advise the Ministry of Education on its policy for rural education.

Chopra relaxed into his chair. He was enjoying the company of Mrs D'Silva. He'd noticed a few members trying not to stare when she walked through the room. She was a fine-looking woman. He smiled at her. He wanted to hear more from Mrs D'Silva.

'And what of the future for your Anglo-Indian community here in India? I'm interested in your views as I have been considering doing a feature for the paper on this very subject,' said Chopra, taking the conversation in a different direction.

'It's a diverse community, as you well know, from the very *pukka* British Anglo-Indians who don't have a drop of Indian blood in their veins, to others who are one hundred per cent Indian and have converted to Christianity somewhere along their family tree. The *pukka* lot are upping sticks and decamping to England or Australia as they are easily accepted for emigration; the others try to battle it out here if they can. I'm one of those who want to make a good go of it here.'

'And is that difficult?'

'Mr Chopra, it's difficult for all our citizens at the moment, isn't it? You said that India was an infant trying to find its feet. But it's particularly difficult for us, as we were so closely allied to the recent rulers.'

'Who made us Indians feel quite inferior,' said Chopra. 'Look at Churchill, see his open disdain of us. We were a nation that was destined to be ruled, according to him. It's a real pity that colonisers have to put themselves in this position of moral and intellectual superiority.'

'But there is a legacy that wouldn't have been possible without Britain and that is the unification of India, which might otherwise still be a collection of warring kingdoms. You do need an external force sometimes to bring about change and the British provided that.'

'Mrs D'Silva, you're now sounding like Dutta, calling for a revolution to destroy the country before he builds it up again,' he said mischievously. 'Would you like another drink?'

Joan looked at the fading light.

'Look, Mr Chopra, it's been very good of you to see me this evening, but I must go now. It's getting dark and I'm meeting someone in town.'

Chopra inclined his head. He thought he would see Mrs D'Silva again. 'Well, thank you for coming.'

'I look forward to reading your next piece in *The Statesman*. If you do discover anything of interest or need me at all, please get in touch with Don Bosco's School. I'm not on the phone. Thank you.'

Chopra stood up and shook her hand, and a bearer came to escort Joan out onto the large veranda. She was greeted by a strong smell of evening jasmine and the screeching of a family of crows in a *peepal* tree, doing battle before roosting.

Joan's faithful rickshaw wallah was waiting outside the club, and she was grateful to see him there as the light was fading.

'Mehmsahib, will you be going to Lindsay Street again?' he asked, thinking maybe that Joan had formed a liking for the place.

'No, not today, just take me to Chowringhee, the Grand Hotel,' she said, excited that she was meeting Phillip there before going home to Liluah.

Phillip had arranged to join her for an iced coffee, which was suddenly all the rage in Calcutta. Pat Tarley too was going to be appearing later on, crooning her way through the evening.

Xavier looked Joan up and down when she arrived to be seated at Phillip's table. 'Madam, have I seen you before, perhaps?' he said as he led her through the seating maze. 'You look familiar.' Xavier smiled like a snake, and he looked appraisingly at her body.

'I was at the coroner's hearing for the case of the Bandle Girl: your wife Agnes, I believe,' said Joan. Xavier visibly shuddered, his composure lost.

'Ah yes, please forgive me, the schoolteacher from Don Bosco's,' he acknowledged.

'Have you heard anything from the police since then?' enquired Joan.

Xavier took the easy way out. 'Bah! Bloody police. What bloody good? That fool Basu came to question me again, here in the hotel, asking me the questions about where I am the week of her disappearance. Then some bloody fool questions about my connections with Lindsay Street painted ladies. Can you believe it? Besmirching my name in front of my employers. Me, I'm only providing introduction service and getting blame for being bloody criminal. Sister Theresa is pulling many strings to stop me getting the sack.' Xavier looked around to see if his employers were watching him.

He and Joan reached Phillip's table.

'Mr Phillip, your memsahib friend is here, please enjoy your evening,' said Xavier, handing over his charge. Phillip felt a little uneasy as he watched the head waiter leave; Xavier had looked at Joan once more and was probably making comparisons with Audrey in his mind.

'That fellow gives me the creeps,' he whispered to Joan.

Pat Tarley, dressed in a black, figure-hugging dress with bright sunflower prints and a boat-shaped neck, caressed the silver microphone like a long-lost lover recently returned from the sea. She crooned through

Doris Day's 'Send Me the Pillow You Dream On', while Joan and Phillip sucked on their iced coffees.

'Phillip, how are you these days?' asked Joan, breaking the silence between them. It was one of those simple questions.

'I came here today deliberately to see if I felt any regret about Audrey. I can safely say that I have none. I have got her out of my system. And may I say that you have been most helpful.'

Joan smiled, acknowledging the compliment. 'Have you always lived on your own?' she asked, speaking her thoughts aloud but regretting her intrusive question midway through her sentence.

'Err, not quite.' Phillip paused a bit and Joan felt even more embarrassed for asking. 'There was a lady in Darjeeling who moved in with me: into the teachers' quarters at the school. We were together for a few months but things didn't work out.'

'Oh, I'm sorry to hear that,' said Joan looking into his eyes, hoping to help him with what seemed likely to be the outpouring of some past affair.

'Living in sin, I think it's called these days. Might be OK in Europe but it seemed to cause quite a scandal in Darjeeling. Her father, you see, was a very *pukka* Britisher: a tea plantation owner. He never approved and it all got quite nasty with threats from some *goonda* policeman over my future safety and a lot of pressure on my girlfriend.'

'That's awful,' comforted Joan.

'Yes, even the greatest love between two people can get strained and soon we were quarrelling. It all ended after

I had a not-too-satisfactory conversation with the principal who said I was bringing down the reputation of the school. The hypocrite! After all the affairs he had with the local women.'

'Oh, Phil, I'm so sorry to have brought up the subject,' said Joan, wanting to hug him in sympathy. Better judgement prevailed and Phillip soon regained his composure, so she reached out and put her hand on his arm in a gesture of friendship. 'Thank you too,' she continued, 'for being such a close, understanding friend. The world seems to be attacking my sanity with all these things happening around me, but I can't bear to be just a bystander.'

'Don't get too involved, Joan, that's my advice. The forces you are dealing with are dangerous and quite beyond your control.'

'Yes, I'll be careful.' And then, as if she wished to change the subject, she said, 'Shall we dance?'

The request took Phillip by surprise. He'd come for a little chat, an iced coffee and the songs of his favourite singer. Dancing had not been on the list of things he expected to be doing. The priests at school had once lectured him about the 'dangers of dancing'. 'The devil lurks at every dance,' he remembered being told by one priest, and the lecture seemed to have had an everlasting effect. Dancing therefore became an opportunity to do something sinful, which he quite looked forward to. But dancing with his closest friend seemed more like going for a walk or taking a cup of tea as they quickstepped around the floor.

'Phillip, this is nice,' said Joan. 'Thank you.'

It was the first time he'd held a woman close since his affair with Audrey had been so abruptly terminated. Joan's Evening Jasmine perfume permeated the air around her. It was a cheap bottle she'd bought from Hong Kong John and it had a Made in China label on the box, but Joan had taken a great liking to it and wore it whenever she was out for an evening.

'I love your perfume, Joan,' is all that Phillip could say, hoping he didn't sound too corny.

'It's only a cheapie from John,' she said as they side-stepped away from the band so they could hear each other.

'It reminds me of happy times,' he smiled.

'Oh, your other conquests? Other women?'

'Joan, I didn't mean that, you know.'

She grinned, amused.

Phillip took Joan back home to her flat. She didn't invite him in for a nightcap as she said she was tired after a long day. She wanted to write her letter to Jonty. As Errol slept soundly in the bedroom next door, she began to craft a suitable reply to her suitor.

My dear Jonty,

I'm sorry it's taken me so long to reply to your sweet letter of proposal. I have been rather swept away with events here in Calcutta.

When I received your letter I was reminded of the day that we spent at the Residency and your stories of my great-grandmother. You helped clarify so much of my past and the connection with my mother whom I knew for just a brief time on this earth.

Jonty, I have given your proposal a great deal of thought and I have been so flattered by your asking me. However, I'm sorry to say that I will have to turn down your kind offer; I could not in all conscience marry you for the economic convenience you would bring to my son and me.

Marriage reminds me of the bond of affection I had with George, my deceased husband. I would need to recreate something as strong if I were to marry again, and if not I'd feel I was letting him down. I hope you will understand.

I trust your sickness will not cause you too much pain, that the doctors are proved wrong and that you recover over the course of the year. Then we will get a chance to see each other again at the Residency next New Year.

Affectionately yours,
Joan

Joan licked a blue stamp marked 'Special airmail delivery' and fixed it to the envelope. It would still take a couple of days. The normal postal delivery could mean a week or ten days, and given that she had taken so long to reply to Jonty's proposal she needed him to know her answer soon.

That night Joan dreamt she was held captive in a forest, with chains attached to her feet and hands. A huge black cat came running out of the darkness towards her. All she could see was its shining red eyes, and she began to run

189

for her life, but the chains slowed her down and she wished she could be free of them. Her yells for help woke Errol, who was confused and scared and had to be comforted back to sleep. After that she slept lightly, her mind full of thoughts about Anil and his cell, Chopra and what he might find out next and of course Phillip. What was going on in his mind? Was she just his friend?

TAMASHA

'Isn't this a bit like celebrating while Rome burns, darling?' said Charles to his wife Edwina. The Smiths had decided to throw a party to celebrate the first anniversary of their time in India.

'No, not at all, sweetie; we're just experiencing normal things that happen in India. Don't be such a drama queen,' she argued.

A large *shamiana* tent had been erected in the garden, festooned with lights of all colours. The guest list read like a Who's Who of the well-connected and influential in Calcutta society, from Chief Minister Roy to media stars like Pearson Sureeta, the cricket commentator and *Musical Band Box* host, and Raj Chopra, who was also a well-established figure in Cal society.

Edwina Smith had found an excellent *durgee* through a woman in her ladies' circle, and the man had arrived to take her measurements, under instruction to make a special outfit for the occasion. She had ordered a scale pattern of a full-length dress from Liberties in London. The dress was to be in a deep indigo satin, procured from Raymond's in the New Market. It was a daring new Chanel design, cut away at the back down to her waist. Edwina had seen a picture of Princess Margaret in something similar at the film premiere of *Richard III*.

The *durgee* was familiar with making Western-style clothing, but had never made anything quite like the dress Edwina had in mind. He took a good look at the pattern and wanted to know if there was a bit missing at the back. When he was assured that this was part of the design, he scratched his balding skull and, with a shake of his head to one side said, 'OK memsahib, we try to please. Can I be taking the measurements?'

He pulled out his tape measure and Edwina stood erect so that he could get the full length of her 5' 8" frame. The *durgee* was a Sunni Muslim who was not comfortable with touching women. So the exercise was conducted with some unease, very outstretched arms and eyes firmly on the tape measure.

They came to the highly awkward procedure of measuring Edwina's bust size. She was a sizeable thirty-eight D cup and cut quite a striking figure when she pulled back her shoulders and stood up straight. The *durgee* paused for a minute standing behind her, pondering how best to approach the difficult task of measuring Edwina's bust without actually touching any part of it.

Eventually he decided on giving her the ends of the tape measure and asking her to pass them across her breast. He then took hold of the two ends from the back and completed the measurement standing well behind her. 'Perfect, memsahib,' he said with satisfaction, and Edwina smiled to acknowledge the daring feat he had carried off.

Then there was the difficult job of selecting the menus. About half the visitors would be non-Indians, mostly Europeans who were not altogether familiar with Indian cuisine. So she asked Philomena to suggest a menu of food that would cater to Eastern and Western tastes. In the end the cook was given a wish list of delicacies that ranged from what Philomena referred to as boring insipid food such as sausage rolls and sandwiches to exciting street finger foods such as *samosas, shami kebabs* and many different stuffed *rotis.*

Live music would also be necessary, and the services of Danny Covelo and his band of top-class Goan musicians were procured. Danny was a well-known saxophonist on the Calcutta cabaret circuit and played the most current songs from Vernon Corea's Radio Ceylon hit parade.

The invitations caused a stir among the well-connected members of Calcutta's upper echelons. Those who had been invited to the Smiths' party wanted to let their friends know, and those who hadn't were keen to let it be known they could not attend the evening as they were otherwise engaged.

Charles and Edwina had applied a simple philosophy in drawing up the invitation list. Only those who had made a noticeable contribution to the continued safe and secure operation of GKW's business would make the list. This would include politicians of influence, lawmakers and enforcers and commercial customers. This therefore included nearly every member of the Calcutta Club (Charles carefully weeding out any particular members he disliked) and Edwina's ladies' circle, whose husbands were inevitably also members of the club.

Guests started arriving at around seven on Saturday evening. They all carried presents of varying sizes, as was the custom for such big events in the social calendar. Edwina and Charles stood by the entrance to the *shamiana* and greeted the guests while one of the servants relieved them of their gifts and laid these in a neat pile nearby. Soon the pile of presents had increased in size to such an extent that one of the other servants had to carry them away to start a fresh collection in their place.

It had been a hot day and the evening temperature had only just dropped below eighty degrees, so the outdoor setting was perfect and Edwina felt very comfortable in her backless dress. She had made a special exception to her invitation guidelines to invite Joan and Phillip as a couple. They chose to come by taxi, an extravagance they felt was worth it to avoid the dirt and grime of the number 54 bus.

'Joan, lovely to see you,' said Edwina, kissing her on one cheek; she was one of the few guests that she had kissed that evening. Most of the Indian dignitaries preferred the *namaste* and both Charles and Edwina had become experts at offering this greeting in a most gracious way.

'Edwina, you look gorgeous,' said Joan.

'Oh thank you. You don't think it's too bold, do you? Inspector Basu can't keep his eyes off me.' She smiled across the room to where the inspector was standing.

'He probably wants to arrest you for indecent exposure but can't summon up the courage. This is such a great party: you've got all the rich and famous here tonight.'

'Are they?'

Joan smiled. 'Even the First Minister.'

'Charles seems to be well liked.' She looked around then back at Joan. 'You look rather lovely yourself, Joan. Where did you get that dress?'

'Oh, it's something my *durgee* knocked up from a piece of silk I bought from Hong Kong John,' said Joan coyly. The bright red, shiny silk dress with golden prints of Chinese parasols complemented her jet-black, shoulder-length permed hair, styled only hours earlier in China Town.

'Where are your boys tonight?' asked Joan.

'There in the far corner,' Edwina pointed, 'trying to overcome their shyness of the adults.'

'I'll go over and join them,' said Phillip, electing to be with the boys where he would feel more comfortable. He was not the sort to mix freely with the social elite of Calcutta and preferred the company of young people with whom he could revert to his teacher role.

'Philomena not here tonight?' asked Joan.

'No, she's asked to take the evening off. But she's worked slavishly to get this event off to a good start. The menus, chasing up invitations, the lot.'

Joan hadn't alerted Edwina to the young woman's political affiliations since Anil's revelations; or the conflict with her role as the family nanny. But with the Movement at the centre of suspicion for the James murder, Joan now believed she had a duty to tell Edwina. However, first she must confront Philomena.

Joan was grateful to hear Edwina change the subject. 'Inspector Basu is still looking this way,' she said.

'He might want to speak about the school. His son is doing well.'

'I'd better go and rescue Charles from the politicians.'

As Edwina moved away, Basu took his chance to talk to Joan. He was smiling as he reached her but she greeted him first. 'Good evening, inspector, lovely party isn't it?' He was wearing full civilian attire: a white traditional Bengali *dhoti*, the end of which was meticulously tucked into the left pocket of his stiffly starched white shirt.

'Miss Joan, good evening. How are you? Many interesting people are coming here tonight.'

'Yes, inspector, like you and me,' said Joan, getting a smile out of Basu. 'And thank you for getting me into the *thana* to see Anil.'

'I have been hearing that you've been making some interesting enquiries in connection with the case of the Bandle Girl,' said Basu.

'How do you mean, inspector? I didn't know you had spies after me?'

'No, I just heard that you have been around talking to Mr Chopra and people like that....'

'Oh, you do have your spies on me. What else have you been observing?' Joan enquired.

'A few other things, but be careful, Miss Joan. You could be getting into the hot water. There are many *goonda* factors creating difficulties for us these days,' cautioned Basu.

'I can take care of myself, inspector, but you know what puzzles me is why the police can't solve some of the crimes that are being perpetrated every day in this city. It's obvious that the job is too big for your department.'

Basu smiled indulgently at Joan. 'Miss Joan, just be careful of Dutta and the Workers' Movement. You could be getting into much *garbar*. He is almost certainly being linked to the murder of the factory manager Mr James, and my CID officers are investigating a possible link with him and the death of the Bandle Girl.'

'Oh, inspector, your people have been busy,' said Joan, surprised by this revelation. 'I thought Anil had confessed to the murder.'

'We are now suspecting that confession as other evidence has come to light.'

'Oh?'

'Miss, I cannot say more at this stage, but please be taking my warning.'

Basu looked uncomfortable and Joan was not sure if it was simply the civilian attire that sat uneasily on a man more accustomed to the uniform of a police officer, or if there were problems of a deeper significance troubling him.

'Joan, you don't have a drink, darling,' shouted Edwina, coming towards her. 'Gosh! You and the inspector look so serious in discussion.'

'Please be excusing me,' said Basu as he melted away into the now-packed *shamiana*.

Edwina took Joan by the arm and led her towards Charles Smith and Judge Bhattacharya, who were in close conversation. 'Tell them I'm just not interested,' she heard Charles say. They broke off what appeared to be a disagreeable discourse for both men and smiled somewhat falsely as they saw the women close by.

'Darling, meet Judge Bhattacharya, he's one of our sweetest friends here in Cal,' said Edwina, literally handing the man over for safekeeping to Joan. 'He's a keen historian and a student of the Lucknow mutiny too. You may have something in common.'

'Very pleased to meet you, sir, though I believe we have met before,' said Joan, recognising the man from the coroner's courtroom a few months earlier. The judge smiled at Joan. He was trying to remember where he'd seen her. Edwina smiled at them both, the perfect hostess. But it was time for her to move back into the room. 'I must insist that I ask one of the bearers to refresh your glass, Batty.' She left the couple together as she turned around to join another group, displaying the handsome shape of her uncovered back and shoulders as she went.

'That lady has some style, don't you think?' said the judge, and Joan felt a little uncomfortable at the way he looked at Edwina as she glided across the floor of the *shamiana,* away to her next attempt to foster social mingling.

'Indeed. So nice to see someone with fresh modern ideas and energy in town.'

'May I say you don't look too bad yourself,' said Judge Bhattacharya, but he looked slightly embarrassed, realising that he may have become too familiar too soon. 'I'm sorry, I hope you don't mind me saying so.'

'I'm not too used to people, especially men, paying me compliments, but it's very nice to hear, so thank you,' she said, putting Bhattacharya back at his ease. The judge's white linen jacket, with a dark blue tie displaying the Bengal Cricket Club insignia, complemented his yellowing, tobacco-stained moustache.

'But you have the advantage on me. I can't quite recall our first meeting?'

'You were the coroner for the Bandle Girl case and my son was the one who discovered the body. Do you...'

'Ah, yes of course, you looked familiar.' He caught himself considering what to say before continuing cautiously. 'Strange case that one. Must have been very distressing for you and your boy?'

'Yes, he was speechless, which doesn't happen often. I saw the body myself and it was in quite a state. But then we do see some distressing things on the streets of Cal, sir. The mutilated bodies of children forced to beg for some *goonda* gang, for instance, or refugee mothers with half a dozen starving children sleeping outside the railway station at Sealdah.'

'Well, quite.'

A bearer, one of the many in starched white tunics and magnificent twirling blue turbans, came with a bottle of Eagle beer and a fresh glass to replace the empty one in the judge's hand.

'So, Edwina tells me that you are from Lucknow and that some of your ancestry has connections with the mutiny?' asked Bhattacharya, interested to hear about Joan's Lucknow connections.

'Yes, on my great-grandmother's side, I believe, although I haven't been able to do much to verify any records as such. I just saw an incredible likeness to her in one of the portraits at the memorial, and someone who knew my mother knew of the connection.'

'I know exactly who you mean: Ellen Fulton and the Raja Tulispur's dash for freedom. How extraordinary to meet you, madam.'

'Thank you. And tell me about your interest in the mutiny.'

'Well, as an amateur historian I've always been

interested in that period of Indian history as it was the beginning of our nation as it is today. That is, we as Indians realising that we had to fight a common foe. So in a perverse sort of way we need to thank the British for uniting us from a collection of squabbling little fiefdoms and princely states.'

'But a lot of blood spilt on both sides. The British weren't ready to give up India and the *sepoys*, although very much superior in numbers, didn't appear to have the arms or the organisation.'

'And arguably, madam, India was not ready for self-government. It would take us another half a century to discover the Mahatma and the maturity and power of non-violent protest as a political weapon,' said Bhattacharya nodding, as if to make the point to himself.

'A point that seems to have been forgotten by many of the current generation of young revolutionaries who prefer the ways of Mao to Gandhi,' said Joan, testing the judge's views on the wave of violent political protests in Calcutta.

'Regrettably! Well, Bengal has always had its own way of doing things. Netaji was out talking to the Nazis to bring about a collapse of the British forces in the East while Nehru was preparing a constitution to lead the biggest democracy in the world. We know how that worked out. Tagore, my hero and the great Bengali poet, thought Gandhi's ideas of rural regeneration completely potty.'

'Have you come across this Dutta character?' asked Joan.

The judge looked at Joan carefully. He was not used to such a direct question from a woman. He was cautious now.

'I'm certainly aware of his activities. Inspector Basu tells me that there is a possibility he might be linked with the death or, as I think they call it, "assassinations" of a few people. The success of the first democratically elected communist government in Kerala has given the Marxists much hope. Except Dutta and his people don't believe in democracy.'

'The inspector seems to suspect a lot of things but can't get around to arresting the right people or solving these unexplained deaths, like the one of Agnes which I believe must still be open.'

'Ah yes, but really that was a very clear case of suicide, I'm sure, but the incompetent Basu just couldn't get his act together, so there we have another open verdict,' said Bhattacharya, sounding quite confident of his position.

The band stopped playing, a large gong sounded and there was the piercing sound of a public address system being switched on. Charles Smith's head appeared at the corner end of the *shamiana* as he climbed a makeshift dais to address the guests. 'Hello, hello, is this switched on?' he began, tapping it until he was satisfied that the audience could hear him and the feedback from the amplifier had been neutralised.

'Good evening friends, *namaste* and welcome to this celebration. My wife Edwina and I are delighted that you could join us this evening to help us celebrate the first anniversary of our arrival here in this remarkable city. We have so much enjoyed meeting our many friends who are here today and wanted to mark this occasion with a special thank you to all of you who have made us feel so welcome in our new home. Yes, I do refer to Calcutta or Cal, as some of you say, as our home because in a year it has begun to feel as if we have always lived here.' There was a small ripple of applause, Edwina smiled and Charles continued.

'I know the city is going through a hard time of political unrest but I'm sure, talking to many of you, that this is just a passing phase. Just looking around me and seeing the incredible talent and hope that exists for the future of this city, and the nation as a whole, gives me great comfort, and it is a pleasure to be part of building a great future. Please join Edwina and me in partaking of the rich and varied delicacies of this marvellous city, prepared by our cook, with a little help from the head chef at the Grand. Thank you everybody and have a lot of fun.' There was an outburst of applause.

'The speech of a diplomat, I'd say, not a businessman. Although I hear he is quite tough with his people,' commented Bhattacharya. He looked at Joan. 'Shall we join them for some *khana* to eat?'

She began to feel a little uneasy talking to the judge. 'I'd better find my escort for the evening, who might be feeling rather ignored. It's been nice talking to you, sir.'

He graciously bowed his head. 'The pleasure has been mine, and please could we meet again? It's been so nice talking to you. Are you on the phone?'

'I'm afraid not...'

A bang like thunder cut through the room. People instinctively bent their heads as if to avoid the aftermath of some disaster, and seconds later the top of the *shamiana* began to fill with smoke. Most of the guests thought they were witnessing a fireworks spectacle, and they all began to look up at the top of the marquee, holding their breath for the next big bang.

Soon people had resumed their conversations and the

clatter of plates and cutlery started up again. Then there was a succession of smaller bangs as balloons began to burst, each one going off like a firecracker amidst yelps and screeches of good-humoured laughter.

But then flames appeared, opening up a hole in the roof of the big tent, and a large sheet of tarpaulin came drifting down to the ground in flames. Someone's sari caught fire and she screamed and fell to the ground with two guests trying to douse the flames. Another piece of burning tent fell to the ground, starting a wider commotion.

Women began to scream and the crowd started to panic, everyone suddenly rushing towards the small entrance that had seemed perfectly adequate for the arriving guests but was completely unable to disgorge over a hundred people all at once. More burning bits of tent began to rain down to the ground and balloons burst everywhere, adding to the sense of alarm.

'Please stay calm, please, please,' shouted Charles, 'we can all get out of here safely.' But he could not be heard now as the screams and shouts drowned out his pleas.

Bhattacharya grabbed Joan by the hand, 'Come on, we've got to get out of here before the whole tent goes up.'

But there was no other way out. Frightened people were now running around the *shamiana* in circles, afraid to stand still. The fire began to rage in the ceiling. Paper Chinese lanterns were now in flames, and bits came falling down on the heaving mass below. A few people had managed to escape and were calling out to their friends or loved ones still trapped in the tent.

'My babies, my babies,' cried Edwina. She thought her sons must be at the back of the throng trying to get out of the narrow entrance, and she tried to move against the tide of people, shouting '*chullo, chullo*'. Joan and Bhattacharya were near the entrance now and struggled to stop themselves from being pushed to the ground. Joan stepped on someone who had curled up in a ball to protect herself from being trampled to death. She tried to get the woman up but was pushed further on by the force of the crowd behind her. 'Come on, we have to look after ourselves first, push forward,' said the judge, still pulling Joan by the hand.

Phillip had still been talking to the boys when the blast struck and, recognising the obvious danger of being at the opposite end to the only exit, he'd immediately begun to look for another way out. He noticed the marquee had been tied to the ground with rope secured to wooden pegs. He shouted to the boys to stand well back towards the walls of the *shamiana* and began to undo the ropes, making a hole big enough for them to crawl through, out into the open. Soon the boys were through. He yelled to some of the other panicking people who were terrified of being burnt alive as more debris rained down.

Phillip worked desperately to increase the size of the opening and pushed the less agile through to speed their escape. In this way the hole opened up further and soon others realised that there was another way out and began to crawl through the hole, making it still bigger and easier to negotiate.

The fire now appeared to have abated and the smoke in the *shamiana* was leaving through the large opening in the roof. The crowd was still coughing and spluttering, some gasping for fresh air. Many had burns as they emerged and those who had been trampled earlier were now being carried by the bearers and laid out on the grass outside.

'It's that bloody Dutta again, I'm sure,' said Inspector Basu, a little worse for wear, having been one of the people who had to crawl out of the hole at the back of the tent.

Edwina was now hugging her sons, not fully believing that they were unharmed, and Charles was running around, fetching water and blankets for the injured. Bhattacharya appeared unscathed in his linen jacket and was calmly sitting on a bench surveying the chaos, sipping the remnants of his glass of Eagle Beer. Phillip found Joan just as she was looking for him and soon a couple of fire tenders arrived. The ambulances from the Woodlands private hospital drew up much later to carry away the injured and those in a state of shock.

Phillip held Joan's hand. 'Are you OK?'

'I'm fine. And you?'

Just then Charles came up to Phillip and said, 'You are the bravest, most decent man I know, sir. Thank you for saving my boys and all those other people from the marquee. I can't thank you enough for what you have done, at much personal risk, I'm sure.'

'Just an instinctive reaction really,' said Phillip, more embarrassed by the praise than pleased.

Attracted by the smoke and the noise, a huge crowd had gathered, together with a number of rickshaw wallahs and taxis keen to cash in on some unexpected business.

'Basu, start getting some statements, will you. Some of these people must have seen something, someone,' called Bhattacharya, more as a command than a suggestion. Basu, feeling he'd just come close to being burned alive, was still in a state of semi-shock. He was sitting on the lawn gazing blankly into space, his white starched shirt and *dhoti* crumpled and soiled with a combination of burnt debris and earth from having crawled on all fours out of the *shamiana*.

But it was a command he had to obey. He rushed to his car to call the Howrah *thana*. There were now a few hundred people outside the walls of the bungalow and Charles, with his servants and bearers, had to keep them outside the gates to clear a way for the ambulance and fire engines to arrive.

There was not much for the fire service to do as the *shamiana* had by now been reduced to a wreck of charred poles and bits of wire. The main casualties were out on the lawn, suffering from burns and smoke inhalation. The woman who had been trampled by the escaping crowd had fared particularly badly and lay on her back, being tended to by an elderly man.

Charles surveyed the scene. One of his servants brought a rickshaw wallah to him. 'Sahib, this man says he saw someone cycling away after throwing something over the wall at the *shamiana*.'

'Did he get a good look at the fellow?' asked Charles.

'No, not exactly sahib, he says he thinks it may have been a woman.'

'A woman? What sort of woman?'

The rickshaw wallah was asked to describe the suspect and seemed unsure of himself. Charles had developed a theory that Bengalis, in their effort to help someone, often felt the need to make up a story to reassure the questioner. The servant translated for Charles.

'Sahib, he is saying that the person had her hair in plaits. Only womans is having this, sahib,' explained the servant.

'You'd better get him to talk to the police,' commanded Charles.

The rickshaw wallah protested at the order to talk to the police, for in his lowly position he could end up in the *thana* and not get out again for days. He might even be forced to say things that he did not agree with.

'Sahib, he wants *baksheesh* now for the information.' The servant conveyed the rickshaw wallah's request.

'Only if he talks to the police,' said Charles, stepping up the pressure.

The rickshaw wallah refused and walked away, muttering and complaining at the request. A few rupees was not a fair price to pay for a few nights in one of the worst jails in the country. Charles wondered how Basu managed to get any convictions, given the poor reputation of his force.

The firefighters were scouring the burnt-out wreck to look for the cause of the fire. Marquee fires were quite common and many a wedding party had been wrecked by them. Usually poor electrical wiring was the cause. But the firemen were trawling through the debris of the Smiths' *shamiana* carefully to make sure they knew precisely how this fire had started and it was not long before one of them was holding up a broken beer bottle in his hands and discussing it closely with his colleagues.

The woman who had been trampled was carried out on a stretcher. The rest of the walking wounded were seen by a doctor and put in taxis to go for further treatment at the hospital. Charles had made it known that GKW would foot all medical bills.

'Very strange business with one of the rickshaw wallahs, darling,' said Charles to Edwina. 'Fellow says he thought he saw a woman speeding away from here on a bicycle.'

'A woman? On a bicycle? How odd!' she said with narrowed eyebrows and widened nostrils, a characteristic trait of hers when she quizzed her husband.

'Never know whether to trust these chaps, who seem to want to be helpful but do make up a few tales from time to time. Wouldn't speak to the police, I'm afraid.'

Joan, who had been helping Edwina recover some of the china and household effects from the debris, overheard the comment and stood still in disbelief.

'By the way, Edwina, where did you say Philomena was this evening?'

'Oh, she didn't say.'

Joan thought again about Philomena's political views, the coincidence of the rickshaw wallah's story of a woman on a bicycle, her affiliations with Dutta and the fire in the shamiana. 'I wondered where she was, especially on such an important evening of your social calendar,' said Joan, leaving a hint of anxious enquiry in her voice and expression.

'Yes, Charles, it is very odd that Philly decided to have today off.'

'She said it was a long-term appointment with her friends from the college. Something they do every year,' replied her husband. 'Anyway, darling, I don't think Philomena being here would have helped stop this disaster or made it any easier. She's better out of it.'

A CID detective had now arrived and Inspector Basu

and his small group of khaki-clad constables were going around talking to the taxi drivers, rickshaw wallahs and other bystanders to see if they would reveal any sightings of a person intent on starting a fire in the *shamiana*. All they got was a lot of shaking of heads and silence.

Bhattacharya and the Chief Minister seemed to be engaged in an intimate conversation. They touched each other on the shoulder repeatedly as if emphasising their agreement and familiarity, the way that Bengali men seemed to do. The judge's wife went up to them and broke up the discussion.

'Charles,' said Bhattacharya as the three prepared to leave in the Chief Minister's official car, 'damn shame this fire tonight. Firemen think it's foul play of some description. CID is checking out anyone suspicious. Expect we'll have the suspects by the morning. Mind you, knowing Basu and his bunch of incompetents, who knows? Joan, are you OK?'

'Oh yes, I'm fine, and thank you for pulling me out of the mêlée,' said Joan, half smiling her acknowledgement at the judge. She wasn't sure she liked Bhattacharya's definitive tone and assumption that a few suspects would be delivered overnight. In high-profile cases such as this it usually meant randomly rounding up individuals and holding them for questioning.

The men left in the black Ambassador and Charles and Edwina went to see how some of their other guests were coping with their transport back home.

'Let's get out of here,' said Phillip, hailing a taxi back to Joan's flat in Liluah.

Back on Joan's veranda they both sat down to unwind from the evening's traumatic events. Neither of them were drinkers but on this occasion Joan poured Phillip a large glass of rum diluted with a local cola, and made one for herself too. That evening they both felt lucky to be alive, in each other's company and back in Joan's home with Errol asleep; a time when being alive and unharmed seemed to be a luxury and a moment to treasure.

'Phillip, I wrote to Jonty with my answer,' said Joan, who had finally told Phillip about the proposal.

'And the answer was?'

'Oh, a polite no, of course. How could it be otherwise?'

'Do you think he'll be offended? I mean in the last days of his life?'

'Phillip, you don't understand. Marriage means a lot for a woman. Well, certainly for me. It's not about convenience, or money. It's a bond of unconditional love which I just don't have for Jonty. Would you marry a wealthy woman if you didn't love her, Phillip?'

'It's different for a man, Joan.'

'Would you or wouldn't you?'

'Well, if she were going to provide for my children the sort of essential things I could never afford, if she did not expect any physical or sexual relationship, and if it were something that would have a finite end in sight, then yes I would consider it,' said Phillip, looking her directly in the eyes.

Joan looked back. 'Men just don't understand women, do they?' she sighed.

The conversation moved on to the people at the reception, the possible causes of the fire, the discussion

210

with Bhattacharya and, of course, Phillip's immense act of bravery, which he put down to survival and commonsense. One glass of rum led to another, slurring Joan's speech a little and making Phillip feel more adventurous in his advances towards her.

'Phillip, I felt very proud of you tonight when Charles commended you,' said Joan.

'And I was just so pleased to see you OK, Joan,' said Phillip, reaching out from his cane chair and holding her hand. Seeing that she didn't seem to mind, he knelt at the bottom of her chair and held both her hands, pulling her down to kiss her on the lips, to which she willingly responded by lingering for a few seconds longer.

Her spine tingled a little, for this was the first time she had kissed a man full on the lips since the night before her husband George had departed on the Dehra Doon Express. She was used to their normal diet of sex most nights and George would sometimes jokingly complain of Joan's voracious appetite for being pleasured more than once on some occasions, especially on a full moon, he claimed. They would lie naked, bathing in the near-incandescent rays of the Bengal moon streaming through the bedroom window, and Joan would run her hands down George's stomach and caress him, to arouse him for another round of love-making, which she never wanted to end. But all this stopped the night George lost his life, until something this evening triggered that same urgent desire.

Each small advance of Phillip's was reciprocated in silence by Joan. Phillip put his face in Joan's lap, still kneeling by her feet. Joan kissed the top of his head, Phillip moved his hands to massage the sides of Joan's thighs and she held the back of his head. And so they continued, one incremental step at a time, undressing each other, wanting each other. She only half-believed they were making love on the floor, the tiles still warm from the evening sunshine. It didn't last long as Phillip tumbled quickly into the abyss of his own orgasm.

'I'm sorry, so sorry, it's been ages since I…'

'It's OK Phillip, don't worry,' interrupted Joan, putting her hand over his mouth to silence his embarrassment. They lay still in silence for a moment; Phillip wishing the building would collapse all over him and end his shame, and Joan wondering how she had allowed their liaison to reach such a bare but uncomfortable intimacy so easily.

THE SAVIOUR

'Arson Blamed for *Shamiana* Blaze' was the main headline in *The Statesman* the next morning. The report read:

What was probably the society event of the summer ended in disaster last night after a fire in the roof of a shamiana in the grounds of Mr and Mrs Smith of GKW.

It is believed that a Molotov cocktail, thrown at the roof of the tent over the walls of the residence, caused the fire. The company has been the target of strikes and attacks by the Workers' Revolutionary Movement, which, it is also alleged, has been linked with the stabbing of Mr James, the factory manager employed by the same company.

More than a hundred party guests escaped with burns and minor injuries. Inspector Basu of West Bengal Police, himself a guest at the party, commented, 'It is a miracle that nobody was killed on this occasion. My department is making maximum effort to catch the culprits.'

On Sunday morning a police Jeep with three constables inside stood guard outside the Smith home. Charles Smith had taken his family to the Grand Hotel for the night as Edwina could not face the trauma of staying one more minute at their place.

Back at school, Joan and Phillip were the focus of attention in the teachers' common room as everyone wanted to know the details of the event and their ordeal.

'Phillip was such a hero,' said Joan, very proud of her friend. 'If it hadn't been for him, there would have been many more casualties.'

Joan had made a special effort to meet Phillip at the school gates before assembly. Her head hurt a little from the alcohol and lack of sleep, but she wanted to see him before school. She didn't want the embarrassment to linger.

'I'm really sorry for last night, Phillip. I overstepped the mark, way above where I should have gone. I'm sorry,' she repeated.

'I, I... don't know what to say.'

'Don't, Phillip. These things are better left as they are. Last night was a lovely evening. I still think you're fantastic and I'm full of admiration for you. What happened was just a devil trying to get out in me. Could we leave it at that and still be friends?'

'But it was I who...'

The assembly bell interrupted their muted conversation and they hurried through the school gates.

In the common room Phillip maintained a modest smile in the midst of the compliments on his bravery, saying that it was nothing more than staying cool and applying common sense. Joan talked about the prestigious guests who were there, mentioning that she had seen Pearson Sureeta and the Chief Minister and talked to a judge. The teachers were most impressed at this sudden injection of excitement into their generally mundane discussions. This was definitely more engaging than Punditji's last visit to the doctor or a report on someone's weekend canasta party.

'They must be arresting the culprits now,' said Punditji. 'Otherwise all the foreign companies will be leaving Calcutta tomorrow.'

'Like looking for a needle in a haystack,' said Joan. 'The best we can expect is that someone innocent will be arrested and blamed by the police, probably confessing after a bit of coercion. Look at our Anil, now in prison accused of the murder of Mr James. I know he is incapable of doing it.'

'I wonder if the Smiths will pack up and go home. I know I would,' said Mrs Costa. 'It's only going to get worse, isn't it? I notice her boys aren't at school this morning: I wouldn't blame them.'

The Chief Minister had indeed called emergency talks to see if the escalating violence towards foreign-owned companies could be stopped and the ringleaders arrested. Dutta had gone underground, only meeting his Movement contacts at secret locations to avoid detection. As a prime suspect he would almost certainly be arrested now and detained, probably without trial, for as long as the police felt necessary. Anil and the others held for the factory protest were still in detention.

After some forensic examination, CID had found two sets of fingerprints on the knife used to kill James. One set belonged to Anil, the owner, but another set, marked in blood, belonged to someone else. This second set did not match any of the other prisoners' prints. Basu was therefore in a quandary: he had a confession extracted from Anil but knew that he was most probably not the murderer. Also, there was a public perception that the police had already apprehended the James killer: to admit that killer was probably still at large would only further damage the already ruinous reputation of the police.

It was about this time that Raj Chopra decided he should seek a secret interview with Dutta in an attempt to make him more visible to the public. Through a few contacts at Calcutta College he managed to get a message to the leader to the effect that the newspaper wished to give him a platform for his ideas. As he had hoped, this offer appealed to Dutta's vanities and within days Chopra found himself being spirited off to a village about a day's drive from Calcutta, blindfolded and hands tied in the back of a truck.

The ride had been rough for more than six of the eight hours of the journey. Judging by the rocking of the truck and the constant creaking of the suspension, this was not the Grand Trunk Road, but some minor, multi-rutted track. They seemed to pass few other vehicles throughout the journey, which Chopra took as a sign of the remoteness of the location. When they stopped for breaks there was total silence, the only sound coming from the crackling radiator of the vehicle as it cooled.

In the evening, starved of any food or water, Chopra arrived with his escort at the meeting point, a mud and bamboo hut collection of dwellings. When he was inside the compound, his blindfold was removed and his hands untied. This was Dutta's new rural headquarters. Chopra was told to sit on a rickety *khatia* bed and was given an earthenware *kulhar* containing milky sweetened tea.

Hours with a blindfold on had blurred the reporter's vision, and for a few minutes he saw only unfocused images of buildings, but then he gradually noticed chickens scratching about the courtyard picking up leftovers; a man dressed in olive-green fatigues squatting on his haunches while chopping up a pile of onions; the collection of mud and bamboo huts around a central courtyard. A young girl kept up what seemed like a continuous vigil of sweeping the hard-baked clay ground.

This didn't look like the hideout of one of Bengal's most-wanted guerrillas. After about half an hour of sitting on the *khatia*, Chopra was getting restless. Then at last a Jeep rolled up outside and two men came through the entrance. One wore grubby jeans and a vest; he sported long, shoulder-length hair and a thin beard. 'Let's talk,' he said.

This was Dutta, the man the police were dying to talk to. Chopra shivered a little with the excitement of being with someone of such immense notoriety, and he pulled out his notebook and pencil.

The other man, who seemed to be Dutta's bodyguard, brought him a stool to sit on and the interview began.

'Sri Dutta, you probably know that I have been interested in the activities of the Workers' Revolutionary Movement for some time. Are you behind the current spate of disappearances, murders and firebombings in the state?' asked Chopra without any formalities or introductions, knowing that his interviewee was not given to such things.

'My Movement believes that the system, this state and also the entire nation are based on centuries of corrupt

217

colonialism, and before that on the feudalism of the landowners and the *Nawabs*, much of which is still in place today, untouched. The systems of government, the police, the railways and other public bodies are all deeply corrupt. Everything is determined by the amount of money you have. What chance is there for those without money and power? Look around the world and you will see there are some people standing up to this kind of injustice.'

'But we have the British to blame for that. Now, surely, with our hard-won freedom we can do something about it? We're still just finding our feet,' said Chopra, hoping to challenge Dutta, who probably wouldn't be used to much in the way of argument from his compliant disciples.

'But no one is doing anything about it, Chopra. Show me where?' Dutta snapped back. And the journalist, rarely for him, was lost for words.

'In China,' Dutta continued, 'Mao is pulling up the old establishment by the roots and trampling out the people who have supported it; in Cuba and South America, Guevara wages an uncompromising war on the corruption of the American imperialists and European colonialists. These are some of the people who wish to build a future for their people based on a new order. They have decided that change needs people with a vision and a dream. My followers and I share a similar dream.'

'But some say that this is not the Indian way, sir. They say that here in India we do things by non-violent means. We have a long tradition of bloodshed and conquests and now we need to grow up and be mature and use the democratic process to bring about change, through the ballot box,' said Chopra.

'Listen, I know that people like you say we are not being realistic. But how can these peasants even begin to understand who to vote for when they are starving every day and their primary purpose is to find the next meal? Some people are a cancer in our communities and they have to be taken out and eliminated. We have our list of these people and more are being added every day: we are serious.'

'What would it take for you to stop your activities?' asked Chopra.

'Nothing will stop us. I have no negotiating point because I do not believe that anything other than total surrender would help us achieve the radical agenda we have set. Everything else would be compromise and we don't compromise. Mr Chopra, your readers need to see life this way. No compromise. We won't tolerate just a little bit of corruption, or a little bit of injustice, or just some starvation of the poor. This might seem idealistic but if we dilute these ideals where do you stop and where do you end?'

'So what makes you think your efforts won't be in vain? The forces stacked up before you are enormous. Consider the suffering and pain people will have to endure.'

'Mr Chopra, all revolutions are painful. Am I confident that we will prevail? Yes. Every day a steady stream of young men and, yes, even some women are joining us. They love their country and cannot stand to see another hundred years of degradation for the people of this land.'

A group of young men and a woman arrived on foot, dragging their tired feet into the courtyard. Their clothes clung to them with perspiration. Some wore red headscarves, one a Lenin hat. They carried long *lathis*, one had a nine-inch knife in his belt and the woman carried a pole on her shoulder with a *chatti* containing what was probably water tied to the one end. They chatted in Bengali to each other and went over to the man chopping the onions to see if they could eat something soon.

'This is the future of the country, Mr Chopra. All these people have given up their comfortable middle-class lives for the Movement because they believe in it. Most of them are college educated, even this woman.' His hands indicated his fellow revolutionaries.

Chopra glanced at the woman, who wore brown slacks and a navy tee shirt. She wore the familiar Mao revolutionary's hat, an essential part of a Red Guard's uniform, her plaited hair just showing under the back rim. She looked back at him in a defiant way, unlike most Indian women who would have immediately diverted their gaze.

'And what is their role in your movement?' asked Chopra, returning his attention to Dutta.

'We have two fronts, an urban one and a rural one. In our cities our Movement is advanced and having effect. Here in the villages we are beginning to educate and to organise the peasant farmers and workers, to get them to understand that we are there to help them in their struggle with the landowners and capitalists.'

'And assassinate and abduct those who get in the way?' probed the journalist.

'Whatever is necessary,' snapped Dutta. 'Whatever, Mr Chopra, is necessary. I think this interview is now concluded. I will get you escorted back to the city.'

'Why did you agree to see me, Sri Dutta? Did you have a hand in the assassination of Thomas James? Did your

220

people firebomb the Smiths' gathering?' continued Chopra, but there was no answer and Dutta said something to one of the young men and disappeared into a hut.

The truck that Chopra came in was nowhere to be seen. He was blindfolded again and told to sit in the back seat of the Jeep that had earlier transported Dutta to the compound. He heard the engine being manually cranked by the driver, and it burst into action: he could smell black diesel smoke, which filled his lungs. Then movement, the dirt track again which seemed to last for hours. He had not eaten or drunk anything all day apart from the sweet, milky tea. His tongue was dry and his head hurt with the constant rocking motion of the vehicle.

The Jeep stopped and Chopra heard the distant noise of traffic. His blindfold was removed and the ropes that tied his hands were cut open. His sole escort, the driver of the vehicle, wore a mask to hide his face, which seemed odd as none of the others had bothered, including Dutta.

'Tell me where we are,' he said to the driver. 'Which way is it to the city?'

All he got was silence. The man got back into the Jeep and rode off, swirls of dust emerging from the rear of the vehicle. Chopra noticed he didn't take the direction from which they had come.

The road, which was about half a mile away, looked busy with lorries and other heavy traffic going both ways. He walked towards it until he was able to stop a truck going in the direction of Calcutta. The driver was taking a load of scrap metal to a collection site on the outskirts of the city.

'*Bhai*, would you give me a lift to the city? I'm going to visit my father, he's ill in hospital,' he said in Hindi.

The driver looked a kind fellow in his thirties. He beckoned to Chopra to jump into the cab. A statue of Ganesh sat perched on the dashboard and a myriad of silver and gold tassels hung from the rear-view mirror up to every corner of the cab. The driver cranked the gear stick and the vehicle rattled into life.

'This is my home, friend,' he said as they trundled forward, changing gears and increasing speed. 'Welcome to my home.'

'You don't live anywhere?'

'Nowhere in particular, friend. You're sitting on my bed and my armchair. This is all I have in the world, my lorry.'

'You're a Bihari, aren't you?'

'Yes, from Patna. I was one of seven children in my family and two of my brothers died before they were five. We never went to school or anything. I presume you did. You look quite well off.'

'Yes, I did go to school, in Calcutta. Did your family not have a house in Patna?'

'*Hah, hah*, my father had a small *maccan* with a few hectares of land and a cow and we grew some rice and managed to feed the entire family. Then one day I remember some *goondas* coming to the house and telling my mother that they would kill my father and rape her if he didn't pay up a loan. My father had borrowed from a rich landowner to pay for the dowry of our only sister.'

'Did your father find the money?'

'No, he had to part with the land and our home for a few hundred rupees and we were all forced onto the streets in the city to make our own way, sleeping near the railway station. I was a coolie at the age of nine.'

'So how did you come to be a lorry driver?'

'One day after many years of carrying boxes and bags I had a lucky break. The driver who drove this lorry asked me to be his *chokra*. I helped the driver load and unload scrap metal from all over the state and by twelve years of age I was about as strong as he was. He became blind and made me drive the lorry until one morning he never awoke. I took on the lorry as he had no known relatives and now I transport scrap for a few rupees a day, which just about covers the cost of the petrol. But at least I have a roof over my head in this cab.'

As Chopra wrote the concluding paragraph of his special report for *The Statesman*, he posed the question: would the driver's life be any better if Dutta had his way? The much-hated leader of the Revolutionary Movement was trying to improve the life of many millions of people who, like the lorry driver, were caught in bonded labour, owned by the wealthy landlords and exploited by the rich, lucky enough to have been born into money. Was it what Dutta was trying to achieve or his methods that were so despicable?

WASTED LIFE

There was no suicide note when Anil was found hanging from a beam in his prison cell. His parents came to collect the body but were told that forensic tests would be necessary before it could be released.

Joan went to visit his family.

'I never knew my son could have done this,' said Anil's father at the family apartment in Belur, a suburb of Calcutta. 'What a wasted life for a boy with such a promising start. Mrs D'Silva, you were always reporting good things about him at school. But after he went to the Calcutta College he seemed to develop grand ideas about changing the nation, said that we were prisoners of our religion and our culture. How was he getting these stupid ideas?'

Joan looked directly at Mr Sen. 'I went to visit Anil a week ago and he was very depressed. Although he confessed to the murder of Mr James, I don't believe he did it. Your son was not a murderer. Someone else did it and was happy for him to be accused.'

'It was those girls he made friends with that I didn't

approve of,' said Sen, apparently unconcerned at that point about his son's innocence or guilt.

'Who were they? Which girls, Mr Sen?'

'The two from the convent, you know, one of which was found dead in Bandle. I knew there was trouble and *garbar* up when that happened. You know, Miss Joan, we Hindus bring our children up in a different way from your community. Mixing with the sexes causes problems which young men cannot handle. They get confused and their sense of control is lost. That is why we keep them apart. It is not natural.'

'But they were just good friends, Mr Sen.'

'No, you don't understand, Mrs D'Silva. It confuses a young man, you know, the power of women, the sexual power. Anil lost his innocence when he went to college because of this social mixing. Your Anglo-Indian community allows this to happen from a very early age so it becomes natural, but for us it becomes most disturbing. I'm sorry to say this but that is how I feel.'

Mr Sen told Joan that the autopsy of the body showed that Anil died in what the police described as 'suspicious circumstances'. Strangulation marks on his neck other than those made by the noose indicated that he might have been killed before being hanged from a beam in the prison cell.

Anil's parents had to suffer a double grief: not only was their son dead, but they also could not cremate him until the authorities released his body. Joan tried to contact Inspector Basu to see if he could intervene, but no one returned the several telephone calls she made. She had called his main office at the central *thana* but she was told by a peon that he was busy, out of town.

225

There was still Chopra. She found his card. They met on the ground floor of *The Statesman* offices. He had been reluctant to meet, but Mrs D'Silva had been persistent. 'Mr Chopra, I've come to see if I can help you further with your investigations into the activities of the Workers' Revolutionary Movement,' she told the journalist after she decided that the press was perhaps the only well-functioning organ of democracy that she could turn to in order to help the Sen family.

Chopra had been finalising his piece for the newspaper following his meeting with Dutta and was under pressure from his editor to get it completed for the Sunday special edition. 'I'm pleased to see you, Mrs D'Silva, but I haven't got a lot of time this afternoon. I have to get some work done,' he said.

'Look,' persisted Joan, 'you need to know a few things that might complete the picture. I was perhaps the only person that Anil confided to in prison. Now that he is dead, we have three connected murders that can be traced to one man: Dutta.'

'But Anil committed suicide, surely?'

'I don't believe that for one moment. Yes, he was in quite a bad way, but the boy was a fighter. You know when you see suicidal people; they keep talking of ending it all. Anil just wanted to prove his innocence and get out of jail. And now we know there is an ongoing investigation into his death. So it's not a clear-cut case.'

'Are you saying that Anil was killed by one of these *goonda* elements in prison because he knew too much?'

'Yes, can't you see you have a much bigger story to tell,' said Joan, staring at Chopra, encouraging him to understand the scale of what she was saying.

Chopra's narrow eyes widened. He had thought he had a good story already, but Joan had given it a whole new dimension. Dutta's bombastic ideals certainly contrasted with the ruthless way he dealt with his own followers in pursuit of those ideals. Was this a man blind to any compassion that might get in the way of his lofty goals?

'Very interesting, Mrs D'Silva, but there's one thing I don't understand and that makes this case all the more important to me. Why would anyone want to conceal Dutta's brutality? Surely, looking at all the events so far, he wants people to know that the Movement is there to make the established order quake. No, if Anil was killed, then there is something else going on. Someone finds it convenient to pin the blame on Dutta, or Anil as his disciple.'

Chopra had a peon bring Joan a cup of sweet Marsala tea, and they talked over it for an hour. Joan replayed the prison meeting in detail, recalling Anil's appalling state after his ordeal with the prison guards. 'He was definitely in a bad way, but he was not suicidal. I taught him for a few years and I'm certain he was a determined young man, not given to despair.'

She told Chopra how Anil had tried to frame Agnes's husband Xavier by hinting he might have driven her to commit suicide. Anil had been trying to protect Dutta from something that went disastrously wrong. Agnes too had died, probably brutally killed, all in the cause of the same man.

Chopra knew this might be the biggest story of his life. 'Mrs D'Silva, it's really quite extraordinary that you, an ordinary citizen so to speak, are so determined to bring this man Dutta to justice. I wish there were more people like you.'

227

'Mr Chopra, I can assure you it is only because of the discovery of Agnes's body and the pleas of help from Anil, who was one of my pupils, that I've been drawn into this. I'd usually be very content to go and teach in school every day and read all about such goings-on in your paper, observing the world going topsy-turvy from a distance.'

'Unfortunately, ninety-nine point nine per cent of the country believes that they cannot do anything about the situation. It's their karma, fate, or whatever to suffer the consequences.'

'And thanks to people like you,' said Joan, putting down her cup after draining the last few drops of the sweet tea, 'we still enjoy a free and powerful press that can provoke and shame the authorities into doing something.' She smiled at Chopra, challenging him. He looked away.

'Like you, Mrs D'Silva, I'm a victim, being caught up in these events as a patriot. I can't bear to see us fritter away the fruits of our early democracy so laboriously earned.'

The peon who brought Joan the sweet tea came and whispered in Chopra's ear. He arose immediately saying, 'It looks like the editor is getting restless about my copy deadline; I'm going to have to buy another few hours' grace. Could you excuse me, Mrs D'Silva...'

'Absolutely fine by me, Mr Chopra, thank you for your time,' said Joan, rising too.

She walked out of the offices of *The Statesman* feeling she had relieved herself of a heavy load that she had been carrying on her shoulders for weeks. It was almost as though she had been to confession and had now been absolved of her sins. Chopra had been her father confessor and inquisitor and companion in the same cause: bringing

228

Dutta to justice. The act of pouring out the events of the last few months to him had for her clarified the connections between these events.

Chopra too mulled over the conversation. He sensed there was a complex web of skulduggery in this case, and that Dutta and his revolutionaries weren't the only villains. There was much more to this that he had to unravel.

Joan was not ready to go back home. Her mind still raced with the thoughts of the last hour's conversation. She thought a visit to the Coffee House, for a cup of her favourite iced coffee, might help settle her down a little. The place was buzzing as usual with a young crowd, and the waiter told her she might have to stand in the queue for around twenty minutes before he could seat her. Joan was considering leaving when she saw Philomena with three young men at a table across the room. She waved to attract her attention but rather than respond, Philomena leaned forward to say something to the men. One of them turned around to give Joan an unwelcoming look, like an unfriendly government official who doesn't wish to converse with underlings.

But Joan wanted to confront Philomena and find out where she had been the night of the fire at the Smiths' party, and she wanted to tell Edwina and Charles about her involvement with Dutta's Movement. She sat at a table on her own and ordered an iced coffee. She felt a bit lost without Errol, who was playing cricket with his friends that afternoon, and who would almost certainly have ordered the Tutti Frutti.

After a short while Philomena and her friends got up;

Joan did the same and crossed the room to where the girl was standing with her back to her. 'Philomena, we must speak. Now.' It was more a command than a request, and Joan went back to sit at her table wondering whether the young woman would respond to the abrupt instruction from a schoolteacher. She did. The friends left the restaurant laughing and giggling; probably, she thought, at the way Joan had delivered her request. Philomena looked slightly abashed, as though she had missed handing in her homework or broken some forbidden code.

'Philomena, I'm going to have to tell the Smiths about you and that fellow Dutta. I owe it to them,' she said, not wasting any time getting to the point. Philomena still stood, not saying a word. 'Where were you the evening of the Smiths' party, when that fire ruined everything?' Still there was no response. 'Look, I've got myself dragged into two murders, probably three, because Anil and you wanted me to help get justice for Agnes. Now I find that it was because of your fellow Dutta that she ended up dumped in the river and now poor Anil too has met his end, trying to protect him.'

Philomena looked up at Joan. Her eyes flared; she was ready to speak.

'Miss, do you have any idea of the lengths to which we will go to overthrow this rotten establishment? How much work needs to be done to root out the dreadful things these people, who call themselves patriots and builders of a new nation, get up to? Go ahead; tell the Smiths if you wish. I'm done with leading a double life. The Movement needs me more now than at any time before.' This was another Philomena: vocal, angry, defiant.

'Did you firebomb that party, Philomena? Tell me.'

'I may have, I don't know.'

'What do you mean, you don't know? People could have died. They, the Smiths, had been so kind to you. How could you?' Joan's voice was taut, heady with a rising anger.

'It was a mere political statement, done to make people aware that their comforts are under attack. The Movement has to be taken seriously. How do you get complacent capitalists and imperialists to believe that times have to change?'

'Philomena, what are you thinking of? What would the nuns make of you? Your community?'

'Don't speak to me of my community, Joan. Remember, I was abandoned as a child by a mother who had no love of me, who couldn't keep her virginity or then her child. How do you think I feel? And the nuns who made us all feel as though we were sinners, unclean. As though it was Agnes's and my fault that we'd been abandoned by careless mothers and irresponsible fathers.'

The waiter arrived with Joan's cup of iced coffee and asked if there was another order. '*Nahi*,' Philomena said, shaking her head firmly and walking out of the restaurant. Joan did not try to persuade her to stay.

The *Sunday Statesman* ran a letter on its editorial page the next day, putting the case for the arrest of Dutta.

Dear Sir,

A misguided and dangerous mind lies behind the spate of personal crimes that have been committed

231

recently here in Calcutta. The leader of the Workers'
Revolutionary Movement, Mr Dutta, has created more
a cult than a political party. The members of this cult
are prepared to give their lives to the cause of Mr
Dutta's idealistic goals, to bring about the downfall of
this democracy as we know it.

In the jungles of South America and on the
southern plains of China other revolutionary leaders
such as Guevara and Mao are at work to destabilise
the fragile infrastructures of those nations. Dutta
plans to do the same from this state of West Bengal
using his fast-growing band of youth, burning with as
much dedication as himself.

I speak in a personal capacity, as a citizen of this
great country of ours, and call for the immediate
arrest and conviction of this man for the many
abductions and deaths in this city. I call on our Chief
Minister to instruct the police to step up their
activities to the maximum to apprehend this man
and bring the current wave of violence and protest
to a halt before we have destroyed ourselves or been
invaded by our enemies across the borders.

Yours,
A Bhattacharya

The same paper carried a feature by Chopra cataloguing
the various incidents from Anil's death in custody to the
James stabbing, the fire in the Smiths' *shamiana*, the
mysterious death of Agnes the Bandle Girl and the
countless strikes and *bandhs*. He pieced together the

events over the last few months to conclude that the state of Bengal was plunging headlong into a crisis of lawlessness and '*goonda* rule' and it was not clear whether or not it was all being caused by Dutta.

'After reading this morning's papers I think we all want to emigrate,' said De Lange, speaking after Sunday mass to a group of parishioners who had gathered for a cup of church tea and biscuits.

'I didn't realise that Xavier's wife was tied up in all that business,' whispered Mrs Costa to Joan, making sure she was out of earshot of Xavier, who never missed Sunday mass.

Father Rector had said mass that morning, and in his sermon he had asked the congregation to 'pray for a peaceful reconciliation to the current political problems and for the soul of an ex-pupil who has taken his life'.

The editorial on the worsening political situation and Bhattacharya's open letter in the Sunday edition had already begun to cause quite a stir at Government House. Chief Minister Roy had summoned his top aides to discuss what could be done to apprehend Dutta. Roy wanted answers and action. Basu was one of those attending the briefing, knowing full well that looking for Dutta would be an impossible task. Basu was asked for answers to questions he knew were beyond him.

'Sir, may I be saying that the fugitive in question has gone underground somewhere in this state and, given the guerrilla tactics they are using, the job will be difficult,' he said, arguing for more time when the minister called for early results.

'Then round up all his sympathisers and give them a bit of encouragement to tell you where he is,' said the minister.

'I'm not going to tell you your job. Go speak to that fellow Chopra and see if he can reveal where he met Dutta.'

Inspector Basu called on the offices of *The Statesman* the next day to interview Chopra. Chopra was used to dealing with policemen. It came with the role.

'I'm not at liberty to divulge any information that might harm my sources. You know that, inspector. And anyway, all I know is that it's quite a distance out of the city in the countryside. But I could help identify one of his followers, a young Anglo-Indian woman I believe. I got a good look at her in his compound. Judging by her clothes and hair she must only spend part of the time in the rural villages.'

Basu considered Chopra's offer of help but felt he had done enough to pacify the Chief Minister for the moment. 'Very well, we may have to take you in for helping the questioning at some stage if we aren't picking up the man.'

Chopra smiled at Basu then proceeded to finish off his cup of tea without showing any sign of concern. He didn't offer to show him out.

Joan helped Errol choose the top ten records for the next week's *Binaca Hit Parade*, a popular programme compèred by Vernon Corea on Radio Ceylon. Every week Errol entered the contest to choose the winners, in pursuit of the hundred-rupee prize: a princely sum for a ten-year-old.

'No, *beta,* I'd put "It's Now or Never" at number one, rather than that noisy racket you like,' she advised her son. 'Elvis the Pelvis is just so popular with everyone, he can't help winning.'

'Mum, I like "Shakin' All Over", it's so jumpy and good. Rock and roll it's called,' argued Errol.

'Well fine, your choice, and don't forget to include a Binaca box top in the envelope when you send it.'

Binaca made toothpaste, terrible-tasting green chlorophyll and normal minty-flavoured varieties. The *Hit Parade* competition did wonders for their sales as most Anglo-Indian families entered every week and therefore had to consume at least one tube per household per week. Friends gave their box tops to Errol to make up his shortage and trusted Phillip had come around to give his to Errol that morning.

Joan and Phillip had not spent any time together since their love-making on the veranda. There was an edge, a tension to their company, but they had both agreed to put the affair out of their minds and not spoil a good friendship.

'See the article in the papers today, Joan? There's going to be a bit of *garbar* now with all this out in public. Chopra will need a bodyguard.'

'I think Dutta knew he would publish something damning. Why else would he have agreed to see him? Dutta wants all the publicity he can get to destabilise the government and put the fear of God into them. He's certainly achieved that now.'

'But you need to be more careful, Joan. Your name isn't actually mentioned in the article but there are a number of references which could point the finger at you.'

'But that's absurd! How do you conclude that?' said Joan, rejecting any sense of danger from Dutta.

'I'm not so sure, look here.' Phillip picked up the paper and began to read.

'References to "a close friend and mentor of Anil Sen",

"a trusted friend of the Smith family" and references to "a witness in the Bandle Girl coroner's investigations" could quite easily lead to you. Remember, Joan, you are the only one who heard Anil declare his innocence in the *thana*.'

Phillip had read the paper more carefully than Joan. She waved the palm of her right hand dismissively. 'What can they do to me? I have no power or influence over anyone.'

But Phillip's fears were well founded. Mrs D'Silva was becoming known to both the authorities and the Movement for her annoying persistence in trying to uncover the dark goings-on in Calcutta's political underworld. Initially caught up in finding out what really had happened to Agnes, she was now entering the dark warren of intrigue surrounding the death of James and now Anil, and she was no longer an innocent bystander.

That evening Joan had a surprise visitor. There was a knock on the door early in the evening and to her amazement it was Jonty, impeccably dressed in white slacks and a navy-blue blazer.

'Joan, I hope you don't mind me dropping by,' he said.

Joan was lost for words. Errol came running up to the door beaming with pleasure; he appeared to be thrilled by Jonty's appearance. But here was the man who lived nearly a thousand miles away, to whom she had written days earlier turning down his proposal of marriage, and who was perhaps due to die quite shortly.

'Jonty, what a surprise!' she said, trying to regain her composure.

'Joan, I thought I might have a short holiday in Calcutta, you know, to see a few friends and get out of the rut in LKO.' Railwaymen never lost the habit of referring to places the way they did when in service. 'Putting up at the Great Eastern in Cal. Invited myself for *cha*. Hope you don't mind.' He turned to Errol. 'And how are you, young man?' he asked. 'Look what I've brought you.' He pulled a grubby-looking, hard-backed logbook from his pocket and opened it up for Errol to see. 'Look, here is a record of all my journeys as a mail driver between 1935 and 1942. All the times, the scheduled arrivals and the delays, with comments on any problems with the engine. It's yours, Errol.'

The boy's eyes opened wide. He was speechless with excitement. There were hours and hours of reading for him here, and of course lots of questions too. 'Uncle Jonty, thank you, thank you,' he kept repeating, staring at the pages and flicking them over.

'Errol darling, have you done your homework for today? Uncle Jonty and I will chat while you go and get on with it,' said Joan.

'But, Mum, please let me stay for another few minutes.' Errol looked to Jonty for support but to no avail.

'Errol, better do what Mum says. She knows best, *hah*!' said Jonty in her support.

The young boy sulked off to the bedroom. Joan made Jonty a cup of tea. He sat stiffly on the sofa. When she returned to the room she knew he wanted to talk.

'Joan, I'm sorry to surprise you in this way but I'm just not going to give up that easily, you know. I'm a bit of a fighter, and though my health may not be that good I have enough puff left in me to get what I want,' said Jonty, declaring his intentions immediately.

'Jonty, I don't know what to say. I'm quite lost for words really!'

'I bought this engagement ring, Joan,' he carried on, pulling out a small blue-velvet box from his top pocket and handing it to his intended bride.

'Gosh!' is all she could manage, and she stared at the small box for a while. Jonty moved to hold her right hand.

'Please, Joan, just open it.'

'Jonty, I really can't at the moment. I really can't.'

'Is there someone else?'

'No, no... Jonty, no. Well, yes, in a way. George, my dead husband.'

'George?' he said, amazed. 'But Joan, it's just your dead husband's memory.'

'Yes George. I can't see myself with anyone else yet. I'd feel I'd betrayed him.'

'Joan, don't be ridiculous. Time moves on, you have to live your new life. And there is the boy's future to secure, his college education and so on...'

Joan stiffened, straightening her back and giving Jonty a cutting look of defiance. It was the one she reserved for people who had displeased her. A pupil got such a look when he had for the umpteenth time forgotten to do his homework, Errol got it for not telling her where he was and the milkman had received the same look when he once tried to sell her watered-down milk. By calling Joan 'ridiculous', Jonty had given up the slender advantage he had gained through surprise, turning up on Joan's doorstep bearing an engagement ring.

'I can manage quite well by myself, Jonty. I appreciate your kindness and your concern, but I do have a job and with my private tuition we can make our way. If Errol wins a scholarship we'll have plenty to go round.'

'This country is a cruel place, Joan, you're never far from the gutter.' Jonty put the ring away. 'You need all the financial cushion you can get to move yourself far away from it.'

'Jonty, you're preaching to me. I'm a woman thirty-two years of age, not a child. I need to love someone to marry him. I don't have any love for you, it's as simple as that, believe me.' Joan's tone was getting more serious as she turned his proposal down yet again.

'*Aste, aste,* slowly now, I didn't ask for love. I don't mean to be persistent but, Joan, I've just got this thing in me, this urge that makes me want to go on and pursue you till I haven't got any life left. You're like the love of my life, just returned after forty years.'

'You'd better go back to your hotel, Jonty, and think things over. I'm Joan, not Dilys. I'm her daughter.'

'I'll go, but please promise to see me. I'll stay here in Cal at the Great Eastern until all my money runs out.'

'I hope the hotel will treat you well.'

'Can I see you tomorrow?'

'No.'

'The day after, please?'

'OK, maybe I'll see you in a couple of days, Jonty. I'm very busy with the school and things at the moment,' she said, standing up to make sure he left. She ushered him towards the door.

She bolted the door of her flat firmly and went to the bedroom, where Errol had fallen asleep reading the railway logbook. That night she drifted in and out of sleep, dreaming about Jonty's proposition, playing through the worst scenarios of marrying a demonic-looking figure, half man, half animal, who enslaved her in a cage and fed her watery rice pudding to keep her happy. She awoke with a start when a centaur's face was moving up to her to try to kiss her on the lips. Her heart raced and, crossing herself, she thanked Our Lady of Bandle that it was just a bad dream.

FAREWELLS

Errol and Joan listened intently to the *Binaca Hit Parade*. Errol had ticked off Elvis in second position, so he hit the roof when Vernon Corea announced 'Are You Lonesome' as the new number two. All that was left was number one, and when they heard 'Shakin' All Over', Joan and Errol joined in a celebration dance around the living room, with Errol singing 'yippee yah yeah!' at the top of his voice.

Errol ran up and down the stairs of the apartment block telling all the people he knew about his win and they all congratulated him as though he had won an Olympic gold for India. 'What are you going to do with the money?' one neighbour asked.

'I'm going to buy myself a bicycle,' he replied without hesitation.

Edwina Smith had announced she was going to depart for England with her sons. She hadn't set foot in her home since the fire.

Joan visited her at the Grand one evening to see how

she was. 'Edwina, we'll be so sad to see you go. You brought a breath of fresh air to us in Cal with your parties and wild ideas,' she said, surprised at Edwina's decision to go back home. She had thought that with Edwina's fine education and her husband's connections, she would have been much stronger.

'Joan, darling, something changed that night of the fire. I'd had so much hope for this city, put so much into making the event a success and then all my dreams were shattered so quickly, nothing but charred wreckage. First there was the murder of one of Charles's close associates; then there was the fire. They say things come in threes and I don't want to be here for the third.'

'I know how it must feel, Edwina. These *goondas* are achieving exactly what they want: to frighten away foreigners with new ideas for a prosperous India.'

'I have two little boys, Joan. I can't possibly afford to take any risks for their safety. How vulnerable are they? Would I be able to forgive myself if anything terrible happened to them?' said Edwina, her eyes filling with tears.

'Is Mr Smith going to stay on?'

'Yes, until the company can find a replacement for him. I think now they will have to find an Indian to take his place, as I can't imagine anyone in their right mind wanting to come out here in the current climate. I think Guest Keith must be already thinking about selling off their operations here, given the appalling strike record and financial losses.'

The two Smith boys roamed around the building aimlessly, sometimes taking a swim in the pool or ordering a soda. The initial thrill of staying in a big hotel and being able to choose anything they wanted from the menus was now wearing thin. There was little for them to do and, being bored with each other's company, they frequently quarrelled over the most trivial things.

'Joan,' said Edwina, 'could Errol come and keep the boys company for a couple of days at the weekend? It would mean so much to them. He could stay over on Saturday night.'

'Certainly, I'm sure he'd love to,' said Joan, delighted that Errol could stay in the Grand, a luxury well out of the reach of her income.

Errol made the most of his weekend at the Grand. He had his first dip in a swimming pool, taking a few tentative dog paddles in the shallow end, which his friends thought hilarious. They splashed and kicked for hours, like strange beasts discovering the joys of playing with water for the first time.

Joan had at last spoken to Edwina about Philomena's suspected association with the Movement, and of the danger she now might pose to her employer's family. This only heightened the Smiths' resolve to leave the city as quickly as they could.

'I don't think we want to dig any deeper into this by going to the police,' said Charles. 'I'm not convinced they will be able to do anything other than arrest someone quite innocent.'

'But, Charles, there is a young woman out there prepared to do anything to harm us, the people who paid her wages and looked after her for months,' said Edwina.

'Disconnect emotion from all of this, Edwina,' her

husband told her. 'We want to exit this episode of our lives in the most peaceful way possible. I'm just going to pay her off with a termination bonus as if nothing happened. Now that we're about to leave for England, there seems no point making ourselves further targets for the Movement and getting embroiled in more police investigations.'

In the hotel, Xavier fussed over the boys, feeding them little titbits from the kitchen every now and then. 'Bet you young chaps are not tasting one of these,' he would say every time the chef produced a new batch of cheeselets or pastries from the kitchen.

For Xavier, the boys created a fresh challenge. They were more fun than the older guests, who were always demanding and treated him as a low-paid servant. The boys sparkled with their boundless energy and needed Xavier to dig into his reserves of interesting things for them to try from the kitchen.

Errol tried every ice cream flavour on the menu, finally settling on the vanilla, which he enjoyed best. The hotel's chef made exquisite finger food, from small hamburgers the size of little biscuits to mince patties and wonderful potato chips with ketchup. By Sunday afternoon Errol was beginning to feel quite sick from this surfeit of nourishment.

The Smith boys enjoyed his company and they tried their hand at every game they could play. In the billiard room they took turns at potting balls, making up their own rules. They tried chess but soon lost patience; draughts seemed a lot easier. Then Errol beat them both at table tennis, his coaching from Phillip giving him a strong advantage.

Errol's imagination and talent for making up games

were unbounded. Growing up on his own he had to invent more hobbies and make-believe adventures than his friends at school, who all seemed to have numerous brothers and sisters. He loved to play 'trains', which involved pretending to be an engine driver hauling the Doon Express at full steam. Soon he had Oliver and Terence involved in the fantasy, whistling and blowing puffs of steam. The veranda of the Grand made the perfect setting for a long train powering its way out of Howrah up towards the planes of Bihar and onwards to the foothills of the Himalayas.

Hide-and-seek was also a lot of fun as there were so many places to sneak away to and not be seen.

'Let's play another game of hide-and-seek,' said Errol towards the end of the day as dusk was approaching. He knew the perfect place to hide, where it would be impossible to be found. 'Can I go first?' he said.

The boys went off to the corner of the inner courtyard and turned their backs so that Errol could disappear. He had just thirty counts to find his spot and they had already begun counting. Some of the hotel guests looked on with amusement, reminded of the game they had all once played in their youth.

Errol dashed out to the front veranda at the entrance to the main Chowringhee Road where two large ferns stood, as thick as the jungle itself. The Grand was like an oasis surrounded by the noise and bustle of Calcutta. A few steps outside the entrance and you were straight into the chaos of a full-blown bazaar. Inside, the tranquil splashing of the fountains and the crunch of walking on the gravel drive were the only noises that broke the silence.

'Thirty!' shouted the boys, and they spread out to look for Errol. First they checked the places that had been hiding locations in past games. The games room was a favourite, under the billiard table. The next most popular spot was the changing rooms off the swimming pool. Then they began to comb the ground floor of the hotel carefully, from the central reception area to its perimeters. Then they tried the inner garden, the kitchens, the bar behind the big sofa, the café and the gentlemen's toilets.

It was just turning six and getting quite dark when Joan arrived with Phillip to pick up her son. 'Where's Errol?' she asked the boys.

'He's hiding somewhere, miss, and we can't find him.'

'Oh well, let's give him another few minutes and then we'll all go and look for him.' Joan looked around at the splendour of the Grand. She turned to Phillip. 'Let's go and find Edwina and have a cup of that lovely iced coffee,' she said, relieved to be inside such a haven of peace.

The boys' enthusiasm for hide-and-seek had begun to fade and one of the hotel guests, a middle-aged American lady, noticed their sagging spirits. 'Well you boys ain't gonna find him in here I can tell you. Try outside on the veranda.'

'We're not allowed out there, Marm.'

'Well that's where he went and that's where he'll be,' she said, disappointed at their lack of enthusiasm.

Knowing now where Errol was hiding and not wishing to break the strict boundary rules set by their father, they sat and waited on two enormous, cushioned sofas in the reception area, sofas so large they seemed to swallow the boys up.

Phillip and Joan found Edwina in the restaurant. She was pleased to see them. 'I'm really so glad we were able to have Errol for the last few days. The boys have brightened up and had a lot of fun. Your Errol does love his ice cream you know,' said Edwina.

'Oh I hope he didn't make a pig of himself,' said Joan, always the concerned mother.

'No, of course not.'

'So you're all set for the journey, Edwina?'

'Yes, our bags are packed and I can't wait to get out of this prison, however pleasant it is.'

Joan and Phillip shuffled uncomfortably. Night was falling over the city.

'We'd better be going,' said Joan. 'Phillip, could you see if Errol has appeared? Thanks.'

Phillip was getting to be quite the dutiful husband. He increasingly looked to Joan and Errol as his adopted family and Joan quite liked having a man around for her son. Their attempt at being lovers may have been cut short but they were now more comfortable than ever before, knowing that sex created difficulties that neither of them was ready to take on.

'He's a nice man,' said Edwina as Phillip left the room, in a way that begged Joan to tell her more about the relationship.

'A very good friend,' said Joan in a neutral tone, not wishing to give anything away and quite content to keep Edwina guessing. The latter's English upbringing kept her from probing any further.

Phillip found the boys, sulking by now, in the huge sofas of the reception area. 'Not found him yet, boys?'

'No, sir, that lady said he went out onto the veranda and we're not allowed there.'

Phillip went out onto the veranda and called out, 'Errol, Errol, come out now, it's time to go home.'

He walked down the short gravel drive, shouted out again and saw no movement. By now Xavier had come out to ask Phillip if he could help. When Phillip explained, they both began to look behind pots, trees and finally the large ferns. Phillip bent back the ferns but there was no sign of Errol.

'He's not here,' confirmed Phillip as Joan came out to see what had been keeping them so long.

'Oh that boy's going to be the death of me!' said Joan.

'Madam, I'll get the bearers to search the hotel inside. Do you think it might be possible that he has gone outside in the Chowringhee for a look at the shops?' suggested Xavier.

'I'll go and take a look outside,' said Phillip, who rushed out of the hotel into the chaos of pan wallahs, rickshaws and general evening mêlée.

New Market shoppers were everywhere and the early-evening neons flickered into life. Mr Wong stood outside his shoe shop and gave a nodding smile at Phillip. 'You in big hurry today, Mr Phillip. No come in and try my shoes?'

Phillip shook his head and made for a narrow alley of shops sporting an assortment of handbags and other leather goods, then into a textile alley, where yards of fabric of every conceivable colour and design lay strewn on the shop counters as vendors tried to entice their customers. Phillip scanned every face to be sure not to miss Errol wherever he was.

Back outside he was accosted by a rickshaw wallah. 'Sahib, I take you to Lindsay Street? Know nice clean Anglo girl.'

'*Achha, achha,* listen,' he said. 'Have you seen a boy about this big, in short pants, come out on his own?'

The thin, emaciated-looking man, who didn't look like he could pull even himself along, shook his head. Then one of the pan vendors, who had heard Phillip, said that he had seen a boy come out about an hour ago and walk along by the arcade in the direction of the toyshop about fifty yards away. 'I thought I saw a woman with him, sahib, but I can't be sure, there were so many people around.'

The Regal cinema had just finished its matinee showing of *Bridge Over the River Kwai* and crowds were shuffling out onto the pavement and the street. Taxis and rickshaws all joined in the crescendo of calls to prospective customers. Phillip grew more and more disheartened about the chances of finding Errol in the human throng.

He hurried along to the toyshop where he had bought Errol's model locomotive. The array of cheap Japanese plastic and tin imitations of Hornby trains and various bits of bric-a-brac was still there. He asked the shopkeeper if he had seen a boy an hour or so earlier but the man shook his head. Phillip walked up and down the arcade asking shopkeepers, none of whom had seen or noticed a boy like Errol. Given that there were at least a hundred people of all ages passing through the arcade every few minutes, this wasn't surprising.

A low, thin cloud of smoke had begun to drift over the *maidan*, rising from the numerous small wood fires started by pavement dwellers who were cooking their evening meal of rice and *dal*. That early-evening smell of burning wood was a part of Calcutta, and the dark *maidan* was now dotted with clusters of red glowing embers. Errol could be anywhere.

Phillip got back to the hotel to find that Errol had not turned up there either. There were clear signs of anguish in Joan's voice when she said, 'Phillip, what are we going to do? Where is that boy? How dare he just walk off like that!'

'Now calm down. I'm sure we'll find him eventually. Even if he's lost he has a tongue, he can tell people where he lives and where he's been this weekend. Don't worry,' said Phillip in an effort to reassure Joan, even though he was himself very concerned about Errol's whereabouts in the darkness that had fallen outside.

Edwina dialled the Calcutta Club where Charles had gone to see one of his friends to ensure that the air tickets and travel arrangements for his wife and sons were in order. He said that he would be back immediately to join the hunt for Errol.

'I think in the present circumstances you had better stay the night here at the hotel,' said Charles when he arrived. 'I'm sure Errol will get someone to direct him here eventually. It's here that he went missing so it makes sense for you to stay here for a while. I'll ask the hotel to get you a room.'

'But I don't have any things with me for the night, I...'

'I'll go back and get them for you,' offered Phillip.

'And I'll get my driver to take you there,' said Charles.

Joan gave Phillip the keys to the flat and some vague instructions for finding a set of pyjamas, her toothbrush and a change of underwear from her wardrobe. The drive to Liluah seemed to take forever and the driver leaned on his horn for most of the way. Sunday evening was particularly crowded along the potholed Grand Trunk Road that headed west out of Calcutta.

Phillip played out all the possible scenarios of Errol's disappearance. Young boys of ten were all over the streets in Calcutta, but most of them were seen working, pulling, carrying or sweeping. A well-dressed boy, unfamiliar with the area, would stand out. It should be easy to get witnesses and trace his path from the hotel. So why had only one person seen Errol leave the hotel? Was there really a woman with him?

Phillip reached the flat and entered, using Joan's key. The entrance hall was dark so he turned on the light to get to the bedroom and find Joan an overnight bag. There was a small suitcase near the bed, which he began to fill with anything that might be useful for a night away. He packed her nightdress, which hung by the bedside, a set of underwear from one of the top drawers of the dressing table and a wash bag from the bathroom. He switched off the lights in the bedroom. He was at the front door when he noticed an envelope on the floor marked 'urgent'. He put it in his pocket to take back to Joan.

Missing

When Phillip returned to the Grand, he'd been gone for almost two hours. The concierge informed him that Joan had retired to the Smiths' suite of rooms and arranged for a bearer to take Phillip there.

Two hours of thinking the worst about the fate of her son had taken its toll. It was as though one moment she was driving along in a comfortable car quite content with herself and then suddenly someone had driven into her at speed, leaving her bruised and battered. Errol, her flesh and blood, was now out there at the mercy of a troubled city. 'Any news, Joan?' said Phillip and she just shook her head and put her face in her hands.

'This is the worst thing that's happened to me since that man came with the telegram about George,' she murmured. 'God, what have I done to deserve this?'

'This envelope was on the floor of your apartment,' said Phillip. 'It's marked "urgent" so I thought I'd bring it to you straight away. Probably not the best thing to be adding to your anxiety,' he added, handing her the envelope hesitantly.

Joan was not in the mood to open any envelope from a complaining neighbour or anxious parent. She took her bag from him.

'Thanks, Phillip, did you find everything all right?'

'Sure, check them if you would and give me a score out of ten,' he said, trying to lighten the depression in the room.

Joan checked the contents but only nodded her head, clearly showing the strain of Errol's absence. She tore open the envelope and pulled out a sheet of paper that had been cut out of the previous weekend's *Statesman*, the page with the article by Raj Chopra about Dutta and the Movement.

There were red circles on it emphasising certain words. At first she was puzzled and showed it to Phillip, who knew immediately what it was and how bad the situation had become.

Phillip winced as he deciphered the pattern of the words that had been ringed. It was what he had been expecting although not in this form. This was going to be a hard night for them all.

the movement is holding him as security behave with silent respect and non interference in our affairs or else

'What is it, Phillip? What does it say?' Joan pleaded, knowing in her heart that it wasn't good.

'Hello. Something the matter, dear?' asked Edwina, hearing Joan's voice from the next room. She looked at the expression on Phillip's face and realised how serious the situation was.

Phillip read the message out loud. As he finished Joan

screamed, collapsed on the bed and convulsed into fits of uncontrollable sobs. 'Jesus, Mother Mary, how can you? How can you?' she kept questioning, her eyes flooding with tears.

'Is this what I think it is, Phillip?' whispered Edwina. He nodded.

The hotel manager, alerted by one of the staff, appeared at the suite to investigate what the commotion was about. He was despatched to get a doctor as Joan struggled with the shock of the abduction note.

'I'll never see my darling again, again... never see him again,' she kept on saying.

The doctor arrived and Edwina convinced Joan to take a Valium tablet to help her sleep. Half an hour later Edwina was able to console her. The crying slowed to silence. Then Joan spoke. 'Crying is not going to get my boy free. Is it?' She had gathered herself, found some strength and decided this was not a time for tears.

'We need to think this through very carefully,' said Phillip.

'That doesn't mean we just sit on our hands and do nothing,' said Joan.

'Do you mind if I tell Charles, Joan. He is very discreet,' said Edwina. Joan nodded, her eyelids heavy, and soon she rested on the bed and fell asleep. Phillip removed her shoes and Edwina covered her with a sheet.

'The problem we face here,' said Charles softly, 'is that there is no two-way communication between you and the abductors. We need a way of setting up that communication.' He sounded like a man who dealt with the abduction of minors every day of his life.

'Do we call the police, Inspector Basu?' said Edwina, offering a more immediate idea.

'Good heavens no. Not that blithering fellow, not if we want to get the boy back,' replied Charles.

Phillip stayed with Joan all through the night, dozing off on the sofa from time to time. A slow-motion movie played in his mind: it showed Errol being led away down Chowringhee, quite happily trusting the person he was with to take him somewhere with the promise of buying a cheap Japanese tin train, and then suddenly being bundled into a car against his will. He could almost see the look of fright on the poor boy's face as this angel had turned demon.

At daybreak he slipped away to get a clean set of clothes and to arrange for someone to stand in for Joan at school.

Joan woke at eight o'clock. She'd dreamed she was being chased by a pack of rabid pariah dogs down the back streets of Calcutta; she was trapped in a dead-end street with a brick wall at one end and a dozen snarling, menacing faces at the other. There was no way of scaling the wall, nor did she have any weapons to frighten or fend off the hounds. Suddenly she found Anil's knife lying on the ground and picked it up to brandish at the dogs, which became more ferocious but did not attack her.

Despite the dream, the sleep had been good for her, but on waking she recalled the events of the evening before and horror flooded back. She wished the real nightmare would end. Edwina came to her room to see how she was and gave her a long hug.

'I'd like to speak to Judge Bhattacharya,' Joan decided.

255

'He's the only one whose advice I could trust.'

'We'll call him right away,' said Edwina, a little taken aback by Joan's choice.

Something had impressed Joan about the judge since the day they met in the coroner's court. She felt she needed a sage rather than a shoulder to cry on. Someone who might make a special sound or whistle that would calm the rabid dogs of her dream and render them docile creatures until she could make her escape.

Bhattacharya arrived after breakfast. 'Mrs D'Silva, I'm very sorry to hear about this,' he said when he had scanned the copy of *The Statesman* with the red-circled words, giving out their message of warning. 'Now we have to ask ourselves one very important question: why did they take your son to silence you and not carry out a much simpler task and just have you eliminated. I hope you don't mind me being so blunt?'

'Sir, that would have been preferable to what they have done. A young, innocent life to bargain with, why?'

'They are ahead of us here. To decide to take your son, Dutta must have something coming up which will need your co-operation. Now, what could that possibly be?'

'I heard Anil Sen's prison confession. He apparently confessed to the murder of Mr James but told me it had been under duress and that he actually believed someone else had taken the knife from him to stab James. He was loyal to Dutta and was protecting him.'

'You see, Mrs D'Silva, that is probably it. And Dutta might just be holding your son to ensure you prove his innocence. Were he ever held in connection with the death and assassination of James, you would be a prime witness for the prosecution, but you could also be a witness for the defence. You take your pick if you want your son. The interesting question for me is how does Dutta know all this? He must have extremely good sources of information in that prison, and among people that you have been quite close to. So be careful whom you talk to from now on. That's all I can say,' said Bhattacharya, raising his eyebrows into a warning frown.

Joan was beginning to see some picture emerging, some pattern to Errol's kidnapping. She was glad to have Bhattacharya's counsel and thanked him again for coming to the hotel to see her. She made a promise to all the saints she could recall that, if they returned him to her unharmed, she would ensure that Errol stayed close to his Catholic faith; she would encourage him to seriously consider a priestly vocation and offered any other manner of oath that played to her religious mind.

Joan went back to her empty flat later that day. The sight of Errol's unmade bed, his clothes in an untidy pile in the corner and his train set on the floor brought her to tears once more. Phillip came and insisted that he sleep on the sofa for another night. That night she awoke startled after another ghoulish dream in which she watched a suitcase opening to reveal her son's body parts, his eyes staring straight at her. And then, later, she dreamed of seeing him running down the school lane towards her, tears streaming from her face as she shouted with joy.

The following morning came quickly. Father Rector visited to offer a few words of support and consolation.

'Prayer is a good way to find peace in these troubled times, Joan. I recommend it highly. I lost my entire family to Franco's butchers when I was a young man. It was prayer that rescued me. There is an excellent story in the Bible on the desolation of Job, the man who lost everything he had and, to make matters worse, was infected from head to toe with sores. But God was only testing his faith and it was this belief that allowed him to get through his pain and suffering. Pray that God's test of your faith will be short and that he gives you the strength to see you through your ordeal.'

Joan appreciated his words. 'Thank you, Father. Right now I need to do something to get my mind off what's happening. This is my son and I feel I must do something to help him but I just don't know what. There is nothing I can do. I'd like to come back to school and take my classes again. I think that would be the best therapy for me right now.'

'Joan, I don't think that would be a very good idea. You need to rest, pray for God's strength. It would not be fair on you or the boys if you came back to school. Rather than take your mind off Errol it would only remind you more of him,' said the rector, smiling slightly and admiring her stoical response to the situation.

So Joan stayed in her flat the next day, imagining the many smiling faces of the pupils in her class. She saw Errol there in her mind and felt almost contented thinking he was there somewhere in their midst as she went through the day. The teachers popped in, offering their well-intentioned support as news got out that Errol had gone missing. No mention was made of the link with the Workers'

Revolutionary Movement and they assumed this was just another opportunistic kidnapping by a crooked gang.

'These *goondas* are just wanting the ransom. Soon you will be getting the ransom letter; then we will have to find the money for you,' said Punditji, attempting to offer some hope to Joan and an easy solution; the whole thing solved by a collective monetary response.

Beyond the grounds of Don Bosco's the city continued to sink further into political turmoil. *The Statesman*'s headlines threatened President's Rule. Along Dalhousie two buses were burned and one of the passengers died in the blaze, unable to get off in time. Another day-long *hartal* shut down all offices and businesses in the city. Some people used the event to run riot through areas of Chowringhee, looting shops that had stayed open. Chief Minister Roy sank further into lethargy as the government in New Delhi put plans into place to take over the control of the state.

The Indian Army's Eastern High Command, based at Fort William, was put on standby to take over policing the city, and hundreds of extra troops were drafted in from elsewhere in the country to reinforce those already stationed in the state capital.

For most people life just went on; they took the troubles in their stride by circumventing them. For Anglo-Indians, however, the situation was a further catalyst, accelerating their departure. It confirmed their fears that the country would soon descend into anarchy and their own difficult position would make life unliveable.

'We've been accepted by Canada,' said De Lange to

Joan. 'We'll be going to Toronto where I've already been offered a job in a factory making furniture.'

'Isn't it very cold in Canada?' said Joan. 'You'll freeze to death.'

'I'd rather freeze to death than be burned in my house or stabbed outside the workshop gates, Joan. You don't know where all this is going to end, do you?'

'And you, Joan,' said Mrs De Lange, 'what about you? Things couldn't get much worse, could they?'

'No, it's pretty bad right now. Couldn't get much worse for me. I can only wait and pray that God gives me back my Errol.'

'No more news then on him?' asked De Lange.

'Nothing so far. I've had Inspector Basu call and tell me to contact him personally if anyone tries to get in touch with me.'

Joan had tried to keep news of Errol's abduction confined to just a few friends and teachers, not wishing to have it publicised for fear of upsetting the chances of his return. Edwina had asked her husband to delay her departure to England until there was some resolution to Errol's disappearance. She had decided that her family was no safer in the hotel so they moved back into their home, having cleared the garden of the fire damage. For Edwina, Joan's suffering was the ultimate trial for any mother and she considered herself fortunate to have both her children safe and close to her.

Phillip spent all his spare time with Joan to keep her company. He too missed Errol's incessant questions, particularly over the bicycle he should get with the prize money from the *Binaca Hit Parade*, or indeed if he should choose something else to buy instead. The one hundred rupees had arrived and awaited Errol's return home.

Phillip moved into Joan's flat, bringing with him a roll of bedding and a pillow. 'I'll sleep on the sofa again tonight. I can't leave you on your own,' he said and Joan had very little energy left in her to disagree.

That evening, sitting out on the veranda, Phillip asked her, 'Have you ever thought of marrying again, Joan?'

She looked out into the darkness. 'I'm not sure how to answer that question. I'd always want to compare the man with George and that wouldn't be fair. Like you, for example.' She smiled sweetly at him. 'You've been really nice to me and Errol but I couldn't see you as my husband because you wouldn't be George. I'm probably embarrassing you now. That wasn't a proposal, was it?'

Phillip looked away. 'Mmn, no, if I were proposing I'd be on one knee or something like that. I'm just interested in what keeps driving you forward in such a self-sufficient way.'

'I had to become that way to survive after George's death. And you know what? I quite like it. I wouldn't like to go back to the days of being the memsahib and having it all done for me. I feel more in control now than I have ever done, despite the tragedy of what's happened to Errol.'

Phillip sighed. 'I feel a bit like that myself. The two women I've had in my life swept me away, made me lose my head. I did irrational things with them as though I was on ganja or something. It was fantastic for those moments but most of the time it was depressing. Now I'm happier in a steady state where, like you, I'm more in control.' He tensed, not knowing if he had explained himself properly. Joan didn't notice.

'But who knows, Phillip, it might all have changed by the morning,' she said with a tiredness in her voice that was a signal for Phillip to find a comfortable place on the large sofa in the sitting room. Joan fell asleep on the veranda.

The next morning Phillip and Joan had breakfast together, but her mind was racing. 'I can't stand it here, Phillip,' she declared. 'I'm going over to Chowringhee to have another look around.'

Phillip knew he couldn't dissuade her, and she said that she should be back by the evening.

When she got off the tram at Chowringhee, she thought a walk around the toyshop and the New Market might uncover something Phillip had missed before. She got to the toyshop and gazed into the glass window, her eyes passing along the rows and rows of tin Japanese cars and carriages; the space where Errol's model locomotive had been was now filled by another that looked very similar. Then she noticed the reflection of someone in a blazer standing a few yards away. She turned around immediately to identify the familiar reflection: it was Jonty.

'Oh hello, Joan, shopping for the young *chokra*?' he said.

Jonty was the last person she wanted to meet that morning and the disappointment on her face showed. Jonty kept up a cheerful pretence. 'Got time for a *cha*?' he said smiling.

'Not really, Jonty, I'm late for a meeting with one of my friends.'

'Oh go on, Joan. Can't be that important. Haven't seen

you in days. Don't know anyone here in Cal, you know.'

'Go back to Lucknow then,' said Joan with an abruptness that didn't seem to affect the elderly man.

'I was hoping we could spend some time together before I go. Not long in this world, you know.'

'Jonty, really! I've given you my answer.'

'I just can't get you out of my mind, Joan. Just a few minutes of your company will refresh me.'

He was now holding the palms of his hands together as a sign of pleading. The spectacle of an elderly man pleading so dramatically with an attractive younger woman was intriguing, and a small group of people stopped to watch. In Calcutta people stopped to look at the most trivial of things, and Jonty and Joan had attracted quite a gathering.

Joan tensed at the extra attention. 'Jonty, there's a lot going on in my life at the moment. I know where you are so I'll stop by at the Great Eastern sometime.' She smiled weakly at Jonty then walked quickly away, hoping he wouldn't follow.

Joan decided to go back home. She felt uncomfortable with the thought that Jonty might be following her around; the idea of being watched by someone was unnerving.

'Why does bad luck come all at once?' she thought.

PRESIDENT'S RULE

This is All India Radio; here is the news, read by Shuba Mirchandani. The Central Government in Delhi today announced the transfer of power from the state of West Bengal to the President of India, for an unspecified duration. The unrest in the state of Bengal has prompted this unprecedented action. Military units have moved out of the Fort William barracks this morning to guard key locations such as Government House and the offices of All India Radio. All strikes have been declared illegal and an evening curfew has been imposed in the centre of the state capital.

In a special statement read to Parliament last night, the President said that 'exceptional measures were necessary to deal with the breakdown of law and order in the state'.

The military, under General Sukminder Singh, set to work on the capital. There was an immediate air of reassurance for the citizens of Calcutta as men in stiffly starched, olive-green uniforms leapt from huge Tata-Mercedes trucks, their polished boots shining in the morning sun, their faces sharp and alert. Instead of *lathis* they sported guns, reputedly with real ammunition. People stopped and stared with admiration at these *javans* who had been fighting to protect India's borders, and were now here to save them from destruction.

Charles Smith was called to Government House to meet the general, where he was reassured that the army would now be responsible for his personal protection and all company assets would be offered twenty-four hour military security.

The measures began to have immediate effect. Rumours began to circulate that at a bus burning in Ballygunge, the army shot and killed six looters. They did not give any warnings or fire tear gas or shots into the air; they just aimed at and shot troublemakers. At a blockade in the docks at Diamond Harbour they rounded up every protester at bayonet point: not one got away.

In a couple of days, the city was back to its normal life of ordered chaos. The rickshaw wallahs returned, trams trundled along the Esplanade, clunking their bells as they went, and the city breathed a huge sigh of diesel exhaust-infused air.

Joan prayed that she might soon see Errol again as things seemed to be getting back to normal. 'I wish those incompetent fools at Police Headquarters would take lessons from the military on how to get the job done,' she told Phillip.

The general was a seasoned fighting man who served in Burma, initially with the British Indian Army and then with a breakaway unit of soldiers fighting for Indian

Independence. He was one of the few in his unit to have survived the 1944 Japanese campaign, managing to escape back to India and obtain a special pardon for desertion, having saved the life of a British Army officer.

In the 1947 war with Pakistan he had commanded a unit on the front in Kashmir and had distinguished himself for bravery by taking an enemy position against all odds. When Chinese troops invaded India from its northern borders he had commanded one of the very few units that held their position in Ladakh.

It was possible that Dutta and the Workers' Revolutionary Movement had met their match.

'Now we have to eliminate the root cause of the problem, the agitators who have been responsible for the collapse of the city,' he told Raj Chopra in an interview for *The Statesman*.

During the three hard decades of his military career the general had acquired some powerful interrogation techniques gleaned from the Japanese, the British and other battle-hardened *javans* in the Indian Army. He put these to use immediately to find the driving force behind the Movement.

Over the next few days of military operations, hundreds of people were snatched off the street at renowned trouble spots or rounded up in house-to-house searches based on CID informants. The press kept silent about any civil rights abuses, having been subject to a blackout on reporting military operations in the state under the powers available to the President.

The notorious Howrah jail had been turned into a reception centre for those arrested, and with around three thousand people jammed into a jail meant to hold a tenth of that number, conditions couldn't have been worse. After a day of thirty or forty people packed to a cell, tempers flared and arguments broke out, resulting in some casualties. These were just left to lie on the cell floor no matter what their physical condition. Sustenance was confined to a slice of dry bread for each prisoner and a *balti* of water to satisfy their thirst.

Singh had several batches of prisoners taken in succession to the interrogation room on the top floor of the *thana*. Havaldars – the sergeants of the Indian Army – dressed in civilian clothes carried out an initial questioning to determine the names and addresses of other accomplices and key members of the Movement. In particular they were keen to identify the whereabouts of Dutta and his close associates.

Singh's havaldars knew that anyone close to Dutta, or with knowledge of his whereabouts, would be unlikely to provide anything worthwhile at the first interrogation. The training these prisoners had received in the Maoist camps would have equipped them well for dealing with the harshest forms of military interrogation. But Singh's techniques were well tested.

His Japanese captors had not believed the Indian unit that had surrendered to them was part of a defecting wing of the Indian Army, numbering some thirty thousand men. To ensure they had the truth from these men, they employed a form of interrogation that had remained indelibly marked in Singh's mind over his entire military career. It was pure psychological torture, ruthlessly effective and the one that he adapted and deployed now in the Howrah *thana*.

The havaldars had been coached by him in what he referred to as the art of *ultai pani*. The prisoners were strapped splayed out on a low *khatia* bed, with their upper body tilted towards the ground at sixty degrees.

'You are scum, you *behan chode* sister fucker, you don't deserve to live. Prepare to die now,' the havaldar would snarl out.

A dark cloth was put over the prisoner's face and cold water poured over it. The perception of drowning was instantaneous and very soon the prisoner would jerk and convulse in a death rattle, yelling a muffled shout of surrender. Answers to the question being posed by the havaldar flowed immediately thereafter. There were no burn marks or scars or any evidence of torture resulting from the exercise and soon the clean, clinically efficient method began to provide a deluge of valuable information that had so far eluded Inspector Basu and the state CID investigators. Names of associates, addresses, employers and so on were all followed up with ruthless efficiency and a dramatic fall in the level of unrest soon followed. Most of the perpetrators were held in detention or dealt with through the crude justice that military rulers were famous for. But still the whereabouts of Dutta, the prize they were all waiting for, eluded them.

General Singh concluded that there were a number of places he might be hiding, in an area that could cover more than five thousand square miles: it would be impossible to search each potential hideaway.

'If you were a *shikari*, havaldar,' he asked one of his men, 'and you had been told to hunt down a man-eating tiger, you wouldn't go looking in the hills for the beast in the faint hope that you might catch sight of it and shoot, would you?'

'No sir, no. That wouldn't be the way. In fact there would be a good probability that the tiger would come and eat you,' replied the havaldar.

'What would you do?' probed the general, always keen to get his men to do the thinking and then refine any innovative ideas himself.

'Sir, I have been reading about Mr Jim Corbett and the man-eater of Kumaon. It was a most interesting book about a tigress here in Bengal, which was responsible for killing and eating more than four hundred villagers. In the book Corbett sahib describes how he tracked the *sher*'s movements for many days to understand its habits and where it preyed on the villagers. They were referring to it as the evil *shaitan* devil and Corbett sahib had to begin to think like the *shaitan sher*. Finding the man-eater was like looking for a needle in a haystack as it never returned to the same site to kill or take its prey.'

'Havaldar, *shabash*! That is a good analysis of our challenge; we have to get into the mind of this *shaitan* Dutta. What do we know about the way he operates, from our interrogations of the prisoners?' said Singh, impressed by the way this very junior military man, from an illiterate Punjabi peasant family, had worked hard at educating himself. This was the sort of endeavour that the army should reward.

'Sir, the first thing we have to be aware of is that this *shaitan* will use any person or situation to achieve his goal, which is the overthrow of the government and us, the army, that keeps the current order. No matter how difficult the task, he believes that it is possible, by creating enough civil disturbance to bring the system down like a pack of cards. We also know that, like the tiger of Kumaon, he works under cover of darkness, varying his pattern every day. You will never find him in the same place for two days in a row. He used to be at most of the major factory *bandhs* and *gheraos* in the city but of late he has managed these operations in absentia. We think he spends most of the time out of the city in places like Behala and maybe Belubari, where there are sympathisers. We cannot trust the CID to monitor his movements as they have been infected with his informers,' said the havaldar, reeling off a string of details that he had diligently recorded from the interrogations of the last few days.

'Who are his associates, havaldar? Who has he been seen with most frequently?'

'Sir, we have information that says he is liking the ladies very much. There is this *larkie*, we couldn't get her name. She may be a Christian or an Anglo-Indian. Chopra, the journalist from *The Statesman*, mentioned her. Also he has a woman bodyguard trained by the Chinese in martial arts, knife-throwing and chopping bricks, who they say can overcome the strongest man.'

'How does he communicate with his followers?'

'Mostly through a network of cells. We've rounded up cell members but they do not seem to know activists from other cells, so the *shaitan* controls information carefully. His disciples keep low just like him, so if he wants to do a job like the firing of the Smith *shamiana*, he passes on the instruction via one of the members of his Revolutionary committee and so down a chain.'

270

'What about beating him out of the bush like they do with tigers? How about offering a *lakh* of rupees to anyone who helps us find him? That should break the back of his closest disciples,' said the General, trying to find a creative solution to the problem of breaking the strict code of secrecy around Dutta.

'Sir, his most loyal supporters come from quite wealthy families already and money is not their motivation.'

'*Achha*, the tiger leaves a path here and there which I believe *shikaris* like Corbett were good at following. What trail do you think we should follow that would lead us to Dutta?'

'Sir, the most interesting will be to follow that fellow Chopra if he gets invited again for another interview. Dutta loves publicity for his cause. Perhaps we should stimulate another one of those chats with Dutta and the journalist.'

And so the general hit upon a plan to force Dutta into making contact with Chopra. Since coming to Calcutta he had spent a few evenings at the Calcutta Club, getting to know some of the city's men of influence. He'd emptied several glasses of Black Label Johnny Walker whisky and water, a drink that was getting more prohibitively expensive by the day, with Charles Smith, the most controversial businessman in town. He'd also drunk the best Assam tea with Inspector Basu, along with a conversation that he found highly dull. But his most enjoyable time had been spent with Judge Bhattacharya, as they saw eye to eye on most issues to do with law and order and the future of the modern India.

Bhattacharya, a keen historian, found General Singh's stories of Burma, the defections of the Indian troops, the various battles with Pakistan in 1947 and the more recent skirmishes with China to be highly entertaining and all in the best spirit of good company.

'So Bhattacharya, tell me now, I'm looking for a big favour,' said Singh that evening when the two of them were well into their fourth bottles of Eagle beer.

'What is that? You want me to help you put away some of these *goondas* based on those shady interrogation techniques of yours I keep hearing about.'

'What's wrong with my interrogation techniques? Don't give me all that intellectual stuff about human rights and things. If we save the innocent life of just one of our citizens, not to say the future of our democracy, won't it have been worth suspending these traitors' rights?'

The tone was good humoured, a gently inebriated debate.

'No, I'm asking for a favour to help me catch this chap Dutta,' said Singh, getting serious and leaning over in the big cane armchair to avoid being heard by the other drinkers on the club veranda.

'I'm all ears,' the judge responded, leaning towards Singh.

'Could you write another comment piece for the papers about the risk we face if the country is held to ransom by people like this Dutta; stress the need for patriots to denounce him and how every living Indian today should fear the reign of terror that might ensue if Dutta and his party were to get the upper hand?'

'Strictly not supposed to, old boy, you know the

independence of the judiciary and all that. Can't show bias you know in case I have to try the bastard one day. Got into a bit of trouble after the last one I wrote calling for his immediate arrest.'

'You can get around that by not naming him but referring to the Maoist movement and the horrors of what's going on in China and what could happen here if we adopt those ways. You know you can find a form of words: you're a judge, it's your business. We'll get that fellow Chopra to interview you and encourage a "right of reply".'

'Mmn, let me sleep on it. I'm mildly interested,' said Bhattacharya, quite taken by the idea but not prepared to commit himself after the best part of four bottles of a strong rice beer. 'Look, why don't we get that Chopra fellow to interview us both, the general and the judge, *hah*?'

'I'll call you in the morning,' said Singh, not letting go.

And so a plan was crafted. Raj Chopra was asked to interview Judge Bhattacharya, the respected citizen of Calcutta, a man of the high court and a person of the highest integrity, and General Singh, the patriot and guardian of the state. They were both asked to give their view of the situation facing the state of Bengal and, ultimately, facing the country.

Chopra's questions were direct and to the point. What was the ultimate conclusion if the Maoist revolution took a hold in India? Did the army have a role to play in arresting the decline of law and order? How long should they be allowed to keep that law and order before the civilian police were allowed to take back control?

Bhattacharya kept his comments at an authoritative, statesman-like level. He quoted from the *Ramayana*,

273

outlining the richness of India's long cultural and religious heritage, the Gandhian ideals of tolerance and non-violence and the dangers of buying into false prophets, even giving the Christian Bible a fair airing. He drew attention to the pain and suffering being inflicted on the people of China and asked readers to draw their own conclusions.

The general talked about the cowardice of terrorists who masqueraded as freedom fighters and needed to be pulled by the roots and eliminated until they could no longer spread their poisonous vegetation. *Javans* were giving up their lives on the borders to Mao's army and here were people who were openly supporting India's enemies.

The Statesman carried the interview on the front page of its Friday edition, with Raj Chopra being credited by the paper as their eminent journalist doing one of the most significant interviews of his life. The item received a mention on All India Radio's national news, drawing attention to the fact that a top judge and a general had spoken out in support of the emergency rule imposed by the centre. Soon the judge and general were being talked about in reverential terms in coffee houses, offices and the teachers' common room at Don Bosco's School.

'You know this Judge Bhattacharya, don't you?' said one of the teachers who came to visit Joan at her home. 'Wasn't he at the Smiths' party when they had the fire?'

'Yes, nice man and a real gentleman,' said Joan. 'He's definitely raised the temperature on the campaign to get Dutta.'

'And no word on your son yet?'

'No, there's still no news. It's driving me mad,' said Joan, almost in tears.

'Let's see what the new day brings. I'll say a little prayer for you tonight and light a special candle to Our Lady of Bandle. She's wonderful at working miracles.' Her visitor was on her way out of the door, but then came back into the room. 'There's a note for you here, Joan.'

The envelope that had been left at the entrance to the flat was marked 'JOAN'. Inside there was a handwritten note, scribbled on a page torn out of an exercise book. The author had not used the elaborate device of a newspaper to convey the message this time.

Dear Joan,

I may have some information that you will find useful in connection with Errol. Please meet me at the Coffee House tomorrow at three in the afternoon and come on your own. Please don't talk to anyone about this, for the safety of both of us.

Philomena

In one corner of the page in a different, immature handwriting were four words:

Mummy I love you

RANSOM

Joan read the note repeatedly, a cold tremor running through her. She put the words 'Mummy I love you', in Errol's handwriting, to her lips and kissed them, her eyes closed. She had to tell Phillip about the note.

She walked to the railway colony where Phillip lived. She knocked on his door but there was no reply. Mr Jones, the landlord, heard Joan's knocking and came out to see her. 'He hasn't got back from the school yet, I believe. Who should I say called?'

'Oh I'm Joan, one of the teachers from Don Bosco's.'

'Well do come in and wait here. Shall I make you a cup of tea? I'm sure he won't be long.' Jones was a man in his late forties, with terrible dandruff and a sweaty smell emanating from under the arms of his Terylene shirt. Joan looked at him, unsure. She hesitated and then, hoping that Phillip was only minutes away, agreed. 'Yes OK, thank you very much,' she said.

Jones disappeared to boil a kettle as his *khansama* had left for the day. Joan sat in the living room on an enormous teak armchair that had probably been appropriated from a railway waiting room, with its long arms, cane bottom and backing.

The shelves were covered with old photographs of railway locomotives, mostly with Jones hanging out of the tender with the fireman, or posing by the giant wheels and piston rods. All the photographs – in stations, in sidings and in motion – were of the same WP7014 locomotive with a destination nameplate 'Dehra Doon' on the front. Jones was obviously one of the drivers of the Doon Express and had been so for a number of years judging by some of the pictures, in which he looked considerably younger.

And then Joan noticed a small picture towards the end of the row that she instantly recognised: the 1955 wreckage of the train that killed her husband George. The picture was just of the locomotive, which had become separated from its tender and was on its left side halfway down a steep cutting, like a multi-legged animal that had fallen and was too sick to stand up again.

'Ah Mrs...' Jones walked into the room with a tray and a teapot with cups.

'Oh, D'Silva, Joan D'Silva.'

He noticed Joan looking at the picture. 'Mrs D'Silva, I see the photo of the '55 crash interests you. That was a lucky escape for me. I was thrown out of the tender as she rolled down the side. The fireman lost his life.'

'My husband lost his,' said Joan in a whisper.

'Oh, I am sorry to hear that. Were you with him?'

'No, he was on work, outstation. I just got the telegram. It took me a while to get over it. In fact I still haven't in some ways.'

Mr Jones sat down. His mind cut back to '55. The crash was very much still with him too. 'It was not a good place to be. We were miles from anywhere; it took hours for any help to come. It was only when the sun started to rise that we could see the carnage. I'm sorry, this must be upsetting you.'

'No, on the contrary, I would like you to say some more. I haven't met anyone who was there on the night; please go on.'

He poured tea through a strainer, the dark brown liquid steaming as it left the spout, filling the air with Darjeeling, slightly mixed with the smell of tired unwashed sweat. Joan breathed it in unwittingly, listening to Jones unravel the night she thought she had lost everything.

By the time Phillip arrived back at his room, she felt as though someone had finally filled in some of the gaps that had troubled her through her many years of solitary grief. She looked up at him. There were tears in her eyes.

'Joan, has Mr Jones been looking after you?' asked Phillip.

'He's been a gentleman, Phillip, and I'm very pleased to have had tea with him.'

Phillip nodded at Mr Jones. Joan stood up. 'Thank you, Mr Jones. If I could call again at some point?'

'Mrs D'Silva, you would be most welcome.'

Phillip led Joan to his room. He could sense she had something to tell him.

'I've had some more news; it's encouraging.' She passed him the letter.

Phillip read the letter a few times over then said, 'So,

this woman Philomena is implicated, *hah*? Have you told the Smiths that their *ayah* is a communist *goonda*?'

'I have now. But she has gone missing and not been to work since the fire. I've only just got the letter and I don't want to do anything to upset the Movement. I'm now completely dependent on her to protect Errol.'

'I'm not so sure that's relevant. It's not her I'd be worried about but the godless people she is being influenced by. What if she is currently plotting to kidnap the Smith boys and, oh yes, the *shamiana* fire, we're sure now she was behind that in some way,' said Phillip. Pausing suddenly, he realised he had probably gone too far towards damping down Joan's excitement and the possibility that Errol might be back home sometime soon.

'I'm going down tomorrow afternoon to see her at the Coffee House. I don't want you to come with me, Phillip, as I'm scared of doing anything that might harm Errol. But I thought you should know, just in case something happens. I've told nobody else.'

'But couldn't we be seen to be in this together? At least two of us have a chance of coming off better than one.'

'No, Phillip, no. I can't risk Errol's freedom. These are ruthless people who don't like to be disobeyed.'

'OK, but Joan, we are going to have to involve the authorities soon. We can't just let this thing drag on without their help or you'll sink further and further into the clutches of these *goondas*. You know the judge told you that the reason they've chosen to take your most precious possession on earth is that they want to use you for something. Please be careful. Just listen, don't agree to anything.'

'I'll be fine.'

The Coffee House was crowded mid afternoon with shoppers and students from wealthy, middle-class families spending their parents' money on iced coffees, cakes and other sorts of indulgences that would have cost Joan's rickshaw wallah more than a week's wages.

The Italian coffee maker whooshed amidst the general hum of people's conversations, which were mostly in English, as the patrons of the Coffee House wished to participate fully in the European experience. The owner of the establishment was a large Parsi gentleman who had lived for two years in London and had spent many a lonely Sunday afternoon in J J Lyons' tea house in Charing Cross, full of admiration for the waitresses who went about their work briskly and efficiently. He resolved to start something similar on his return to India but felt that tea would not be appreciated, not being different and exotic enough. Hence the idea of the Coffee House was born.

Joan looked around the tables but could not see Philomena. She would probably be the only young woman there sitting on her own wearing a frock. So Joan joined the queue of people waiting for a table, still looking around her in case she might have missed Philomena.

A waiter came up to her and said, 'Memsahib, your friend is already here, can I take you to the table?'

Joan nodded and followed the waiter to the far corner of the restaurant. As they approached, she noticed the back of a woman with a single plait of black hair, wearing a purple *salwar kameez*. The *salwar kameez* was quickly being adopted by most young modern Indian women as the universal dress of progress and prosperity. When they got to the table, the woman rose to greet her, and to Joan's surprise and relief it was Philomena.

'Hello, Philomena, I didn't recognise you. New image, *hah*?'

Philomena smiled and nodded, looking around her. Gone was the dowdy hand-me-down convent dress. Gone was the self-cropped hair. Philomena looked like any fashionable, middle-class student from Calcutta College rather than someone's nanny.

'Good afternoon, Joan, thanks for coming. You've probably got many questions to ask me, so can I first reassure you that Errol is OK and he's been doing his arithmetic and eating his favourite *ponga* kebabs from Calcutta's best restaurant,' said Philomena.

'You've seen my boy?'

'Yes, Joan, just this morning. He is fine, I can assure you.'

'Philomena, you took him, didn't you?' said Joan, controlling her voice, which she felt could break into a scream at any moment.

'I did and I'm also able to bring him back to you, but there are a few things that need to be done before we can secure his total freedom.'

'Philomena, what is going on here? How can you still be involved in this terrible outfit, the Movement? You, with your loving upbringing from Sister Theresa. How could you?' Joan couldn't hold back the tears of rage mixed with sorrow.

'I've already told you, you have to believe in a cause in life. A meaning for being here on the planet. I've found that meaning and it's turned me from some unwanted orphan into a person who is respected and valued.'

'Respected and valued by some gangster *goondas*,

young *chokras* who only wish to cause mayhem. These aren't people to feel valued by!'

'Dutta is a man of huge substance. He will be the saviour of this country, and many people like me believe in him. He is the way forward. Those that want the old order see him as a *goonda*; we see it differently. When taking out a cancerous tumour the patient has to suffer pain.'

The waiter arrived for the order, interrupting a conversation that was rapidly escalating into an argument. They both ordered iced coffees to get the waiter out of the way, and Joan knew that she needed to find out quickly how she could get Errol back to her. Having a furious political argument with his captor was not going to be the best way of doing this.

'So what do I have to do then to get Errol back?'

'Joan before I tell you, I have to ask you something.' Philomena paused. 'Do you agree that we live in an unjust and unequal society based on the single most chance event of our lives, where and to whom we were born?'

'Yes, in some ways, but it may also be down to our destiny.' Joan was losing patience with Philomena.

'Joan, that destiny stuff is nonsense; it comes from religion which Marx described as the opium of the masses.'

'Philomena, I've read my history books too. Let's assume I agree with you, what do you want me to do?' she snapped, tired of Philomena's political enlightenment.

'There are people here in the establishment in Calcutta who need to be dealt with, people who support and perpetuate the system of injustice, people who can be bribed to do anything, no matter how unjust. These are people who are not the capitalists alone but the police, officials in the railways and, most importantly, the judiciary.'

'And what does being dealt with involve?' said Joan, leaning over.

'Being neutralised so that they cease to be a negative influence on the course of history,' said Philomena.

'I don't understand why you need me. I'm just a teacher. I have no power or influence over anybody. You have taken my son and I should be turning you in to the military now.'

'Joan, that is the last thing you should do when you are so close to getting your son back. That would antagonise the Movement and jeopardise his return.'

'So what is this thing you want me to do?' said Joan.

'Neutralise Bhattacharya.'

Joan put down her coffee slowly, staring at Philomena, 'Neutralise Bhattacharya? What do you mean? How do I neutralise him?'

'Assassinate him and you will be doing us a great service,' said Philomena, continuing to look Joan in the eyes.

'That is impossible. He is my friend. He is one of the nicest people I know. Why are you asking me that?' Joan stammered out in response.

'Joan, this man is nothing but evil, believe me. He is bad for the future of our country. The judge has been responsible for the execution of many of our brave comrades while he allows corrupt officials and killers to go free in exchange for big bribes. How do you think he is able to afford his expensive lifestyle in a bungalow in the richest district of Calcutta on a state salary? Bhattacharya is our number one enemy and you are the best person we know with access to him. You must help us.'

Philomena sat back to gauge Joan's reaction. The look of fear on her face made Philomena speak again.

'It is a simple task: we have a delayed poison that takes a while to act. You will not have to witness the death or pain of your victim and it will be untraceable by a doctor as it simulates a heart attack. The declared cause of death will be heart failure. Many enemies of our revolution die of the condition because of their exorbitant lifestyles while thousands of our peasant children die before the age of five because of malnutrition.'

Joan pushed her coffee away and looked beyond Philomena into the distance.

'Can I have some time to think about this?' asked Joan, trying to retreat to a safer place.

'It's best you act now rather than think about it. The more you try to think and rationalise the idea the harder it will become, believe me. Your sole concern should be the survival of your son.'

Joan felt like slapping Philomena hard to stop her easy words. She resisted. 'And how do I know he will be given back to me? How do I know? How can I trust you and Dutta? A man who does some of the most unscrupulous things?' said Joan, beginning to feel more angry than hysterical.

'Errol is innocent. He has done no harm and will come to no harm. You too, Joan, would become an honoured friend of the Movement. As a fellow woman, I can assure you that Errol will have my complete protection. Of course I can't assure that if you do not do as we say. Dutta is not a man to be crossed. But on the other hand as a friend he is very generous.'

'All my life and my beliefs have been built up around the most important commandment: "Thou shall not kill". You know that, Philomena, the nuns must have taught you that. Killing is a sin in whatever form. Taking one life to save another is not something I could find it in myself to do.'

'In war we kill freely and the church sanctions that with impunity. Christians have killed people who go against them for centuries and it's all been sanctioned by the Pope himself. From the crusades to the annihilation of the South American Indians by the Conquistadores, all these have had the official sanction of the church, so don't give me that. And, didn't the church stand by silently in Germany while six million Jews were exterminated?'

'Why not pick on the general or on Inspector Basu, why Bhattacharya?'

'He's our number one enemy, Joan. It's as simple as that. I have the poison here in a capsule,' she said pointing to her handbag. 'All you have to do is slip it into the judge's tea and walk away. That's it. We will never bother you again. There's no gun or knife or weapon of any description. Walk out of here with the capsule, call on the judge on some pretext, take tea with him and then walk away. We've made it easy for you,' said Philomena, becoming more and more convincing.

Joan thought through the consequences of her actions. If she declined to accept the offer she would put Errol in more danger.

'Give me the capsule.'

Philomena smiled. She reached into her bag.

Joan stared at Philomena, her face hardening. 'When will I get Errol back?'

'He will be returned to your flat in Liluah.'

Joan took the pill from Philomena's hand.

ASSASSIN

Joan walked across the *maidan*, a square mile of flat, green, open land in the middle of the city. Young men and boys were playing games of cricket, all with dreams of playing for India one day, Bedis, Umbrigars and Mankads in the making. A few cows grazed on the thin strands of grass that grew on the otherwise barren ground, and a Muslim boy, wearing a white skullcap, led a goat on a rope to what was probably a bloody fate at the sharp end of a butcher's knife. A man on a lady's bicycle rode slowly in the bright sunshine, weaving through the batsmen and bowlers, going nowhere in particular.

Joan wandered through this open space, walking away from the constant honk of car horns in Chowringhee, playing back her meeting with Philomena. The heat of the afternoon sun forced her to sit under the shade of one of the few remaining banyan trees. Could she really take the life of someone she only vaguely knew, in exchange for her son?

Burying her face in her knees as she sat against the tree, Joan closed her eyes and cried, seeing the picture in

286

her dream of Errol running towards her, arms outstretched. Then she chilled at the next dream memory: the suitcase with his remains, his severed head, eyes open, an arm. Could it be that these people would be so bloody just to make a point? There was no way she could bear to see her Errol die at the hands of these murderers.

Philomena had seemed so matter-of-fact and clinical throughout the conversation, coldly making her demands for the head of a judge. How had an apparently good convent girl got buried so deep with such heartless people? Stories of brainwashing by the Maoists were rife but this was a quite extraordinary example.

She thought about the consequences of her actions. Killing the judge might mean that she would get away with the murder but could she live the rest of her life knowing what she had done? The option of talking to the police or the military was worse and the picture of that suitcase loomed larger than ever.

Joan felt that she had moved towards the edge of a cliff; the brief respite to think through what she was doing had only bought temporary relief. Then she noticed the man on the lady's bicycle again, circling back to where he had come from, talking to another man on a bicycle. Was she being watched? She closed her eyes for a few minutes to calm herself, but this only made those images of Errol flash past her faster and faster. When she opened her eyes a few minutes later, the men were still there in the distance.

So Joan decided to walk on towards the racecourse, taking out her parasol for shelter from the biting sun which had begun to make her sweat. The navy-blue cotton dress had not been a good idea, but in her heavy mood that morning she had rejected her brighter clothing options. There was not a scrap of wind to help her cool off and she longed to be back in the air-conditioned comfort of the Coffee House. In the distance the men began to walk slowly in the same direction as her. They were indeed keeping an eye on her movements.

Joan began to prepare in her mind for her meeting with the judge. What would she say when she called on him? What if he was out at the club? 'Please God, could he be out?' she said to herself.

The judge had once talked about the famous Bengali poet Rabindranath Tagore and encouraged Joan to read his works, most of which had been translated into English. Tagore was an extraordinary reformer who believed that it was easy to blame the British for the demise of Calcutta and that its inhabitants needed to cure themselves of the disease of poverty through education. His poetry had won him a Nobel prize.

The poet would be the perfect foil for Joan.

The men with their bikes were still following her, keeping a good distance away, and Joan would be at the judge's house in ten minutes if she walked at the same slow pace.

She recalled Philomena's attempts to demonise him. Was he really as corrupt as she said? The judiciary were well paid compared to most, but the real wealth resided with the established family dynasties, the Marwaris, the Parsis, the Bombay merchants and the foreign business community. Bhattacharya did live in a large, Victorian-looking building which, unlike others of similar vintage, was beautifully maintained, with painted railings and surrounding flower gardens, all in the middle of this expensive metropolis. Few officials lived in these conditions, it was true.

Joan still could not see herself committing murder, despite any doubts about the possibly illicit life of the judge. But she ploughed on, hoping that something might push her over the brink. She prayed for something dreadful to reveal itself to justify her actions. But nothing came.

Finally she came to the house where the large iron garden gate was shut to keep out undesirables. A *chowkidar* saw her approach and came to the gate, acknowledging her with a 'Memsahib?'

'Is Sri Bhattacharya in today?' she enquired.

'Memsahib, I will go to check with his wife,' he replied diplomatically.

'Please tell Sri Bhattacharya I've come to see him about some books,' she said.

She waited by the gate, looking around under her parasol for the men on her tail. She couldn't see them but they could be lurking at any one of a dozen places just out of sight. A dachshund came running up the gravel drive yapping at the world. Then Bhattacharya himself appeared at the door to the house and shouted out, 'Come on in.' He was wearing a loose shirt and *dhoti* and held a cigarette in his left hand.

This was it. Joan turned around for one final look behind her, the *chowkidar* opened the gate and she was soon in the house.

'Mr Bhattacharya, good afternoon, I've come for a small favour,' she said to justify her sudden appearance.

'Oh, Joan, it's lovely to see you, do come and join us for

a cup of tea; Anjali and I were just about to ask the bearer to make a pot of *cha*. Come onto the back veranda, it's cooler out there facing the racecourse at this time of day. What news of your son?'

The veranda was tiled in black and white Italian marble squares, and furnished with large Javanese cane chairs and straw blinds to keep out the sun. It suddenly felt a good ten degrees cooler than out in the heat. The gardens were awash with canna lilies of every hue, and a very modern sprinkler system swished away, creating a perpetual rainbow to add to the explosion of colour.

'No further news, Mr Bhattacharya,' said Joan, lying. As her intentions were considerably more dishonourable, she could not feel bad about a little lie.

'Oh, Joan, do call me Batty, like my friends do, it's easier,' said the judge, apparently uncomfortable with the formality. His wife came onto the veranda and gave Joan a *namaskar,* bringing a little more formality to the meeting. Joan had not met her before. 'Joan, this is Anjali. I don't think you've been introduced,' said the judge.

Anjali wore a blue cotton sari which covered a gently rotund frame, quite typical of middle-aged Bengali women of her social standing, who expended little in the way of physical effort with servants doing most of the daily chores. 'I've heard about your boy,' she said. 'I don't have children but I know how you must feel, the maternal instinct is in us all.'

'I'm just getting on with life and hoping that I might see him again one day. That's all I can do,' Joan replied.

'Now what is this about books, Joan? How can I help? Your pupils aren't going to be taking over the judiciary soon, are they?' said Bhattacharya.

'I want my boys to understand a little about the great poet Tagore. Our literature curriculum is heavy on the likes of Longfellow, Yeats and Walter de la Mare but not a mention of India's most awarded poet,' said Joan.

'Ah yes, Tagore was never quite understood by the British, despite his extensive tours to England, setting up Dartington Hall and being knighted. It was only Yeats who really appreciated him and he was Irish.'

'Do you have anything that would serve as a primer on Tagore for me to begin to appreciate him in a way that my boys could?'

'I have just the work, Joan. Let me go to the library and pick it out for you.'

The bearer had brought the tea on a silver tray; there were three white porcelain cups with silver rims and a matching pot. Joan could smell the aroma of the heavily scented orange pekoe, which contrasted so sharply with Mr Jones's sweat-infused Darjeeling.

'We'll allow the tea to soak for a while,' said Anjali. 'Tell me, what class do you teach at school?'

'I teach Standard Ten and Eleven. I have done for the last five years and it's very enjoyable.'

'You know I've always wanted to be a teacher but never had the courage to do it. I was convent educated in Assansol and remember my school very well. Most of the nuns who taught me have now sadly passed away.'

'Anjali,' called Bhattacharya from inside the house, 'could you come here a moment and help me?'

As soon as they were both out of sight, Joan was immediately aware of the opportunity this presented for her to put the capsule into a cup of tea for the judge. She was still not committed to going ahead with the murder, but now that she had the opportunity something drove her on. Going back outside without the mission accomplished, and seeing her grim reaper followers on their bicycles pedalling away for their revenge on Errol, was not an option she could face.

Joan poured the tea into all three cups, added milk to make the liquid opaque and slipped the capsule discreetly into one of the cups, the one furthest from her, stirring it a few times before Bhattacharya and his wife reappeared holding a couple of hardback books.

'I think we have something here for you,' said the judge, looking very pleased with himself. '*Gitanjali*, the greatest piece of poetry ever written I believe, and a beautiful short story "The Fruit Seller from Kabul", which your pupils will enjoy.'

'You know, Joan, *Gitanjali* is so beautiful, he read it to me on our wedding night as it was the first time we were on our own.'

'My poet's vanity dies in shame before thy sight. O master poet I have sat down at thy feet. Only let me make my life simple and straight, like a flute of reed for thee to fill with music...'

Bhattacharya read slowly in the rising and falling rhythmical singing voice so typical of Bengali poetry.

'It was so romantic,' said Anjali, looking at her husband and making him a little embarrassed at this outward sign of affection in the presence of a stranger.

'But let's have some *cha* now. Oh, you've poured it out already, so efficient!'

Joan picked up the cup destined for the judge and Anjali noticed some floating tea leaves. In her haste to pour the cups, Joan had forgotten to use the silver strainer. 'Give me that one, Joan, he doesn't like tea leaves in his tea,' said Anjali, taking the cup from Joan quickly and handing her husband one of the other cups.

Joan's heart stopped for a second; the poisoned cup was in the wrong hands as Bhattacharya sipped his tea and Anjali cleared the tea leaves with a teaspoon from her cup. She was raising it to her lips when Joan leapt up and knocked the cup from her hands with the clear intention of stopping Anjali from drinking the tea. The judge and his wife both looked aghast at the sudden act of sabotage. The bearer came onto the veranda having heard the crashing china and was rushing back for something to clear up the brown liquid that had begun to form little rivers along the black and white tiles.

Joan sat down on the floor, put her hands in her face and said, half crying, 'I'm sorry my darling, I'm sorry darling baby. I just couldn't, I just couldn't.'

The cruel images of Errol now flashed in front of her like a film strip slipping in a projector's tracking mechanism, throwing out jerking images on a cinema screen. She continued to sob silently.

Anjali was the first to sense that this was not an ordinary display of remorse for wanton damage to her best china. She knelt down on the floor and put her arms around Joan. '*Achha, achha*, we're not bothered about a broken cup now, Joan. Tell us what's going on. It's your son, isn't it? I'd be dying myself, you know, if they'd taken one of my own. We know how you must feel. Let's get you up on the chair and you can talk to us.'

Joan just kept shaking her head. Bhattacharya and his wife helped her off the floor to one of the cane chairs. She had lost all strength in her body. 'Batty, you told me they would come looking for me to do something to get my Errol back and they did.'

The judge and his wife exchanged glances. 'And is that upsetting you?' he said. 'Can we help?'

'Oh, I just feel so horrible about it, going so far with such a terrible thing.'

'And what did they ask you to do?' said the judge.

'To take your life,' she replied.

'His life?' said Anjali with some disbelief. The judge looked blank, almost as if he knew or suspected something already.

'Yes, they gave me a poison capsule to put in your drink.'

The judge considered his words carefully. 'I'm always expecting some *goonda* to come after me or send in some hit man to eliminate me; this is sadly an everyday occurrence in India today. But I must admit I would not have expected it from you.'

'But Batty, it's not surprising. I'd have been driven mad if they had my son, poor *beta*,' said Anjali, defending Joan's sorry condition.

'I'll never see my Errol again, never again. You can't believe the terrible images that flash through my brain of what they might do to him.'

They got Joan a glass of water to calm her down and she gradually revealed the extent of her deception: the meeting in the Coffee House, the men on bicycles outside and the intended effects of the capsule.

'It's quite simple then,' announced Bhattacharya, giving the two women no idea what he meant.

'What is simple, Batty?' said his wife.

'I'll just have to die, in the manner they're expecting. I'll have to simulate a heart attack, you'll have to call Dr Sinah, and we'll announce my sudden passing away to the press. Simple!'

'Batty, I'm not quite getting the full story here,' said Anjali. She was quite used to her husband's more weird ideas but was not totally in tune with this one.

'Well, if I feign death and you tell the world about it, then there is some chance of Dutta releasing Joan's son. Right now his life looks to be in certain danger.'

'But how long can you go on being dead, Batty? Be reasonable.'

'Let's try for a couple of days and see. What's the harm?' He looked across at Joan: the woman who had come to kill him.

And so, after much discussion, Joan was despatched back home to wait for her son and hopefully see him returned. Bhattacharya and his wife put in place an elaborate deception to temporarily fake his death. Dr Sinah, a close friend of the family, was called to certify death by a sudden stroke and, in a special request from the judge's wife, all mourners were asked to keep away from the house to minimise the trauma inflicted on her by this sudden loss. Fortunately the close family was scattered to all parts of India and abroad, so they could afford to extend the deception for at least forty-eight hours.

Raj Chopra was called to interview the widow Anjali. She spoke of the fine upstanding man he was and of his fight to rid Calcutta of the *goonda* element as well as of his love for Tagore. She told how, in the last hours of his life, he had given a schoolteacher from Don Bosco's a copy of his favourite poem *Gitanjali* for the boys in her class.

The front page covered the interview, the doctor's verdict and a picture of the grieving widow. Letters of sympathy began to pour in. Well-wishers left garlands and flowers at the gate of the house, which the *chowkidar* had to clear every few hours because of their abundance. Bhattacharya was clearly a very popular man.

When Joan had emerged from the Bhattacharya home she still could not see the men on bicycles and thought they had gone. The pictures of Errol running down the lane, arms outstretched, now flashed through her mind more frequently and she felt a large burden of guilt had been taken off her. When she returned home she thought she might see her son waiting on the doorstep, but he wasn't there.

How long would it take for him to come back home? Would they ever return him?

CORNERED

'The *shaitan* is cornered, sir,' said the havaldar, talking into his field radio. 'The house has been surrounded by the entire platoon now.'

General Singh was pleased to hear the communication at Eastern Command. '*Shabash*, please give my compliments to the lieutenant. Don't let any of them get away. Your orders are to shoot to kill.'

'Sir, the bait is still inside.'

'Yes, yes I know, so be careful, but don't let any of them get away on any account or take any hostages. Please tell that to the lieutenant.' The general's orders were heard loud and clear on the radio speakers.

The painstaking plan to corner Dutta was reaching its final stages. Chopra was the bait. His interviews with the judge and the general in *The Statesman* had incensed Dutta enough to demand a right of reply. Chopra had received his orders to turn up for an interview and hear the real story about the corrupt judge and his friends. The general had ordered a twenty-four surveillance operation on Chopra immediately after the publication of the article, sure that Dutta would try to contact the journalist.

Chopra had been in the business of newspapers for many years and was fiercely against any intrusion or control of the press, no matter what the justification. Right now, to his displeasure, under President's Rule all sorts of freedoms were being sacrificed in the name of security. The press was being gagged every day and manipulated to put a positive picture on the progress being made in the battle to eliminate the troublesome elements in the state. Chopra knew that he had been used to portray a favourable image of the judge and the general but he did not suspect that he was being manipulated by the authorities to help lead them to Dutta.

The day the news broke about the death of Bhattacharya, a man on a lady's bicycle rode up to an apartment in Park Street and put a note through Chopra's door, telling him that Dutta wished to see him for a right of reply. He should wait for a rickshaw wallah to call at six o'clock that evening to take him to an undisclosed destination.

Chopra felt uneasy about the planned meeting. There was a lot he didn't like. Firstly, it was in the evening when it got dark, and he always felt uncomfortable going on these types of assignments at night. The night was a time when he felt least in control. Waking in the middle of the night he hated the loneliness and stillness of the dark, and prayed for the morning to come. *Goondas* worked at night, preying on people's homes; cruel juntas knocked on doors and knew no justice. The dark was a time to avoid being vulnerable.

But Chopra had no means of dictating his choice of meeting place and so he prepared to be picked up at six o'clock that evening.

The rickshaw wallah arrived at the appointed hour. He looked better fed and better dressed than most of his trade, wearing grey shorts and a tee shirt quite unlike the bare-chested, *loonghi*-clad, emaciated people-pullers of Calcutta. He didn't say a word, just shrugged when spoken to by Chopra.

They set off down Park Street and were soon diving into little alleyways, then along Russell Street and Sudder Street. The rickshaw wallah seemed to know that he was being followed as he kept looking behind him in an attempt to throw anyone off his tail. After around fifteen minutes of this cat-and-mouse ducking and weaving in and out of alleys, Chopra was asked to switch rickshaws and continue on his way. Dutta was taking no chances.

Havaldar Kaul had also been thorough in his plans to track Chopra. He had chosen bicycles as his preferred vehicles of pursuit; they were flexible so that one could give chase at any speed between five and twenty miles an hour in the grinding, congested streets littered with people, cattle, dogs and other assorted obstructions. Given that the fastest you could go anywhere in Calcutta was no more than ten miles an hour, two wheels were good. Havaldar Kaul's men had no problem keeping up with the rickshaw wallah and picked up the switch of vehicles without difficulty.

After another few minutes of riding in the new rickshaw, they came to Clive Street where Chopra was asked to transfer to a taxi; an old Ambassador which, in terms of distance, had probably circumnavigated the earth a few times. The taxi stalled at first and the driver had to get out and hand-crank the engine into action. This gave the tailing cyclist enough time to commandeer another car into service in pursuit of the taxi.

There followed a long journey into one of the burgeoning new suburbs of Calcutta. Here Bengalis, tired of the problems and squalor of the city, had decided to build new homes on fresh plots of land in Behala. Potted roads and poor infrastructure were made up for by the open spaces and traffic-free environment, where children could play freely.

Many of the homes in this area were still under construction or had been recently completed. Electricity, water and other services had yet to be connected and no doubt, given the complex red tape and ponderous way in which public services worked, it would take years for these houses to be fully linked up. In the meantime, these wealthy residents sunk their own tube wells and installed their own generators and sewerage arrangements.

There were no street lamps, so Chopra had no idea where he was being driven. He had not been told to wear a blindfold this time. Far behind, Kaul's men tailed the taxi until it stopped outside a large, modern, single-storeyed house, surrounded by walls on all sides.

The taxi turned its lights out and the darkness surrounded them.

There were a few people in the house that night, gathered around a table in a square room that was probably destined to be the kitchen. The only form of lighting was

300

the flickering flame of a candle, which partially illuminated the faces of the small gathering sat cross-legged on the floor. The house had the antiseptic smell of fresh plaster and whitewash, indicating that builders and decorators had only recently departed.

In the faint yellow glimmer Chopra immediately recognised the young woman he had seen on his first trip out to the village location a month earlier. Philomena wore trousers like the others, and her plaited hair was done up under a dark cap with a large peak. Dutta entered the room from another entrance and said, 'So, Chopra, we meet again.' He didn't volunteer a handshake or a *namaskar* and Chopra didn't offer one either, guessing that real revolutionaries didn't have time for traditional rituals.

He switched on a small Sanyo tape recorder, which he had recently acquired from a friend who'd brought it back from Hong Kong. It was the latest in battery-powered wizardry and Chopra had used it a couple of times with considerable success. He had found it more reliable in recalling verbatim statements than his shorthand notes had ever been.

But Chopra was also an old-school journalist and his many years in the profession had made him rely on his notebook, both as a prop and as a shortcut to drafting the final piece for the paper. After many years of writing pieces for *The Statesman*, Chopra had become well practised in the art of annotating interviews. He had also perfected the skill of drafting his entire editorial during the interview, leaving very little amending for the subeditors. After his last interview with Dutta, Chopra had given his shorthand notes to the editor to work with and really had little to do afterwards, other than incorporating the new information he had received from Joan. Chopra had become a consummate professional at his trade.

'I wanted to see you to put the record straight about Judge Bhattacharya, one of the members of the establishment here in the state of West Bengal, and to explain why the Workers' Revolutionary Movement had to execute him,' said Dutta, sitting down on the floor next to Philomena.

'He died of a heart attack,' countered Chopra.

'One of our agents poisoned him,' said Philomena.

'I want to tell you why, Mr Chopra,' said Dutta, wagging his forefinger at the journalist. 'Bhattacharya was like a rotten mango, enticing on the outside, but abhorrent to taste. A case in the courts never got a favourable judgement unless he had been paid off. Many of our compatriots are in jail today with fabricated evidence supported by the judge. Nearly every *goonda* knew Bhattacharya well and he covered his tracks perfectly with that British sense of good taste and judgement. Pah!' He spat on the floor in disgust. 'We had to change that, and a few months ago we set a trap for the judge. He was, as they say in English, a bit of a ladies' man. Lindsay Street was a favourite place for him. One of our fellow revolutionaries volunteered to act as a trap to capture him with his pants down, so we could expose the man for what he was.'

'And what went wrong? I'm assuming you are referring to the girl washed up in the marshes? The Bandle Girl.'

'Yes of course, she died for the cause, murdered.'

'How?'

'We had intended to abduct Bhattacharya at one of the

houses in Lindsay Street. He had been introduced to Agnes as one of the new, freshly ripened fruits waiting for the judge to pluck.'

'And what went wrong?'

'She was a casualty of the war.'

'Are you saying that the post mortems and the pathologist's reports were all fabricated to make it look like an open verdict?' said Chopra.

'Of course, and Bhattacharya made sure he was the judge on the case.'

'Where's the evidence?'

'I was there. She was murdered.'

'But not you?' countered Chopra. Philomena glared at Chopra. He turned back to Dutta. 'Tell me about the James murder. You have been accused of that.'

'We did organise the *bandh* and James was pushed to the ground, but no one was under instructions to kill him. There is a Bombay man who has been trying to force GKW to sell up their business to him. We believe he ordered the execution of James to frighten the company into submission. Anil was hanged by insiders in the *thana* because he knew the real murderer. Bhattacharya would have tried his best to return a suicide verdict on Anil, just like he did on Agnes. He would have used his connections and a chain of bribes to get the verdict to protect the system.'

Chopra kept scribbling away as fast as he could in the dim candlelight. Suddenly, the group was disturbed by Errol, who had entered the room and was rubbing his eyes. Philomena got up and walked over to the boy.

'Errol, go back to sleep, we have to be up early in the morning,' said Philomena.

'*Jao, jao,*' said one of the men. Chopra was about to ask what a ten-year-old boy was doing with them in the middle of the night, but then there was a crack of gunfire and one of the windows shattered. The group scattered. Philomena grabbed Errol, pulling him down.

'The guns, the guns, grab the guns,' shouted Dutta. There was a collection of submachine guns, mostly 9mm weapons and Sterlings that the Movement had acquired through its supply lines from the Ladakh region.

A voice cut into the house from outside, loud and amplified.

'You are completely surrounded by the Indian Army. You have two minutes to come out with your hands up and surrender.'

Dutta hissed instructions to his men: 'This is what we do. Our only chance of survival is to scatter in different directions. It is pitch dark out there; they're not going to be able to pick us all up. In here we'll all be killed for sure.'

'Let the boy go first,' pleaded Philomena.

'*Nahi,* he is our insurance policy, our shield,' Dutta shot back.

'They won't respect his life. They want your head at all costs,' argued Philomena.

'That's a risk we'll have to take,' barked Dutta. 'They won't kill Chopra and the boy.' He turned to Chopra, pointing a gun at him.

'You, I and the boy go together. I'll have a machine gun to your head until we get in the vehicle.'

Philomena pulled Errol close to her. He looked frightened. 'Errol, go out the front door now with Mr Chopra. Your mum is out there to pick you up. She's come

304

with the men from the army to see you. Quickly,' shouted Philomena.

Errol was barefoot and still in the same clothes he was wearing the night he was taken. Hearing that his mother had come for him with the army immediately raised his spirits and he walked out of the front door with Chopra towards the wall and the iron gate. Dutta was behind them, a Sterling machine gun in his hands. Searchlights blinded them as they walked forward, shielding Dutta. The men surrounding the house had their weapons ready.

The havaldar in command saw the boy, 'Wait, there's a young *larka*. Hold it. Hold it.'

Errol continued to walk towards the bank of searchlights in front of him, expecting to see his mother come running out towards him. He broke into a run, pulling away from Chopra. Dutta panicked, grabbed Chopra by the arm and fired a few random bursts of his machine gun into the air. The searchlights blinded him. Errol was clear. He ran into the light and quickly reached the row of Jeeps and men in green military fatigues.

A *javan* grabbed him. 'Ma, Ma, where's my mum? Please take me to my mum,' he cried.

The soldier picked him up and thrust him in the back seat of the Jeep. 'Is your mother in the house?' said the havaldar.

'No, I was taken from my mum a week ago, we live in Liluah, near Don Bosco's School,' said Errol excitedly, not quite believing that he was being rescued by the Indian Army.

'Quiet now, *chup*,' the havaldar admonished him.

Dutta was walking towards the escape vehicle holding the submachine gun to Chopra's back. He was still banking on a respected member of the press providing the perfect cover as a hostage. The taxi that Chopra had arrived in was now only a few metres away.

'Drop your weapon now,' called the havaldar. Chopra waved a white handkerchief. Dutta ignored the instruction. 'Drop your weapon, give up now, it's your last chance.' The instruction was repeated in Hindi.

The havaldar told the marksman to fire his Enfield. Just one shot. Dutta recoiled. Chopra broke away but Dutta fired. Chopra slumped forward. Another shot thudded into Dutta and he was still.

The havaldar ordered a full salvo of fire from his soldiers into the house. More glass shattered and the line of Jeeps advanced to close the ring surrounding the house. The occupants had worked out that it was useless for them now to try to make a run for it; the sheer, overwhelming odds meant certain death.

Errol watched all this from a distance, not fully realising the brutality of what was going on. The excitement of guns going off and the noise of the gunfire masked the reality of real people being killed. It could have been just another game with his friends but this time with real uniforms and guns and live bullets.

Philomena and the other remaining occupants of the house had realised that the army was under a 'take no prisoners' order, so they decided to stay where they were and fight it out. Philomena had trained for such occasions.

She knew there was a strong probability that grenades would soon be thrown into the house to flush them out, so she left by a back door to hide in the garden behind the high walls.

She was happier out in the open where she felt she might have a chance. The glow of the searchlights outside was getting nearer as the vehicles advanced closer to the house. The dark was punctuated by a few shafts of light from the advancing troops and she noticed a small external shelter which she headed for, crawling on her belly.

This turned out to be the generator hood, just big enough to take the Merlin single-stroke diesel. Philomena's slim, five-foot-four frame was just small enough for her to slide in behind the engine, legs first. She pulled the hood back over her just as the bombardment of the property began.

The havaldar did not know exactly how many people were in the house so he had to approach with caution. 'Try the four-pounder on the front wall,' he said to a *javan* wielding one of the two field guns. The first shell punctured a four-foot hole in the wall and the second one demolished it completely. The troops were through.

Two of Dutta's men in the compound returned fire but fell silent in seconds. Three *javans* entered the house, spraying a few bullets in the dark, but were soon shouting out that the house was clear.

'The *shaitan* is down, General Sahib!' said Havaldar Kaul into the radio a few minutes later. 'We have control. No casualties on our side.'

'*Shabash*, Havaldar. Promotion to lieutenant for you

next, old man,' came back the reply from the delighted general. 'And the bait?'

'Bait's down too, sir.'

'I'm sure you did all you could to save him from the *sher*. We'll inform the family. Make sure the area is cordoned off by the police to keep the public and nosey-parker press, etc, away. Pull back your men to barracks once you have secured the area and get a good night's rest. I want good publicity photos of the *shaitan* for the morning press. The country needs to know that the state of Bengal is back to law and order.'

'That's copied, sir,' said the havaldar. 'We also have this *larka* who says he was kidnapped by the gang. He's about ten years old.'

Philomena lay motionless in the generator enclosure as men swarmed around the area. She heard more vehicles arrive and more voices. Her limbs got cramps and the pain was intense but there was not much she could do. Survival was her first priority. Gradually the noises died away, vehicles seemed to start up and fade away and the place fell silent.

It must have been a few hours later that Philomena summoned up enough courage to ease the generator hood open.

REUNITED

Joan slept lightly for the second night after the arranged killing of Judge Bhattacharya. She had hoped that Errol might turn up on her doorstep all through Sunday. For this reason she had stayed away from mass, hoping desperately that he would come knocking on her door at any moment.

The *Sunday Statesman* carried the news of Bhattacharya's sudden death on its front page, with a picture of his grieving wife. There was a glowing obituary of him as one of India's most outstanding patriots, speaking of his ceaseless desire to rid Bengal of those who were bent on the destruction of the country. The lead editorial spoke highly of him:

Bhattacharya, a man of the highest moral virtue, was consumed with the desire to punish those who believe that the ancient traditions and culture of our sacred motherland should be eliminated.

Various people of high standing, including Chief Minister Roy, paid tributes to him.

Joan felt certain that the news would bring freedom for her Errol, but as the day went on she became more despondent. Was Philomena just another ruthless killer like the rest of the Movement? If Errol were never to return, could she ever lead a normal life again? Her situation was made worse by not being able to talk to or confide in anyone about what she had done.

She slept on the sofa in the front room in case she fell into a deep sleep and didn't hear Errol at her door. As she drifted in and out of consciousness, the dream of seeing Errol running down the lane, arms outstretched, repeated itself, providing the little comfort that she needed to sustain her sanity. Then suddenly there was a firm knock on the door.

Joan was up in an instant. Havaldar Kaul was standing outside in his olive-green fatigues. 'Memsahib, is this your son?' he said, half smiling, with one hand on Errol's shoulder.

Joan froze for a moment, not believing what she was seeing, but then she burst into a shout of joy, flinging her arms around Errol. 'Darling, darling, are you all right,' she said repeatedly, feeling his arms, his chest and his face as if he were not real but some temporary apparition.

'Memsahib, would you sign this handover form?' asked the Havaldar, ensuring that the paperwork was in order.

'But what happened, how did you find him, where was he?' blurted out Joan, only half wanting to know.

'I'm sorry but that is all operational information which I cannot divulge at this stage. Someone from Eastern Command will be able to help in the next few days.' With that he said goodbye and left.

'Mum, I'm really tired, can I go to bed please?' asked Errol, and he did. After the days of suffering, the pain of being separated from the person she loved most on this earth, he was back; and all he wanted to do was go to sleep.

As Errol slept, so did Joan. When they awoke at midday, Joan gazed at Errol as if in admiration of a newfound prize, making the boy feel quite uncomfortable.

'Ma, I'm back home now, I'm OK, you know,' he kept saying.

His story of the rescue was sketchy but Joan didn't care. She had her precious son again and now she could go back to living a normal life.

The news of the Behala siege and elimination of Dutta and his 'key lieutenants', as described by *The Statesman*, spread through Calcutta the next day. Offices and government establishments seemed to be in a festive mood as people congratulated the army, themselves and the nation for having conquered the destructive forces of the Movement.

Babus sipped sweet tea by the bucketful all day, extolling the virtues of the army and debating the future of Marxism in Bengal, the ineffectiveness of the ruling Congress Party and the effect on the price of *beckti*, the most coveted fish in Bengal.

The Statesman's lead editorial again covered the story:

The state of Bengal and the nation can now get on with the business of building a great country once again, undeterred by the foreign forces of destruction that have brought such havoc to our daily lives over the last year. Regrettably one of our most-loved and talented journalists, Raj Chopra, lost his life in the skirmish; we join his friends and family in mourning his loss.

The front page carried a picture of Dutta's body, laid out on the ground outside the house in Behala with the triumphant Havaldar Kaul bending over him, resting on the Lee Enfield that brought down the *shaitan*. The photo caption read 'The *shikari* of Behala'. The same photograph was syndicated throughout India, so everyone could see how revolution didn't pay.

On page two the second piece of good news, which added to the sense of celebration, was that Judge Bhattacharya had literally 'risen from the dead'. To the great surprise of his wife Anjali, he had awoken from his death sleep by calling for a cup of tea and some refreshments at midnight, just about the time she received a call from General Singh to tell her the news of Dutta's execution.

The judge had fallen into a rare deep coma caused by a mild stroke, which had been known to deceive doctors. This phenomenon had been observed once before, just as the funeral pyres were about to be lit at Ballyghat for a middle-aged man. He had woken up to the joy of his grieving family and horror at his narrow escape from being burnt alive. Bhattacharya had awoken to the delight of his wife Anjali and commented favourably on the flowers that had been laid out around him.

Now the judge was back to his normal self and doctors had examined him and satisfied themselves that he was in the best of health. The stroke had not damaged his muscular movements or affected his memory, and he was expected back in court, handing out tough but fair justice to the *goondas* that crossed the line into criminality.

Joan's little flat was brimming over with people and well-wishers towards the end of the day as the news of Errol's release spread to the teaching staff at the school and beyond. They brought sweets and flowers to celebrate, and Errol had to recall umpteen times how he had been taken away by Philomena on the pretext of showing him the toyshop in Chowringhee, but was then pushed into a car and driven off into the countryside, being moved every night to avoid detection. But he had been looked after well, fed his favourite *ponga* kebabs most evenings and bought comics to keep him occupied during the day. Over the week he had read all the famous works of Dickens in the *Classics Illustrated* series, several back issues of the *Beano* and the 1960 edition of *Boy's Own*.

Chopra's body was handed over to his wife Kay. His wallet, a bracelet and the small reel-to-reel portable Sanyo tape recorder were also included, with the tapes of the night's interview wiped clean. The authorities appeared to have missed a small notepad, which Chopra had kept buttoned in the back pocket of his trousers. His shorthand notes were indecipherable to Kay, but she thought they might contain something of interest.

Joan went to visit Kay the day after the siege to offer her condolences. As a Burmese woman living in Calcutta, Kay did not have many friends and spent most of her time with her cats. She was on her own when Joan arrived; Chopra's body had already been cremated in the morning.

'Kay, we owe a debt of gratitude to your husband for the bravery he showed in trying to uncover the truth,' she said, handing her a card of condolence.

'Please, you come into the house and have some jasmine tea with me?' requested Kay.

Her flat was simple and sparse. Joan shifted uncomfortably in her seat while Kay left the tea leaves to impart their perfume and colour to the hot water. Kay wanted to show Joan something though. She pulled out the notebook from a biscuit tin and put it on the table for Joan to see. 'I find this in the back pocket of Raj. It is only thing they forget to mess with. It is dated on night of the shooting, two days ago. This is all I can read, other all writing in shorthand.'

'I can't read shorthand either,' said Joan. 'I know someone who does though. Would you trust me to have it deciphered?'

'Yes, OK, but need to be careful. Raj had enemies who don't like what he wrote about.'

Joan remembered that Phillip had learned to read shorthand at college; he had wanted to become a journalist himself before he took up teaching. She said her goodbyes to Kay, and then went directly to Phillip's place in the railway colony.

Phillip flicked through the pages then began to examine each one in more detail. 'This is rather incendiary stuff, Joan. I'm not sure we can go to the papers with this at the moment.'

'Why? Aren't we a free country? I have heard of news blackouts and military censoring in times of emergency, but the fact that Chopra would have recorded comments from a known villain should be of public interest.'

'Yes, but from what I can read here, these notes claim Bhattacharya had a hand in the Bandle Girl murder and

314

covered it up to make it look like a suicide.'

'How could that be possible?'

'It's what Philomena told you.'

'I didn't take it seriously.'

'Also according to Dutta, the murder of Thomas James was arranged by a business rival, who had been trying to buy up the GKW factories on the cheap. A hit man was contracted to make the killing look like the work of the Movement. Again the judge received some payment to ensure that, if the case came to court, Anil would be convicted. Someone on the inside finished him off to save them the trouble.'

Joan was torn between conflicting emotions. 'I need to talk to him, find out the truth. This can't be right but if it is he can't just get away with it.' She really didn't think it could be possible that the judge was involved in the Bandle Girl murder, but she wanted to speak to him.

'Now just be careful, Joan. Think this through. You've just got Errol back. Do you want to embark on another dangerous trail and put him and you at risk again?'

'But, Phillip, I can't just sit here and not do anything. Where's your sense of justice?'

'We're still in an emergency and under President's Rule. The press, everybody, is under the strictest control. Bhattacharya will get his friend General Singh to have you locked up straight away and that's the last we'll hear of you. Let's wait and see if we have a better idea,' said Phillip.

Over the next day Joan reflected on the new evidence. She had respected Chopra. Why would the journalist have recorded these claims by Dutta without any comment of his own if he had not believed these to be genuine? The poisoning incident at Bhattacharya's had seemed to be all too easy. Was it just a trap set up by the general and the judge over a whisky at the Calcutta Club one evening? Bhattacharya seemed to have known that Joan would come for him after Errol's disappearance when he warned her that she would be asked to do something to earn him back.

Two days later the Delhi government announced that it would be handing power back to the Chief Minister, having succeeded in restoring stability in West Bengal. All India Radio announced:

General Singh of Eastern Command called on the Chief Minister Roy to hand over military control to the civilian police force. The Chief Minister expressed satisfaction with the effective way in which the military enforcement agencies had dealt with the criminal gangs that terrorised businesses and caused disruption to the people of West Bengal.

'Phillip, I'm going to Bhattacharya. I finish my last class at three. I'll go then,' she said after assembly that morning.

'Joan, there are a few things we need to do before you go and see the judge.'

'Like what?'

'Like tell someone else in confidence. Spread your risk a bit. Just in case. And I'm coming with you as your bodyguard.'

'Phillip, don't be silly.'

Phillip frowned, apparently offended at the notion that he was not manly enough to be taken seriously as a protector of women.

'I didn't mean it that way,' Joan added hastily. 'You can come, provided you stay in the shadows.'

When Joan turned up at Bhattacharya's house she was told he was not at home. He might be at the club or with General Singh at Fort William, celebrating the end to President's Rule. Joan wanted the benefit of surprise so thought she might go first to the Calcutta Club. The judge had not been there all day, so she asked her rickshaw wallah to go to Fort William. But the guards at the gate were not going to let a civilian through without a pass, much as Joan might try to persuade them that she had been personally asked by the general to call on him.

It was then that the rickshaw wallah said, 'Memsahib, let's go to Lindsay Street. People like Sri Bhattacharya are sometimes going there at this time for drinking and making fun with the girls.'

Joan looked at Phillip and shrugged her shoulders, 'We've nothing to lose, I suppose. *Achha chullo*,' she said.

The rickshaw wallah took them directly to Madame Jessica's. 'Phillip, I think you should go and have a look around first before I go barging in,' said Joan.

Phillip rang the silent doorbell three times because that's what he had seen in a movie about the red light district in Casablanca. Jessica appeared in seconds, popping her head out of the top window to see who was at her front door. 'Yes?' she enquired. Phillip looked up. His confidence was draining but he had to keep going.

'Hello, a friend of mine told me to visit if I was in Cal,

317

said you'd welcome it?'

'I'll come down and let you in,' she said, looking pleased to see a newcomer.

Phillip waited and then the door opened.

'Good evening, do come in,' said Jessica, taking Phillip by the hand and ushering him into her lounge with the faded sofas. There were two people there, a woman in huge earrings and a backless black chiffon dress, almost a carbon copy of Jessica, cradling a man who had his back to Phillip. The room was filled with a combination of cigarette smoke and the smell of cheap whisky.

'Where are you from then, Mr Handsome, I like your lovely green eyes,' said Jessica, still leading him by the hand to a sofa in another corner of the room.

'Oh from out of town, I'm visiting people at the Grand.'

'Oh yes, now there's a place with a bit of history. Not the same today, however. They've let it go a bit. Now can I get you a drink?'

'Well, how much is a glass of beer?' asked Phillip, who wasn't sure he'd be able to afford Madame Jessica's hospitality.

'We can settle up later. What's your name?'

'Er... Phillip,' he said, not sure if it was right to give his real name.

'Now that's a nice name, what do you do, Phillip?' said Jessica, opening a bottle of Eagle beer.

'I'm a teacher actually,' he said, again unsure if telling the truth was a good thing.

The man on the far side of the room turned around. It was Bhattacharya. Probably the mention of being a teacher intrigued him, and he wished to know who he was

318

sharing the room with. He recognised Phillip straight away from the night at the fire.

'We've met before, haven't we?' he said, sitting up and freeing himself from the arm that was draped around his neck.

'Yes.'

'*Achha!* Yes the fire, *ha*?' Bhattacharya was now feeling a little uncomfortable as he sat at the edge of the sofa. 'And you were a friend of that Joan D'Silva, *ha*?'

'That's right and she'd like to speak to you, sir.'

'Oh yes, sure, tell her to come around and see us sometime.'

'She's here actually, waiting outside for you.'

'I don't think she'd be welcome here.'

Phillip got up and walked to the door. He flung the bolt open. Jessica got up to shut the door but Phillip blocked her way. Joan, waiting in the rickshaw outside, saw the door open and immediately crossed the street to enter the house.

'I have to leave now,' said Bhattacharya, attempting to get past Jessica and her colleague.

Phillip pushed him hard. He slumped back into his seat. Joan D'Silva barged into the room. She looked at the scene. People were waiting for something to happen. 'Mr Bhattacharya,' said Joan, all five feet eight inches of her standing in his way. 'Please sit down a minute.'

'Joan!' he said. 'This is the last place I'd expect to see you. Ah, don't tell me, you want me to swallow something else. I have to go now. Please let me pass.' The judge scowled as though he was about to be attacked by a ferocious, mad dog.

'You're not going anywhere,' said Phillip, straightening his back and puffing out his chest. Joan was pleased that he had come along after all.

'You people are making a big mistake. Do you know what this could mean? Apprehending a member of the judiciary against his will? I could have Basu lock you up and forget about you forever.'

'Don't give me that menacing talk,' stormed Joan, incensed. 'We have the last notes of Chopra's interview with Dutta, and you are implicated in many of the recent crimes in this city, not least the Bandle Girl case, and you have indulged in practices that a man in your position should be ashamed of.'

Bhattacharya tried to look unconcerned. 'The desperate ramblings of a madman, minutes from his death, and a journalist out to sensationalise everything?'

'Chopra had no reason to make up the story in that house in Behala and Dutta knew he was risking his life by having him there.'

'You can believe what you want, but I know nothing of these allegations,' Bhattacharya hedged. 'What am I being accused of?'

'You were involved in the death of Agnes and you received money from a businessman to ensure Anil was accused of the murder of Thomas James. That never came to court and someone murdered Anil. We need to know how Agnes died because you were one of the people present when she was killed.'

'That is not true, I was not there. You have a fertile imagination that's going to get you and your friend here into a lot of trouble.'

'So you did know her then?'

'Certainly not. What would a man in my position be doing with a girl of her sort?'

Joan looked around at the room and also at Madame Jessica.

'What are you doing here now? Listen, we've corroborated our stories from more than one source, so I'm looking for the truth. A real confession from you. And if we don't get it then I'm going directly to the editor of *The Statesman* with what's in these notes. I've already lodged a photographic print of Chopra's notes with two different reliable people in sealed envelopes, just in case you decide to get your *goonda* friends to take care of us.'

Joan was taking a gamble to see if the judge could be pushed into telling the whole story.

'You're such an amateur. Have you no idea of the people I know, the power I wield? I could make you and your *Chutney Mary* friends disappear forever.'

Something tripped a switch in Jessica's brain, '*Chutney Marys, ha*? Happy to come here every week and get what your women don't give you and yet you treat us like filth.'

'Filth is what we expect from people like you,' said the judge.

Jessica turned to Joan. She had heard enough.

'I'll tell you the real story about Agnes, Mrs D'Silva.' She smiled contemptuously at the judge. People like him had been treating her badly all her life. Now she would tell the truth. 'Dutta's men came here and said that I would have to collaborate in their operation or my place would be burned down. Bhattacharya picked up the girl Agnes at the Grand one evening and she brought him here. She was a good-looking Anglo girl but had never done this sort of thing before. When they got here, Bhattacharya was surprised to see General Singh, who was also out for a good night. It was then that Agnes's friends, who were supposedly there to abduct Bhattacharya, rushed in. But the general had a bodyguard. There was a fight. Agnes fell head first as they were attempting to flee; she hit her forehead on a big stone on the pavement. The men fled. Singh called his havaldar to get her body removed. I believe he had it dumped in the river.'

'What, the fall killed her?' asked Joan.

'I don't know. I know she was out cold. That's all I know.'

Bhattacharya had kept silent through all this and now continued to look down at the ground in silence. Mrs D'Silva turned to him.

'Judge, sir, either you resign your position tomorrow morning, first thing, or we publish Chopra's full account in the press a day later. You have your choice. You know who the public is likely to believe.'

Bhattacharya tendered his resignation the next day after visiting the Chief Minister's office. With President's Rule ended he could no longer persuade his friend General Singh to block publication of Chopra's interview with Dutta. Bengalis always favour dead heroes over live ones and the journalist had been much praised for his bravery in leading the army to the hideout in Behala and losing his life in the process. Bhattacharya would not now be credible if he argued the case that Chopra was a liar when he was being praised everywhere as a patriot.

A statement from the Chief Minister's office cited

reasons for his resignation as ill health and concern that the judge had not fully recovered from his coma. The Minister thanked the judge for all his patriotic endeavours in helping to make Bengal a safer and more law-abiding place for its citizens.

Inspector Basu was delighted at the news of Bhattacharya's resignation. He had detested the way the judge had always put him down. 'Mrs D'Silva, I'm being very pleased with the way of recent events,' he said when she called at the *thana* to see him.

'Inspector, I think you should perform a fresh autopsy on Anil Sen to be sure how he really did die,' said Joan, in an effort to allow the Sen family to finally cremate their son.

The fresh autopsy revealed death by strangulation and not by hanging.

Anil Sen was killed by a seven-millimetre-thick cord being tightened around his neck to collapse his windpipe. This would more than likely have been performed by at least two persons, one to hold him down and the other to perform the act of strangulation. The victim was already dead when he was hanged from the ceiling in the cell.

Joan read the pathologist's report and closed her eyes for a moment, thinking of those last desperate moments of the young man, who would have put up little resistance given the abuse he had received.

There were no witnesses and Basu told Joan it was highly unlikely that the murderers would be apprehended so long after the crime. And so Anil's body was reunited with his family for cremation.

His mother cleansed the badly bruised body and dressed it in white. One last time she touched and stroked the person who had once been a part of her and of whom she had been so proud, her only child. She stayed at home while her husband accompanied the funeral procession to Ballyghat, where a funeral pyre had been built by untouchables, especially assigned to this sacred task.

Mr Sen lit the fire around the pyre by going around it anticlockwise with twigs of burning grass. Soon Anil's body was consumed by flames that reached high up into the air. Mr Sen looked into the flames with sadness, but now his son was at peace, his spirit finally released from his tortured body. In the final act of release, one of the mourners raised a bamboo pole and cracked open the skull to end any chance of entrapment. Mr Sen winced at the crude crack of the bamboo against his son's skull, but found comfort in the thought that he was at last in peace.

Joan watched from a distance and joined the mourners as they walked away from the pyre with their backs turned towards the cremation site. 'Mrs D'Silva, thank you for all you have done for our son,' said Anil's father, still humble and respectful despite the atrocities that had been committed against his own child.

LOOSE ENDS

Just across the Bengal–Bihar state border, in a village settlement, Philomena sat down to eat an evening meal of rice and *dal*. She had been reunited with a couple of fellow associates of Dutta. She felt lucky to have survived the siege at Behala, where the generator enclosure had saved her life.

After hours of lying with cramp in the stillness that followed the army retreat, she had ventured to lift the housing and drag herself outside into the dark. She could see the police cordons surrounding the house but found it quite easy to slip between them into the blackness of the night.

Hitching a ride on a succession of goods trains travelling west, she had managed to distance herself from the state capital. For a few *annas* she had procured a soiled sari from one of the refugee women sleeping rough on the station at Sealdah. Moving only at night, she had found her way to the safe settlement.

'Fellow revolutionaries, our leader is dead but the fight must go on. Sadly we will have to lie low for a while to regain our strength. But the need for a revolution is now more important than ever. The government may have won this battle but the long-term war against injustice has only just begun,' she said, and they all agreed.

Soon after the story of the siege of Behala had been published, Edwina Smith called on Joan. 'Have you considered the implications of all this for your safety?' she asked her friend. 'It's not going to be long before some very unpleasant people are after your blood. You're going to have to get out of Cal, Joan. You aren't safe here any more.'

'But where can I go, Edwina? I have nowhere. My brother-in-law in Lucknow will be retiring soon and I'm not sure I'd be any safer there.'

'Joan, Charles and I could help you emigrate to England. We know the High Commissioner here and he could process you a passport quite soon. You have English lineage down your maternal line and we could find you somewhere to stay in London while you get on your feet.'

'Edwina, that's very considerate of you, but I don't think I see my future in England, really. The cold weather, the cold people and Errol; how would he cope in that environment? We'd be so cut off from everybody.'

'Now, Joan, it's not all that bad. Charles and I aren't so dreadful, are we? Consider the alternative. You don't want to live through another episode like the one you have just experienced, do you?'

And so after a while Edwina had convinced Joan that she should at least try to see if she could get her papers processed to emigrate to England but keep her decision private until things were more certain.

'Phillip, there's something I want to talk to you about,'

Joan said one evening after school. 'I believe Errol and I might be in danger after everything that has happened.'

'Yes, I've been thinking that too. There must be more than a few people feeling aggrieved. The Movement, or what's left of it, couldn't be all too pleased that Bhattacharya suddenly arose from the dead and the judge himself hasn't exactly come out of it well. And what happened to Philomena? Errol was sure she was with him in the house at Behala and yet there was no mention of her in the death toll. She is very dangerous.'

'Phillip, would you be disappointed if I upped and left for good?' asked Joan.

'Very much so! But it's not that bad now, is it? I could come over and sleep on the sofa at night, if having a man in the flat would make you feel safer,' said Phillip, uneasy about Joan's sudden intention to leave. 'Where would you go? There aren't many places you'd be safe from these *goondas*.'

'It would have to be somewhere quite far away, like England for example,' said Joan, giving Phillip the news in dribs and drabs.

'But that's easier said than done. It's impossible to get in there now, they're clamping right down on Commonwealth immigration.'

'I may have a way. In fact it does look quite possible. I just wanted to know how you'd feel. You've been such a good friend to us; you're almost part of the family.'

'I'd be devastated, Joan.' That was all he said; there were a few moments of silence and then Joan hugged Phillip long and hard.

'I may have to go,' she finally said. 'You'd understand, wouldn't you?'

Joan knew she would miss Phillip's reassuring presence; his mentoring friendship with Errol had improved the boy's confidence, he had always been such a good companion and throughout the dark days of Errol's disappearance he had been a continual source of comfort. Still, other than that one night, Joan had never crossed the uncertain line from friend to lover.

Phillip, the thorough gentleman, had never presumed that he could cross that line unless invited to do so. After the episode with Joan, his pride had taken quite a while to recover and he was eternally grateful to spend his weekends with a woman like her, no matter how platonic their relationship, to nurse back his confidence.

Mrs De Lange had once remarked about their friendship, 'Any wedding bells in the air yet, Joan?' To which she had received a firm shake of the head accompanied by pursed lips, leaving no doubt as to her answer.

Finally a letter did arrive from the British High Commissioner's office in Calcutta, asking Joan to present herself, with Errol, for an interview. Joan wore her dark-brown frock for the occasion for she had heard how the British liked dark colours and she didn't wish to be seen as a *Chutney Mary* in anything too bright and colourful. Errol sweltered in his Sunday-best blazer and tie, accompanied by knee-length short trousers and well-polished brown shoes from the Chinese cobbler in the New Market.

A young man sitting behind a teak desk introduced himself as Leonard Painter and reached out to shake Joan's hand. 'Do sit down. So this is Errol?' he asked, looking expressionlessly at the boy, the table fan on his desk blowing a few strands of blond hair over his forehead. Errol made an effort to force a shy little smile.

'Your application to emigrate to Britain is being assessed by me and I will have to ask you a few questions, to assure the High Commissioner that you qualify under our asylum programme.'

'I do have English lineage on my maternal side,' said Joan.

'I'm afraid that you would only qualify for a British passport if your father was British, Mrs D'Silva; the paternal side you see. Now I hear that you are afraid for your personal safety and that of your son.'

'Yes, are you familiar with the recent events in Behala and the Workers' Revolutionary Movement?' she asked, wondering if the man, who had surely not yet turned thirty, had read the papers.

'Yes, indeed, I do know about those events, and the letter of recommendation and guarantees I have here from Mrs Edwina Smith set the detail out quite clearly. I just needed to ask. And what economic means do you have, Mrs D'Silva?'

'None, Mr Painter. But Mr Charles Smith has said that he would be able to get me some office work in his firm's UK headquarters, so I should be able to have a salary right away.'

'Yes, but how are you going to get to London, Mrs D'Silva? A passage on the cheapest crossing is at least a few thousand rupees and probably twice that by air. And you have your son to think about.'

'We'll find a way. I have some furniture to sell and a few personal items of jewellery which my husband gave me on our wedding day.'

'I see, yes, and you believe that will be enough for your passage? And your accommodation when you get there?'

'Father Rector at Don Bosco's has arranged something through the Salesians in a place called Battersea,' said Joan.

'Mrs D'Silva, Britain is a very unforgiving place for immigrants without any money. You will need something to get you started and without any relatives there you'd be a burden on the state. I don't think we can discuss this any further until you have proof of at least a couple of hundred pounds to get you and your boy started. I hope you are successful in raising the necessary funds,' said the official, standing up at his desk to shake Joan's hand as a signal that their appointment had now ended.

Joan knew that finding that money was impossible. Her total assets, including her twenty-four carat wedding ring and her few sticks of furniture, would not amount to much. She had written to Gerry asking for a loan, but had not received a reply. A couple of hundred pounds in rupees was more than a year's salary for most of her friends and acquaintances. Father Rector had promised her five hundred rupees, payable after her first year in work, if she fell short of her target, and Errol still had his winnings from the *Binaca Hit Parade* competition. But she would still be at least a thousand rupees short.

Back at Diamond Harbour, Hong Kong John, who had not been seen for months, walked off the boat carrying his sack of silk fabrics, watches, lighters and all manner of fake jewellery to flog to the Anglo-Indians in Elliot Road and the railway colony in Liluah. His gold-plated tooth flashed in the morning sun, accentuating the ear-to-ear smile on his face; a permanent feature of the jovial Chinaman.

Soon he was at Joan's door, beaming and promising 'new things all, new things all, miss!' His hallmark expression gave hope to everyone that Hong Kong John was bringing the latest in fashion ideas from Asia's most exciting metropolis.

A long procession of stray dogs followed this stranger into the area, yapping and barking his arrival. The local *durgees* rubbed their hands in the joyous expectation of plenty of fresh business from the memsahibs who relished the feel of the smooth silks and the look of the exciting oriental designs in deep Mandarin red, China blue and lime green.

'John, we haven't seen you in ages. I thought you were dead,' said Joan.

'No, missy, I been sick, but OK now. Please see new things all from Hong Kong,' he said, taking the huge sack off his back and laying it on the ground, spewing out items of every hue.

'John, I don't think I can buy anything today,' said Joan, sorry to disappoint the man.

'Missy, new things all, new things all. You lookie lookie. No buy.' And John was opening up rolls of fabrics and boxes with watches, undeterred by Joan's uninterest in his wares.

'John, really, you're wasting your time.'

'Please, missy, please. Help me. No more memsahib. All gone away,' said Hong Kong John in a plea to one of his most loyal customers for a fair hearing.

'John, we may not be here long ourselves,' said Joan. 'But here, take five rupees for your trouble, you've come a long way and you can call it *baksheesh* for the years you have been coming to me.'

Joan wished she could reach out to relieve the man of some of his wares but knew that anything she bought would be of little use to her if she did leave for Britain. As Hong Kong John limped back down the stairs with his sack of goods strung over his shoulder he waved goodbye, probably for the last time.

Phillip visited that evening with a book of pictures taken from past issues of *The Illustrated London News* for Errol to look at.

'Joan, I've got a solution to your money worries. Will you promise not to fly off the handle if I tell you?' he said cautiously.

'Yes, go on, sell my body? No thanks,' she said with a smirk.

'I've had a word with Father Rector and he says that in principle the school may be able to advance me a loan if I guarantee to pay it back over a three-year period. Now that's only about sixty rupees a month and I can easily manage it with a bit of cutting back.'

'Phillip, how could I take all that money from you when you're not even a member of my family? I wouldn't hear of it,' said Joan, attempting to refuse but secretly quite encouraged by the prospect. It was never polite in Anglo-Indian circles to accept generosity without at first refusing. A second helping of supper would always be turned down then followed by reluctant acceptance and subsequent enjoyment.

'Oh please do accept this. I see you as family, you

332

and Errol are my adopted little family. I don't have much else. You can pay me back as soon as you've got on your feet in England.'

Joan paused, looked at the ground in contemplation and then up at Phillip. 'Let me give you a hug for saying that.'

'Then will you accept my offer?'

'Yes, OK. Thank you very much,' she said with a big smile.

'Darling, Errol *beta,* we're off. We're off in the air,' she yelled, grabbing her son and swinging him around, much to his surprise. 'We've got the money to go to England and we can go by one of those shiny new jet planes, darling. Isn't that wonderful?'

'Mum, are we going for good, won't we ever come back here again?' said Errol, not as pleased as Joan to hear that he would be leaving.

'Maybe one day, darling, but we need to be getting away from the *garbar* here for a while.'

'But, Mum, I won't see any of my friends again. What will happen to the *khansamin* when we go? And Phillip, how will we see him?'

Errol was not happy with the prospect of moving to another land and Joan did all she could to hide her own discomfort at the prospect of going to a place where the people were known to be unfriendly and where she would not have Phillip, Punditji, Father Rector and others to rely on when she needed them.

'Let's go and celebrate your departure. I'm sorry, I mean your new life,' said Phillip bravely.

'But Phillip, you'll be all right without us, won't you?' said Joan.

'Mmn, I'll be much happier knowing that you're safe out of the way of these *goondas*,' said Phillip, still with his brave face on.

They caught a taxi to Young's Chinese restaurant, which was always a treat. 'We'll miss these butterfly prawns in England,' said Errol as the steaming dish of gorgeous, pink, gently battered crustaceans appeared on the table.

'Oh, there are plenty of Chinese restaurants in London, Errol,' said Joan, 'but, true, probably none like Young's.'

Just then a man came walking up to them in a blazer and shouted out the words, 'Joan, good to see you.' Her heart sank. It was Jonty. 'Errol, how are you?' he said turning to the boy but ignoring Phillip.

Joan was quick to introduce Phillip, 'Jonty, this is my boyfriend. How are you?'

Phillip almost dropped a butterfly prawn onto his lap at the mention of 'boyfriend' and rose to shake Jonty's hand. Errol too looked a little perplexed as to how 'sir' was now his mother's boyfriend.

'Oh, I've got splendid news. Guess what? I've met the most wonderful woman, here in Cal.'

'Woman?' asked Joan, amazed. 'Who?'

'Oh, a Calcutta girl, you wouldn't know her. She's a distant cousin. I'll bring her over.'

And a woman in a black lacy dress, about twenty years younger than Jonty, came over to the group. 'Jessica,' gasped Joan, astonished to see the woman from Lindsay Street out of her normal surroundings.

'Oh, hello darlings, didn't know you knew each other,' said Jessica, holding a smouldering cigarette in a long black Bakelite holder.

'Can we join you?' said Jonty.

Phillip and Joan looked at each other trying not to smile. Errol was the first to break the silence. 'Uncle Jonty, how long ago did you say you drove the Doon Express?' And they all sat down together to finish off their butterfly prawns and the rest of the steaming hot dishes, accompanied by the constant chatter of Jessica's stories about the appalling state of Lindsay Street and Jonty's litany of near-disaster episodes driving the Doon Express.

There couldn't have been a better antidote to Joan's guilt over refusing Jonty's proposal. Jessica would now benefit from his undivided attention as long as he lasted out on earth.

That night on the veranda, after Errol had gone to bed and Joan had packed the last precious piece of pottery, which she was determined to take with her, she and Phillip spent their last night together watching the full moon light up the dark Calcutta sky. They sat in silence thinking about their future lives, and their feelings towards each other were uppermost in their minds.

Phillip's act of generosity had taken Joan by surprise. Never had someone acted so spontaneously on her account in return for no particular favour. Phillip would certainly have to make some sacrifices to afford to pay back the loan and Joan resolved to send him what she owed as quickly as she could, but the completely unselfish gesture had moved her. For the first time since her husband's death she felt another man was coming close to touching her heart.

Phillip wanted to savour these last moments with Joan.

She was everything he wasn't: headstrong, fiery, inquisitive and with an unrelenting desire to see justice done. She had been a resolute friend all through his early days at the school and his difficult relationship with Audrey. Although he had felt some shame as a failed lover, that sense of embarrassment had long gone.

Tomorrow they were going their separate ways. Neither of them knew whether they would see each other again and nothing was said about their future plans to reunite. This last night was the perfect chance to enjoy each other and the wonderful golden twenty-four carat moon.

They sat with their arms around each other and there was a moment that Joan ached for a deeper physical encounter but the thought that it would make their parting more difficult restrained her. Instead they just gazed into the night until tiredness and sleep took over.

There was a small farewell party at Dum Dum Airport to say goodbye to Joan and Errol as the sleek cream and blue BOAC 707 touched down from Singapore. The crowd of spectators cheered as the plane landed and Errol felt excited at the prospect of boarding the passenger jet bound for a strange and alien land he only knew about from postcards and films.

Dum Dum Airport was a dingy affair; it had been built by the British to service the growing demands for air connections in the thirties and the art-deco terminal had never been expanded or modernised since. Indian Airlines flew a collection of old Dakotas up to the tea plantation owners of Assam and the northeast, and there was a three-times-a-week connection with BOAC's Asia service.

There was an announcement for passengers to proceed through passport control and Joan put her arms around Phillip and kissed him for what she believed was the last time. Errol shook his hand. 'Look after yourselves now and don't forget to send me a postcard of London Bridge when you arrive,' said Phillip.

At this moment she was suddenly full of doubt about her decision to leave her home for a place where their futures were so uncertain. But the assurance that they would be getting far away from the Movement, and from an aggrieved Judge Bhattacharya, made Joan believe that, for now, she was doing the right thing.

Joan and Errol waited in the departure lounge for a while. Joan recognised one of the other female passengers whom she had met at a De Lange canasta evening. 'Hello, Mrs Lowe, didn't know you had decided to leave.'

'Oh, my husband is in London already. He went there six months ago to get settled with our son. And you...?'

'Oh, there's just me and Errol,' said Joan, patting her son on the head, an act that the boy was beginning to detest.

There was an announcement on the loudspeaker. 'Flight O13 to London. Calling all passengers. There has been a technical delay. Engineers are assessing the situation and we will give you more information shortly.' An hour later, there was another announcement. 'We regret the delay to Flight O13. It appears that the aircraft has irresolvable technical problems. Passengers will be taken back to Calcutta for the evening to await the boarding of a relief aircraft in the morning. A member of BOAC staff will be with you shortly to give you further details.'

'Ma, what are they saying? Can't we go? Where will we go now?' asked Errol. The passengers had erupted into a combination of moans of anger and despair. This was not what one expected of the efficient, modern jet age.

A member of staff explained to Joan and the other passengers that they would be taken to a hotel in Calcutta for the night and brought back to the airport in the morning when another plane from Hong Kong would be re-routed to pick up passengers.

Errol first spotted Phillip as they came out of the terminal. He ran straight up to his friend and threw his arms around him in an uncharacteristic gesture of reunion. 'Sir, sir, we're not going to London after all.'

Joan followed and said quietly, 'You stayed, Phillip.' And he gave her an extra big hug.

'Welcome back, so soon. I missed you both,' he said.

GLOSSARY

This is a glossary of some of the common Anglo-Indian words used in this story. In some cases their usage may by now have become extinct. The author has therefore interpreted them as they were used at the time in which the story is set.

achha	OK or good
anna	Former monetary unit, equal to one sixteenth of a rupee
aré yar	'Oh come on', 'you know'
areh	'Oh!' Common expression prefacing a sentence used mostly to ease speech
aste	Slowly
ayah	Indian nanny, also sometimes acts as a general servant
babu	A Bengali clerk of varying seniority. Also commonly used to show some respect, as in *babujee*
badmash	Bad people
behan chode	Swear word. Literally someone who has sex with his sisters
bhai	Brother
bakri	Goat
baksheesh	Tip, sometimes also used as a bribe
balti	Bucket
bandh	A closure or lock-in, usually initiated by union action
beta	Term of endearment for a child
bhageera	Panther, used to refer to someone sly and deadly

bidi	Very pungent, cheap, hand-rolled Indian cigarettes made for the masses
Biryani	Richly prepared rice described more fully in the text
Blighty	Anglo-Indian word for England, adapted from the Hindi *bilaith*
burra	Big, important
bus, bus	Expression: 'stop doing that!'
challo/chullo	'Come on' or 'let's get going'. Often repeated to communicate a sense of urgency
chameli	Literally means jasmine. Used here in conjunction with memsahib, it was used to denote Anglo-Indian women who made their living as high-class prostitutes
chappals	Sandals
chat	Spicy street snacks
chatti	Cheap, porous earthenware pot used for storing water. Evaporation off the surface keeps the water cool
chokra	Young boy, usually a servant
choli	Blouse worn with a sari
chup	Quiet
chota	Small
chota hazri	Breakfast, derived from Hindi and Urdu words. Now appears to have lost its usage
chowkeedar/ chowkidar	Manservant who doubles as a security guard, provides peace of mind, especially at night
Chutney Mary	Anglo-Indians considered this a derogatory term for a woman from their community

cow sway	Burmese dish made with noodles in a soupy, tangy coconut broth
danda	A robust stick used to attack or defend
dhobi	A popular Anglo-Indian word for a laundry-man
dhoti	Male garment to cover the lower half of the body, draped from a single sheet of material
didi	Bengali word for sister
Diwali	Annual religious Hindu festival of light
durgee	Tailor
engrajee	English
gainda	Marigold
garbar	Trouble
ghat	Place for Hindu rituals such as funerals by the banks of the river
ghee	Clarified butter used commonly in cooking
gherao	Being surrounded by union or political activists
goonda	Collective description of someone bad. Used to describe a range of unsavoury types from a troublesome gang to a group of corrupt people
gussa	Angry
ha/hah	Yes
hartal	Strike, civil disobedience
hijiras	An openly transgender group of people at the margins of society who sometimes castrate themselves and make their lives as singers, dancers or prostitutes. Referred to in the *Kama Sutra* as the third sex
jaldi	Quickly
jao	Go

javan	Collective name for an Indian Army soldier post-independence
kala	Black
khana	Food or meal
khansama/ khansamin	Servant cook, usually a dishwasher too
khatia	Low bed made with straw matting on a wooden frame
koftas	Meat balls
kookri/kukri	A short fighting or hunting knife, often used by Gurkhas
kulfi	An Indian ice cream, cone shaped and made in an ice bucket
kulhar	Disposable earthenware cups used to drink tea
kurta	Loose-fitting collarless garment that looks like a shirt
kya hai	'What is it?' or 'what's up?'
larka	Young boy
lakh	One hundred thousand
larkie	Young lady
lathi	Long heavy bamboo stick often used as a weapon by police. Sometimes called a *danda*
loonghi	Sheet of material that acts as a garment or loincloth for men
maccan	House
maidan	A playing or recreation field, the most famous of which is probably the Calcutta *maidan*
misty dohi	Bengali sweet curds, particularly famous in Calcutta

molu	A special type of fish curry, a treat for Anglo-Indians at the time, but may now have died out. The author was only able to resurrect the recipe from his mother's handwritten notes
nahi	No
nallah	Open drain normally by the roadside, usually emitting unpleasant smells
namaskar	A respectful greeting made by holding the palms of one's hands together like the less formal *namaste* used all over India
nawab	An Urdu word to mean a Muslim ruler
paratha	A rich, flat, unleavened bread made from flour and *ghee* and rolled in layers before cooking
pilau	A rich rice dish usually spiced and cooked with *ghee* and water
pongas	Flat bread rolled with fillings to provide a snack. Good Anglo-Indian substitute for the sandwich
puchka	Puffy, fried, hollow, crispy morsel, filled with spiced tamarind water and chickpeas. Delicious!
pukka	Proper, genuine
puri	A small, round, flat piece of unleavened bread, deep-fried
roti	Collective description for all bread
shaitan	The devil, satan
salla	Common swear word, used here with *behan chode* which literally means someone who sleeps with their sister

salwar	Loose-fitting trousers worn by women with a *kameez*, a blouse
samosa	Popular three-cornered crispy snack stuffed with spiced potatoes
sepoy	British Raj term for Indian soldier
shabash	Well done
shami kebab	Patties made with ground-up chickpeas and lamb with spices
shamiana	Large marquee usually festooned with decorations
sher	Tiger
shikari	A hunter
tamasha	A drama or spectacle, often of some significance and usually associated with fun
thana	Police station
tonga	Horse-driven carriage
ultai	Upside down. Used here with *pani*, water

PARTHIAN

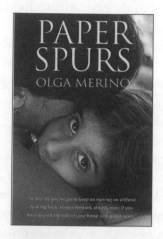

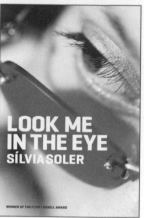

www.parthianbooks.com